THE MAN
WHO WANTED
TOMORROW

THE MAN
WHO WANTED
TOMORROW

Brian Freemantle

STEIN AND DAY/*Publishers*/New York

For Victoria,
who knows so well the
love with which this book is dedicated

First published in the United States of America, 1976
Copyright © 1975 by Innslodge Publications Ltd.
Printed in the United States of America
Stein and Day/*Publishers*/Scarborough House,
Briarcliff Manor, N.Y. 10510

Library of Congress Cataloging in Publication Data

Freemantle, Brian.
The man who wanted tomorrow.

Reprint of the ed. published by J. Cape, London.
I. Title.

PZ4.F8565Man3	[PR6056.R43]	823'.9'14	75-15704
	ISBN 0-8128-1870-9		

(I)

The wind, soon to carry the first snow of winter, scurried over the lake, flustering tiny waves against the shore with urgent, popping sounds.

A vast wedge of blackness was cast over the water by the huge mountain that rose directly over the north-west of Lake Toplitz, and on which, in the daylight, were visible the scars of the successors to the V-1 and V-2 rockets that were still being tested there at the German Navy's secret underwater missile-centre as Hitler put the Luger to his head in the Berlin bunker.

There was light, though, on the eastern section, where the moon could reach, and it was here the first man broke surface. He trod water and turned a full circle, searching the complete darkness of the land. Then, in a patterned bunch, the other frogmen came up, with no sound.

They stayed, as if uncertain, a formal rectangle of men. After several minutes, without any indication of gestured command, they began moving awkwardly towards the shore. Their grouping was unusual, two separate lines each of three men, moving parallel and about three feet apart. From the slowness of their progress, it was obvious that between them they were supporting something of considerable weight. Near the edge, where it was possible to stand, the leaders ducked into the water, removing their flippers to walk easier. They paused, free of the water, to allow the two following to do the same.

The shotgun blast was deafening. It was fired only feet from the man who had first surfaced, completely decapitating him, and immediately there was the roar from another shotgun. The spreadshot killed the second man instantly and wounded the skindiver behind him, who died anyway within seconds in the cross-fire of machine-pistols. The fourth swimmer had a knife quite uselessly in his hand when the first shotgun, reloaded now, caught him in the stomach, almost separating the head and chest from the lower torso. The fifth frogman ran blindly towards the shore, into a curtain of fire being directed into the lake with mathematical precision, and was lifted from the water by the force of the bullets.

It lasted exactly one minute and thirty-two seconds. Then, abruptly, it was quiet again.

The dead men were hauled further on to land, their bodies scuffing through the pine-needles with a hissing sound. Unhurriedly, the mouth- and headsets were removed, so those men not mutilated could be examined under heavy torchlights kept off until now because the killers wore infra-red nightsight glasses for complete visibility. The spectacles had given them a grotesque, frog-like appearance.

'There were six.'

'Yes.'

They all turned towards the lake, quiet and barely stirring now under the persistent wind. The lights jabbed out, showing nothing. For several minutes, they searched the shoreline, seeking another body, and two men waded along, level with the shore, the water up to their knees.

'Who fired, ahead of the command?'

'I did.'

The confession was immediate. The man stood stiffly to attention, knowing of the discipline. There was a momentary pause, then the shotgun blasted again, but quieter this time because the leader had only used one barrel. He had purposely fired into the man's face, so there could be no identification.

8

'Strip them.'

The leader played the light over what the frogmen had hauled from the lake.

'Two boxes,' he said, needlessly.

'There were more. They wouldn't have swum in that formation with just two boxes.'

The flashlights spread out over the lake again and the obscenity was brief.

'Verdammte Scheisse.'

The men stirred with the odd embarrassment of soldiers hearing a superior officer swear. Quickly the leader gave an order and they formed up in a rectangle similar to that in which the swimmers had come ashore. Clothing from the dead men was piled on top of the boxes.

There was military precision in the way the group moved off through the woods.

$\left(2\right)$

The Russian scientists, few of whom had travelled extensively, filed off the special Aeroflot Ilyushin and gathered in small groups, waiting for guidance from the Minister of Science like chicks awaiting the lead of the mother hen. The minister, Alexei Mavetsky, was familiar with New York and strode confidently down the finger at Kennedy Airport, greeting the American officials from Houston and the Russians from the United Nations. They were flying on to Texas the following day, after a U.N. reception.

'Not what I expected,' said Sergei Damerov to the man keeping step beside him. Damerov, the rocket-propulsion expert, was an untidy, fat man who bulged his clothes like a tyre slowly deflating from several punctures. He spoke in nervous, bronchitic gasps, constantly worrying the floss of tangled, grey hair, and laughing immediately he expressed an opinion, as if he expected rejection of his views and wanted to indicate they should not be taken seriously.

He laughed now, glancing sideways for reaction, but the other man ignored him, the inevitable cigarette jutting from his mouth in its black malacca holder. He limped slightly, from a long-ago accident to his left leg.

'I said, not what I expected.'

The limping man turned, his face, as usual, quite expressionless, and Damerov's deep-felt jealousy immediately surfaced. Vladimir Kurnov was the most self-controlled man he knew, thought Damerov, who despised his own nervousness. They had worked together for nearly eighteen years and never once had he known the man betray anger or happiness. Or any emotion, for that matter. It was Damerov who had christened the other man the Robot, giggling to the point of tears when he discovered that Kurnov had learned the nickname. But Kurnov had just stared at him, with those opaque eyes. And walked away, neither smiling nor frowning.

Odd, thought the rocket-expert as they entered the V.I.P. lounge, that even without raising his voice Kurnov inevitably succeeded in getting his own way. Probably his psychiatric training. Damerov wondered if he could hypnotize people into obeying him. That could be it. The tussled man stared up into the empty eyes turned towards him. They could easily hypnotize someone, he decided.

'What *did* you expect?'

Like the eyes, the voice lacked expression. The monotone of his speech was one of the initial reasons for Damerov's choice of nickname. Immediately faced with a question, Damerov sought a path to safety.

'Oh, I don't know,' he shrugged, sniggering dismissively. 'It's supposed to be such a vibrant, exciting place ... full of action ...'

'It is,' cut off the other man, with the curtness of an adult irritated by a child's prattling. Kurnov looked at his watch, pointedly. 'You've been on the ground exactly sixteen minutes, and we haven't even left the airport yet. How on earth can you judge what sort of place it is?'

Damerov was in full retreat.

'No, of course not. Stupid of me. Then again, I haven't travelled as extensively as you,' he capitulated, annoyed at himself. It *had* been a stupid thing to say. Kurnov had turned away, however, ignoring him. The minister was slowly beckoning the party forward, introducing them to NASA officials and scientists with whom they would be working on the joint Soviet–American space link-up.

He gestured to Kurnov, who moved obediently up to the group.

'Vladimir Kurnov,' announced Mavetsky. 'Our leading expert in behavioural patterns and stress factors ... in fact, some people have even said the world's expert ...'

Kurnov waited patiently while the translator went through the introductions, then said, 'I speak English.'

The NASA director, Melvin Sharpe, shook hands and smiled. 'I've particularly looked forward to meeting you, Comrade Kurnov.'

'I've looked forward to coming,' replied the Russian, easily. His English was good, with hardly a blur of any accent.

'I tried contacting you during your last visit,' the American went on. 'But somehow my messages never seemed to get through.'

He stopped and smiled again, inviting the question. Kurnov looked at him, his face blank.

'We found your papers on human stress quite extraordinary. Our people learned a great deal from them,' offered the director.

'Yes,' said Kurnov, flatly, indicating the praise came as no surprise.

'We had no idea you would be so far advanced,' said Sharpe.

'Painstaking attention to detail and slow progress, rather than dramatic performances, have always been a factor in all Russian research,' said Kurnov.

Sharpe looked at him curiously, seeking an implied criticism of America's over-publicized space exploration. But the statement had no rudeness, he decided. It was as if the man had read aloud words written by someone else. Kurnov returned the look, waiting for the director to take the lead again. The American studied the man before him. Kurnov's hair was cropped short, militarily, high above his ears, and his face, almost completely free of lines and shaved to a pink, polished look, gave no indication of his age. So devoid was it of any expression, the director realized, that it would never be possible to guess what thoughts the man might be having. He was nearly six feet tall, but slighter than most of the other thickset, bulky Russians in the party, and his suit, although a nondescript, undistinguished grey, appeared better cut than those of the men around him. The matching grey tie was tightly knotted into a crisp, white shirt, with just the correct amount of cuff protruding. Kurnov would always wear white shirts, decided the director, because he would always conform, even to the conservatism of his dress. Instantly the American doubted his own assessment. He found the man unsettling, without being able to isolate the reason for his discomfort. Perhaps it was the man's demeanour. Kurnov stood before him almost to attention, but at the same time there was a casualness about the stance, the sort of insolence a parade-ground sergeant would have recognized and been angered by, knowing the challenge to authority could never be proved.

The only obvious weakness visible in the man showed in the nicotine-tanned fingers on his right hand.

'I'm sure our joint association will be fruitful,' said Sharpe, accepting he would always have to lead the conversation.

'I'm sure it will be,' agreed Kurnov.

Arrogant bastard, thought the American, as Kurnov fitted another cigarette in his holder.

'I know our psychiatrists are most anxious to discuss with you your views on how to resist mental collapse,' Sharpe tried again.

'Yes,' said Kurnov, unhelpfully, as if he already knew.

The director determined to unsettle the man and get some reaction from him.

'Certainly, from our experience in Korea, our psychiatrists weren't able to concur with your assertion that there could be developed a mental attitude that could resist any predictable pressure,' said Sharpe. 'There's always a breaking-point.'

Kurnov shrugged, as if the conversation bored him. 'I know all about Korea,' he said. 'Child-like brainwashing. The understanding of the mind has moved on considerably since then.'

'Could your cosmonauts keep their stability, knowing for instance that they were lost in space, with no chance of recovery?'

'I think so,' said Kurnov, not bothering to conceal the edge of contempt.

Sharpe flushed, trying to control his annoyance.

'And you, doctor,' he said, accepting the impertinence of the question before speaking. 'How well do you think you could withstand concerted mental torture? Have you ever asked yourself that?'

Kurnov stared at him, letting the surprise show to increase the other man's embarrassment.

'No,' he said, curtly. 'I rarely waste my time on fatuous conjecture.'

The confrontation was broken by Mavetsky bustling Russians and Americans together for a group photograph. Kurnov immediately moved away, not bothering with a farewell to the American, who stood frowning after him.

The minister and Kurnov sat alongside each other in the Zil limousine taking them into Manhattan.

'I'd have liked you by me during the photographic session,' rebuked Mavetsky, who was a vain man and knew the Americans regarded Kurnov as the most important member of the party.

'The people who mattered were where they should have been,' said Kurnov, carelessly. 'I'm a scientist, not an actor.'

'From where you stood, I wouldn't be surprised if you weren't obscured completely,' smiled Damerov, hopefully, from the jump-seat facing both men. Mavetsky looked sideways at Kurnov, but the other man stared out at the Manhattan skyline as the vehicle went over the Triboro Bridge, not bothering to answer.

At that moment, four thousand miles away, one of the foresters employed by the Austrian government, to ensure that Lake Toplitz and the surrounding area remained permanently sealed against Nazi fortune-hunters, strolled down to the shoreline, wondering at the tree trunks apparently stripped of bark. When he realized they were six naked bodies, he whimpered, biting at his lower lip in fear, then ran yelling back through the woods, convinced he was about to be shot, too.

A week later, the Israeli government announced that five members of the Mossad, their secret service, had been murdered in Austria, discounted as irrelevant Vienna's protests at the illegality of the mission and demanded the fullest investigation into the crime.

Because of Russian pressure, the United Nations were immediately convened in New York to formulate a censure motion.

And in Jerusalem, two Israelis who had stumbled ashore together from the Exodus as two bewildered, frightened children, and grown into inseparable friends, had their first serious argument in twenty-five years, then parted angrily, knowing there would be more disagreements.

(3)

Only the trial of Adolf Eichmann in 1968 for the geno-
cide of the Jews had created similar interest. To ensure
the necessary security for the government leaders who
attended, and to accommodate the world's press, the
main committee-room of the Knesset in Jerusalem had
to be set aside for the conference.

Golda Meir attended, as an elder statesman, with
President Katzir. Moshe Dayan was there, too, flanked
by General Mordechai Gur and Yitzhak Rabin. Also
present were two of the country's High Court judges
in case the questioning became centred on international
law. A Brigadier Shimeon Cohen was introduced as the
man who would conduct the conference, assisted by a
clutch of Information Ministry officials behind him.
The beige-washed room had been wired for simultan-
eous translation, and available to every journalist was a
headset linked to interpreters housed beneath the committee-room, watching the conference on closed-circuit
television monitors. The floor was ribboned with
electrical wiring, both from the translation service and
from the television teams from America, France, Germany and England who were transmitting the conference
live.

With difficulty, a junior official quietened the room.
The conference began with a surprise, for although she
held no office it was Golda Meir who rose to speak,
waiting patiently for complete attention.

'Israel', she began, glancing at the notes in her hand,
'does not deny the illegality of sending into another
country a commando squad.'

She paused, with a politician's timing.

'The expected result of that mission, like that which resulted in the capture in the Argentine of Adolf Eichmann, was judged worthy of that offence.'

The only sound in the huge room was the noise of television cameras and the subdued whisper of radio reporters.

'It is no secret', she continued, 'that in the final stages of the Second World War, the inner caucus of the Nazi Party retreated to what they hoped would be their Alpenfestung, their Alpine fortress in the Austrian mountains around Bad Aussee. Eichmann initially fled there, with a fortune in gold and opium. Kaltenbrunner, Himmler's Gestapo chief who was later executed at Nuremberg for war crimes, scuttled there, too, with over £1,000,000 in gold and foreign currencies.'

She paused, sipping from a glass of water.

'Little, if any, of that treasure has ever been recovered,' she took up again. 'It was either buried, or thrown into Lake Toplitz, about which there are many legends of the size of the fortune hidden beneath its waters.'

There was another pause, for effect.

'The Israeli government', said the gravel-voiced grandmother, 'are not interested in the gold and jewellery taken from the 6,000,000 Jews being herded into the gas ovens and crematoria of the Third Reich.'

She stopped, for the point to be assimilated.

'But other things lay hidden in Lake Toplitz. From the information gathered over many years by our various intelligence services, the Israeli government know that also in the lake are full details of the coded Swiss and Beirut bank-accounts containing the millions upon which the Nazis exist today ...'

Another pause, which everyone realized was preparation for another surprise.

'... And also the new identities of the top Nazis, with the details of the prepared documentation under which

17

they live, free from arrest from anyone.'

She moved back, about to sit down, then glanced up, enjoying the denouement.

'With those accounts and files, we could economically strangle every Nazi who escaped in 1945. That was why Israel decided to violate Austria's sovereignty ...'

The final pause.

'... And to expose all the surviving Nazis in their hiding places.'

She sat down and immediately the clamour erupted as everyone began yelling questions. It was almost ten minutes before the flushed Brigadier could restore order.

'Six bodies were found in Austria,' took up the soldier, shouting to make himself heard. 'All, as you know, had been mutilated, some beyond recognition ...'

He hesitated, choosing his moment. The conference had been planned for the maximum impact, which was why someone with the international fame of Golda Meir had opened it.

'There were six men sent upon the mission,' he resumed. 'But one of the bodies found at the lake was not a member of the commando squad. One body had not been circumcised.'

He stopped, letting the significance register.

'One body was that of the assassin group that waited for our people to come out of the lake with the evidence that has been outlined ...'

Again the hesitation.

'Which means one member of our squad escaped.'

The uproar burst out again, but lasted only minutes because the Brigadier had gestured to a room off the main committee-chamber and then stood back as a man, huddled in a wheelchair, was pushed into the room by two white-coated doctors. Behind them came three other men, supporting what had once been a German am-munition-box. It was blackish-green from the fungi that had accumulated during the thirty-year immersion, and the metal bindings and clasps were dark with rust.

'The survivor, Lev Shapiro,' announced the Brigadier, theatrically. 'And one of the boxes recovered from Lake Toplitz.'

Shapiro looked desperately ill. His skin was grey and waxy, sweat-filmed with the effort of appearing before the conference. The towelling robe he wore bulged with an enormous dressing over his left shoulder, and the sleeve of the dressing-gown hung limp and empty by his side.

'The conference involving this man will last exactly five minutes,' declared the Brigadier. 'He is appearing here against doctors' advice. There must be no inquiries how he escaped: obviously he was helped, once ashore, but the Israeli government have no intention of disclosing details of that rescue operation.'

A microphone was moved in front of Shapiro, but his voice was too indistinct, and one of the attendant doctors leaned forward, bringing it closer to the man's lips.

'We arrived in Austria a week before the dive,' started Shapiro. He spoke in short bursts and the sounds as he sucked in air echoed through the microphone. 'We knew that, because of the treasure-hunters, the area was sealed by the Austrian authorities. It took us three days to conceal sufficient diving equipment in the surrounding woods to make the dive possible.'

The Brigadier moved the water carafe towards the man and gratefully he sipped from a glass held by one of the doctors.

'We had an area, marked on a waterproofed map, where the boxes were likely to be. We dived on the fifth day. We had been trained for six months to work as a team, signalling every move by hand signals or body pressure.'

He paused, breathing deeply.

'That first night we found nothing. It was a dreadful anticlimax. We had practised so hard and planned so

19

completely, yet it had never occurred to us that the map references would be inaccurate ... the most obvious thing and no one had thought of it ...'

He stopped, apparently thinking.

'What happened then?' prompted a journalist in the front.

'We made mistakes,' confessed the commando. 'The boxes not being there confused us. Although we had been warned against doing so, we used lights to try to locate them. Still we didn't find them. But we must have alerted people ashore.'

He tried to straighten in the wheelchair, wincing at the effort. Gently one of the doctors helped.

'The following night', continued Shapiro, 'using the point where the boxes should have been, we started an organized sweep of the lake, moving towards the eastern shore and marking each section we covered on the map with wax pencils. Once we had to return to the shore to replenish our air supply. It was extremely cold. We began thinking we were going to fail again.'

For the first time he smiled, a painful expression.

'Thirty minutes after beginning the second dive, we found them. It was almost as if they had been arranged for collection. They lay there, neatly side by side. Four of them.'

He stopped.

'Tell us about the surfacing,' demanded someone in the middle of the conference hall.

Shapiro sighed. 'We put ropes through the side-handles of the boxes,' he said. 'It was completely dark, of course. We weren't using the lights now. In the formation that we had practised, we surfaced. The boxes were heavier than we had expected. We had prepared two possible landing places, neither of them where we had put ashore the previous night. But the weight could have made the rotting wood break and we would have lost forever what we sought, so the leader ignored the instructions and decided to land in the same spot we had used before. It was the nearest point of land. That was our second mistake. They were waiting for us.'

Again he stopped, gesturing for more water.

Shapiro's head was pressed forward on his chest and his voice was only barely discernible.

'There was no warning,' he said. 'It was a perfect ambush. We were cut to pieces. I only survived because I was last in the line and still up to my waist in water ...'

He glanced at his empty sleeve.

'... I was hit four times in the shoulder,' he said, shuddering. 'I've lost my arm.'

His head sank back and the doctor on his right seized his wrist, checking his pulse, then spoke to the Brigadier who again shielded the microphone.

'The last question,' announced the chairman, pointing to a man with his arm raised at the back of the hall.

'The box,' said the man. 'Tell us about the box.'

Shapiro looked up, with difficulty. 'It was the one I found,' he explained. 'As well as putting the rope through the side supports, I was holding the handle. At the first shot, I ducked, kicking backwards. I didn't realize immediately that I was still holding the box. My air was still on and I just swam out into the lake, taking the box with me ...'

His voice began to slur and both doctors turned to the Brigadier, who nodded. There were no protests as the man was wheeled away.

Immediately the Brigadier opened the box. The wood, which had been completely waterlogged, had begun to curl away from the metal rimming as it had dried. Slowly he began unloading its contents, creating on the table before him separate piles of looted French gold Napoleon pieces, adding twelve solid gold bars stamped with the hallmark of the Third Reich, a glittering hill of diamonds and rubies, several jewel-encrusted cathedral chalices and hedges of sterling and dollar notes.

'The money is forged,' he said, dismissively, as he unpacked. 'Part of the millions created by professional criminals imprisoned at the Sachsenhausen concentration camp, near Berlin, money with which Hitler intended to flood the West and undermine the economy of both America and Britain.'

The room was completely still, as over 150 people stared at the fortune laid out in front of them.

'You are looking at loot worth £1,000,000,' announced the Brigadier, simply.

He stood back from the table, as if unwilling to come into contact with it.

'The Israeli government are tomorrow sending everything this box contained to the International Court at the Hague, for whoever considers they have a legal right to begin proceedings to establish ownership.'

He stopped, picking up some of the jewels and tossing them contemptuously inside the amunition container.

'We have no interest in this,' he said. 'It is not the box we sought. We are confident that from the bottom of the lake, in one of the three other boxes, was evidence that would have identified every surviving Nazi. Accepting the importance of what we tried to establish, the Austrian government have provided us with a detailed report of the forensic evidence available at the scene of the shooting. The boxes, as you have heard, were extremely heavy. The shoreline is soft and muddy. Very clearly visible, under scientific examination, were indentations caused by three boxes ...'

He paused, turning to Golda Meir, who rose again.

'We have one,' he added. 'Other evidence at the lakeside indicates the assassins recovered two. Which means one has vanished!'

Realization of the point of staging the conference swept over the journalists.

'That box could contain what we want,' she took up. 'Its contents would enable us to locate Leopold Gleim, former head of the S.S. in Poland, last heard of living as a Moslem in Egypt. We would know the whereabouts of Heinrich Willermann, who took part in the sterilization and freezing experiments in Dachau. We would know definitely if Hans Eisele, who carried out human experiments in Buchenwald, and later acted as a judge in Prague, is living in Egypt ...'

She paused, sipping from a water glass.

'It would also tell us how the Butcher of Auschwitz, Dr Josef Mengele, is managing to live in South America ...'

There was another pause.

'And it would make it possible for us to get from the sanctuary they now occupy two scientists whom the Israeli government regard as equal to Eichmann, Mengele, or Bormann, for crimes against the Jewish people. We want to locate Dr Otto Grüber. And Dr Heinrich Köllman. These two men worked under Mengele in Auschwitz. Later, working as a team, they moved to Bergen-Belsen and Buchenwald. Their experimentation involved testing human reaction to cold, to prepare for the German assault upon the Russian front. They immersed Jews in water which froze solid, to assess their resistance. They force-marched women and children, some dressed, some stark naked, through snow and ice to establish susceptibility to frostbite ...'

She paused, as if uncertain whether to continue. Then she added, 'They starved them, trying to reach the point where, in such extreme conditions, the victims would resort to cannibalism to survive ...'

Another pause. 'And succeeded in reaching that point ...'

She began talking again. 'These two men, working almost under the personal direction of Adolf Hitler, were engaged upon every conceivable form of human experimentation ... Hitler personally entrusted to them the task of creating a biological blue-print for his super-race. About both very little is known. We have established that Köllman definitely survived. About Grüber we don't yet know that. Both were known to be working in Buchenwald when the Russians advanced, and Moscow refuses to answer all inquiries.'

The room was satiated with detail and sensation, and the journalists stared numbly towards the table behind which the officials sat. The woman fingered the gold bars lying before her.

'You have heard that this is worth something like £1,000,000 ...' She looked up towards the television cameras. '... We accept that the missing box may contain nothing more than that which you see before you today ... loot from the crematoria. We have gambled and lost the lives of five Israelis. To recover the box that could contain what we want, the Israeli government are prepared to pay, wherever and in any currency or method demanded, the similar sum of £1,000,000 ...'

In another part of the Knesset building, Uri Perez glanced away from the television monitor upon which he had watched the conference, now bursting into a further flurry of questioning.

'Well?' he demanded. The tension of their argument still existed and he spoke with odd formality to the other man, to whom he had once felt closer than the family he had lost in Buchenwald and Dachau. His companion, a burly giant of a man, overflowing from his chair, his stomach bulged over his army webbing-belt, shrugged.

'Not bad,' offered Arron Mosbacher, turning down the volume on the monitor. They could read a transcript later.

'It sounded pretty good to me,' encouraged Perez, with just a trace of truculence. He could not lose his irritation at Mosbacher's objection to what was happening up there in the committee-room.

Both men had been attached to the Mitzvah Elohim,

the Wrath of God group formed from the Mossad to combat Palestinian terrorism, until they had been seconded to the Austrian assignment. Mosbacher had immediately argued against the proposal, and as the planning had progressed Perez, who had overall command, had twice considered recommending Mosbacher's transfer. He had withheld from doing so because of their association and now wondered if he had made a mistake. He didn't want to make another. A month before, he had stood with Mosbacher on the far side of the Austrian lake and seen men with whom they had lived daily for six months destroyed in less than two minutes of gunfire. Mosbacher's opposition since that massacre had grown with Perez's feeling of guilt.

'It'll be a miracle if there's the reaction we expect,' warned Mosbacher.

'We invented miracles,' reminded Perez, attempting the lightness that had once existed between them. He was a slight, studious man, dwarfed by his companion. A brilliant scholar, with honours degrees from Oxford and Harvard, he desperately wanted to leave his country's security service to take the Chair of Psychiatry at the Hebrew University in Jerusalem. Twice the government had refused his request to leave the umbrella of Mossad, knowing there was no one to equal his ability to organize spectacular intelligence operations.

'There are too many uncertainties,' argued Mosbacher, who was seriously worried about his friend. The idea was insanity, he thought, created by a man who had known only success and had thus become over-confident. It was odd, Mosbacher had often recalled, that it had been he, the older by two years, who had led Perez by the hand on to the beach at Haifa when the refugee boat had nudged ashore, and the two orphans had been shoved on to the beach to avoid British patrols. Then he had been the leader. And remained so for several years. But later the role was reversed. Was he jealous at the change-over, wondered Mosbacher? No, he dismissed, immediately. Even though he now considered the ability was wrongly channelled, Perez was unquestionably the more intelligent of the two.

The Israeli cabinet had selected the two men very carefully, regarding the realistic objectivity of the bigger man as the perfect balance for the impetuous brilliance of Perez. No one was aware of the strain that had grown between them, leading to the mutual doubt.

'There's little to lose,' said Perez, regretting the sentence as he spoke. Immediately Mosbacher picked it up.

'We've already lost five people.'

Embarrassed, Perez said, 'Other people are making sacrifices. Which no one seems to appreciate.'

Mosbacher looked sadly at the younger man. The tendency for self-pity supported his doubt about the man's mental ability to carry through the operation, he thought.

'Everyone realizes what you are doing personally,' he said, soothingly.

Perez snorted, unconvinced. Mosbacher was a fool, he decided, angrily. The plan—his plan—was going to succeed. He knew it would. He'd enjoy having Mosbacher apologize, in the coming months.

'Shapiro stood up well,' said Perez, seeking neutral ground.

'Yes,' agreed Mosbacher. 'Which reminds me. Shouldn't you ring the hospital?'

Sighing, Perez nodded, then dialled a number on a security-cleared line. He was connected immediately, upon identification, to the hospital director and for several minutes became engrossed in detailed conversation. Replacing the receiver, he said to Mosbacher, 'Another three weeks. And he's unsure about that.'

Mosbacher considered the period, then humped his shoulders. 'We don't really have any choice, do we?'

'No,' agreed Perez. His see-saw outlook dropped in

another direction and optimism bubbled to the surface. 'That'll be long enough,' he said, confidently. 'You'll see.'

'It'll have to be,' said Mosbacher, gloomily, realizing that now the conference had been held, they were irrevocably committed.

In his Houston motel-room, which was securely locked, Vladimir Kurnov sat before the television-set carrying live the C.B.S. coverage of the Jerusalem conference. He was tensed forward on the edge of the chair, the habitual cigarette forgotten in its holder. After the coverage, there was a studio discussion among several alleged Hitler historians about whether the £1,000,000 offer would lead to the recovery of the document-box.

The programme ended, and Kurnov realized suddenly his cigarette had almost burned itself out. Quickly he lit another from the stub he extricated from the holder, then pulled the smoke deeply into his lungs. He turned away from the set and began pacing the room, head slumped forward. The dull ache started in his left leg, as it always did in moments of stress.

Once he stopped and, with supreme irony, muttered several times, 'Verdammte Scheisse.'

Three of the men who had formed part of the assassination squad died very quickly under interrogation in the specially sound-proofed cellar beneath a block of office buildings in West Berlin's Ludwigsfelderstrasse. Another went insane and was shot, because he could not answer questions sensibly, thus making it pointless to preserve his life. The leader endured the questioning for five days, repeating again and again they had only recovered two boxes and admitting there had been an insufficient search of the shallow water-line to detect a third. Satisfied the missing box had not been secreted for blackmail purposes, the questioners shot the leader and the other survivor of the killer squad, then walked upstairs leaving others to incinerate the bodies.

'So,' said the man who had asked most of the questions, 'there is definitely a missing box.'

Max Frieden had been the Standartenführer for the area covering Buchenwald when the war ended. But he had been far away when the Russians swept in. By the time Eichmann and Kaltenbrunner and the rest had arrived at Bad Aussee, Frieden had already 'vanished', equipped with a new face and a perfect set of genuine papers, seeing in the rebuilding of war-ravaged Berlin a far greater chance of prosperity than the mountains of Austria. He was an indulgently plump, small man who enjoyed entertaining children at Christmas and birthday parties and prided himself as an amateur conjuror, for which he now had plenty of time to practise, having established one of the most successful property-development empires in the city. Apart from the Berlin apartment, there was the country lodge in the Bavarian mountains outside Munich, and soon he intended purchasing a villa among friends on the outskirts of Madrid. Despite the fact that he was a millionaire, however, he still regarded the years as Standartenführer from 1939 to 1945 as the best of his life. He still recalled with pride among intimate gatherings of friends that, during those six years, he considered he had been personally responsible for the deaths of at least 3,000 Jews.

'Definitely missing,' agreed the second man. 'And it could be the most important one.'

Manfred Muntz had served the entire war as a colonel on Frieden's staff and gone underground with him in 1945. A tall man, with distant eyes, he had a tubercular cough and was constantly bringing a handkerchief to his mouth.

'We've had the shoreline searched. And the surrounding forest. There's nothing,' he added. A month earlier, the two men had examined the contents of the two boxes recovered after the assassination, cursing that they hadn't even the luck of the Israeli survivor. Their boxes had contained nearly all counterfeit money.

'This could be the end of us all,' said the fat man. He looked up suddenly. 'Have warnings been sent out?'

'Yes,' nodded Muntz, one of West Berlin's most successful commercial lawyers. 'To Egypt, Paraguay, Uruguay, the Argentine, Ireland. And here.'

'If we only knew who had the bloody thing,' said Frieden, 'we could outbid the Jews easily.'

'Have we the money here?' asked the consumptive lawyer.

The man who loved children nodded towards the large wall-picture showing a Berchtesgaden mountain-scene, behind which was hidden a wall-safe.

'Four million pounds sterling in gold arrived from Zurich last night,' he confirmed.

At that moment, in a Jerusalem hospital, Lev Shapiro died from the injuries sustained in the dive in Lake Toplitz, coupled with the strain of appearing at the press conference.

And Perez and Mosbacher had their second serious argument.

(4)

The mornings were always bad. It had been natural at first, she supposed, that awakening moment of fear as she lay in the empty bed, tensed for the sound that would mean there was someone else in the apartment, a man in uniform with a warrant for her arrest. But she had expected it to dissipate gradually, like that momentary hesitation when she had to sign her signature and had always paused, very slightly, at the need to concentrate upon the new name of Gerda Pöhl instead of Gerda Köllman. Now she signed any form unthinkingly, because she *was* Gerda Pöhl. But the mornings never began without that cramp of apprehension. She even prepared her clock in its expectation, giving herself ten minutes longer in bed than was necessary, to recover. She lay, as was her custom now, while the fear drained, then got up. A woman of strict regime, she bathed immediately, then strained her heavily greying hair back into its accustomed bun at the back of her head. Patiently, she massaged her face for fifteen minutes, convinced such daily attention had kept it free of any lines or signs of strain. Finally, she washed her face again, in cold water this time, then dressed with care.

It was difficult to dress as she would have liked, thought Gerda. How different from the old days, the good times when her darling Heinrich had had such a standing with the Führer. Then it had needed three trunks to contain what she needed for just a weekend at Berchtesgaden. Several times the Führer had complimented her upon her appearance, which had made it even more important to be dazzling on the subsequent occasions they had been invited. And how *dazzling* she had been, always. All that had been necessary was for her to sign the purchase-bill at any of the couture houses in Berlin or Paris or Rome and the garments arrived always within a fortnight. And what dresses: the finest silks, material woven specially for her, even her own designs. They had all envied her, she knew. Frau Himmler, Frau Goebbels, Eva Braun. Such a mousy girl, Eva. She would never be able to understand what the Führer saw in her. It was said, of course ... but no, that didn't matter. No one questioned the Führer, not even now.

She chose the black suit, carefully picking at the nap on the elbows and the seat of the skirt, trying to remove the shine of wear. It would be at least another six months before she could afford a replacement, despite the good salary Herr Muntz paid her. The apartment was far too expensive, she told herself again. But she refused to abandon the good address. She had so little left. She couldn't lose everything.

A good man, Herr Muntz, she decided, neatly making her bed. It had been a long time before she realized he was an ex-Nazi and that her wage represented not only the reward for her undoubted efficiency, but a pension that was rightly hers as the wife of such a leading member of the Party. They had never discussed it openly, of course, even though their relationship had become closer over such a long period. Once, many years ago, Gerda had even wondered if Herr Muntz wished to take her as a mistress. She had prepared herself for the approach and had decided to accept the role, after the initial, fitting hesitation. After all, there was no one else with whom she could have considered any sort of passing friendship, let alone something deeper. But she had been wrong, she reflected, with nostalgic regret. Herr Muntz's interest had remained decorous, his behaviour towards her indicating a shared secret but always stopping short of intimacy.

She sighed. Perhaps, through the Nazi survival network, the Organisation der Ehemaligen S.S. Angehörgen in which she was convinced Herr Muntz had high office, he knew dear Heinrich was still alive. Immediately she corrected the thought. Heinrich was definitely dead. It had taken her several years to face that reality. It had been different with Heini. When their son had been killed, the body was returned from the western front and there had been a proper funeral, with a grave in St Thomas Kirchhof cemetery, which she visited, surreptitiously, every Saturday, disguising the attention by pretending to grieve at the adjoining burial-place. But with Heinrich there had been nothing. He'd just failed to return, and no one seemed to want to answer questions about him. For years she had cherished the hope that he would trace her, even though she had abandoned her real identity. But it wouldn't happen now, she accepted. Heinrich had died, she was convinced of it. He had loved her, passionately. She knew that. Had he been alive, anywhere in the world, he would have contacted her.

She pushed the recollections away. It was ridiculous to regress so constantly. But where else did she have to live, she asked herself, except in the past? She made her coffee and drank standing in the window, looking down at the early-morning workers bustling along Duisburgerstrasse. Eight-thirty chimed, as she knew it would, as she emptied the cup. She washed it and left it to drain, carefully brushed her matching black coat, affixed her veiled hat into place and, carrying the briefcase containing the neatly completed conveyancing agreements she had brought home to type the previous evening, she stepped briskly out on to the busy street. From inside the café fifty yards away, near the Kurfürstendamm, Uri Perez saw her emerge. He had the appearance of a man at least thirty-five years older than he was, a bent, almost crushed figure, the ancient black homburg that had covered his white hair carefully on the seat beside him, the black overcoat, of a fashion long since dated, buttoned tightly across his chest. Just visible was a suit once blue but now greying with age and over-use, and the shoes, although of obvious good leather, were worn down and scuffed. In another six months, his appearance would be that of someone used to wealth who had finally arrived at the doorstep of complete poverty. Even now a few people in the café gazed at him sympathetically, as he huddled over coffee that had grown cold. Uri didn't follow the woman. There were four men in the street who would alternate their surveillance as far as the office and three more who would relieve them during the day. The Mossad had known of Gerda Köllman's existence for over fifteen years and had a file upon her so exhaustive it contained details that even she would have had difficulty recalling. They knew of Muntz, too, but not just how strong a figure he was in the Organisation der Ehemaligen S.S. Angehörgen. Both were viewed dismissively as bait, expendable except for the attraction they might have for people who really mattered.

Since the Austrian shootings and the Jerusalem conference Gerda Köllman had become important, but still only as bait, so now she would be watched, by a rotating team of a dozen men, to report the slightest deviation from the rigidly established routine, charted so minutely in her file.

Uri rose, paying his bill, never thinking of leaving a tip, so well had he been schooled in his assumed role. Sadly, the waitress watched him shuffle out, feeling no rancour.

Herr Muntz was already in the office when Gerda arrived, which surprised her. Since his cough had grown so bad, he had delayed arriving until 10 a.m. and sometimes later. On several occasions in recent months she had urged him to seek proper advice, once, in her concern, almost blurting out that his new identity was sufficient to conceal any hospital case-history.

'Guten Morgen, Herr Muntz,' she greeted.

'Guten Morgen, Frau Pöhl,' he responded. Her identity documents showed her to be the widow of a sergeant killed during the siege of Leningrad. The man had, in fact, been her cousin, but in the confusion of immediate post-war Germany, it had been easy to blur the association. She even received a small pension.

'I have the documents I took home last night,' she said, efficiently.

The man began to thank her, but was overcome with a paroxysm of coughing. It took him several minutes to recover and Gerda hurried him into a chair and poured him water.

'You should seek treatment, Herr Muntz,' she said.

'Yes, Frau Pöhl,' he agreed, groping for breath. Always there was a barrier of formality between them, but now he stopped, looking up at her. Gerda shifted, embarrassed under the look. It was very direct and most unlike him.

'Frau Pöhl, a favour please.'

'Of course.'

'Lock the door, so we can't be interrupted.'

'The door?'

Uncertainty flooded through the woman and she was reminded of her thoughts that morning that he might once have considered her as a mistress. But surely not now? Surely now he was too sick to ...? She blushed, but moved to the door. As she returned, hesitantly, he was talking to the outside office, instructing them that no calls should be put through while he was in conference. He indicated a chair beside the desk and she sat demurely, knees tightly together, hands in her lap. Why hadn't she worn the other suit? she thought angrily. The brown tweed was only two years old and far smarter than the black. He was clearly embarrassed, poor man.

'Frau Pöhl,' he started, awkwardly. 'We have been together now for many years ...'

She nodded and smiled, encouragingly.

'... Ours has been a fruitful ... a happy relationship ...' he groped on. 'During the time I have known you, I have developed a very deep feeling ... a very deep feeling of respect ...'

There would be no sex, she decided, realistically. But that didn't matter. She rarely felt the need, any more. It would be a union of companionship. They could have meals in discreet, quiet restaurants. And spend evenings at the theatre or opera. She would need clothes, though. She would make that quite clear to him. She would not want to embarrass Herr Muntz with her shabby appearance. She would make him visit a physician, immediately, she decided: she might even make it a condition of their relationship.

The man was staring down at his unmarked blotter, seeking the words to continue.

'You are an intelligent woman, Frau Pöhl. You must have realized, many years ago, that despite your unquestionable efficiency, the salary I paid you and the increases I have allotted annually were more than could have been expected by most women in your position.'

Gerda began emerging from her reverie. The morning feeling of dread stirred deeply within her.

'You must know, Frau Pöhl, why I sought you out, all those years ago.'

He waited for her to say something, but the woman just stared at him, dumbly. How old she looks, thought Muntz. And quite ugly. No wonder she had had to cover herself with all those expensive clothes years ago. He hadn't known her then, of course. But there had been many stories, jokes even. It was said the Führer called her the 'painted clown' and enjoyed having her at Berchtesgaden because she amused him with so many changes of costume. Only Goering changed clothes more frequently, it was said.

'I know your real identity, Frau Pöhl,' he blurted, suddenly. 'I was a dear friend of your husband.'

The office and the man blurred before her and Gerda strained to prevent the tears.

'Don't be frightened,' said Muntz, hurriedly, seeing the emotion. 'There is no danger. No harm can come to you. Believe me. You're quite safe.'

'But why ...?'

'It was time, Frau Pöhl. It was time for us to say openly what we have known for many years ...'

An outburst of coughing broke the sentence.

'... I want us to be better friends.'

She stared at him, all thoughts of liaison buried now beneath the fears that fogged her mind, like a child's toy turned upside down so that imitation snow obscured the picture.

She began to cry, very softly. Muntz came from behind his desk and put his hand on her shoulder. How bony she was, he thought, distastefully.

'Frau Pöhl, please don't.'

'I don't understand,' she said, her voice muffled by her handkerchief. 'I'm frightened, Herr Muntz. Very frightened'.

With difficulty, he took her shoulder again, keeping his touch soft this time.

'There is no need,' he reassured. 'I'm your friend. You know that.'

She looked up at him, through reddened eyes. Her hair had come away from the band and straggled over her face. No wonder Köllman had had such a reputation among the women in the concentration camps, thought Muntz.

'Why, Herr Muntz? Why now?'

The man returned behind the desk, preparing himself. It wasn't going to be easy, he knew.

36

'Things have happened,' he began badly, but confident she would not have heard about the Toplitz incident or the Jerusalem conference. He knew she had no television and rarely read newspapers. 'Not important things, you understand ...'

The cough came and he was glad. He was being very clumsy.

'... You know the witch-hunts that happen, from time to time ...'

'... But it's never involved me in the past ...'

'I know,' said Muntz, quickly. 'But now it does.'

The fear squeezed her, like a band being tightened around her body. She began to shake violently. Muntz gazed down at the desk, his hand shielding his eyes. Oh God, this was awful. He shouldn't have had to do it. He was sick. Everybody knew that. Other people should have done it.

'Frau Pöhl,' he tried again, his tone sterner. 'Please. Control yourself.'

Her feet drummed against the floor in her nervousness. The woman pressed her hands upon her knees, trying to subdue the noise. She was hunched, as if she were hollowed out and about to collapse inwardly, he thought.

'I've said I'm your friend. There's no risk. You'll always have protection from me.'

She nodded, half hearing.

'What do you want me to do?' she asked, and he sighed, inaudibly.

'You are a neat woman, Frau Pöhl, a woman of strict habits who would notice anything unusual.'

She looked at him, curiously, recovering further.

'I want you to tell me if anything ... anything at all happens that you find strange ...'

'I don't understand ...'

'No matter how unimportant it may seem. If the baker from whom you buy your bread takes on a new

37

assistant ... if the postman suddenly changes to someone you don't recognize ...'

The band tightened around her again.

'Me?' she demanded, speaking with difficulty, because suddenly her throat seemed to close. 'You mean they're after me ...?'

Again the handkerchief came to her eyes. Damn, thought Muntz, damn, damn, damn.

'No, Frau Pöhl,' he said, trying to keep his voice level. 'I can assure you that there will be no official investigation of you ...'

She wept on, unhearing.

'Frau Pöhl,' demanded her employer, sternly. She looked up.

'Frau Pöhl, it's not you that people will be seeking. It's your husband.'

The woman stared at him, uncomprehendingly, her mouth half open. She wore dentures, he saw. Her face would collapse at night, making her even uglier. She was shaking her head, a stupid half-smile on her face, moaning unintelligibly at first, then forming the sound into a single word.

'No ... no ... no.'

She would soon become hysterical, he realized. He went around the desk and stood before her, glaring down. It was like the old days, he thought. They had been frightened of him then, always, cringing away, whimpering their terror. The uniform had helped, of course, but he'd had the stature that went with it. He reached out, seizing the bony shoulders and shook her, roughly. Her head wobbled, as if unconnected to her body. He couldn't slap her, he thought. He might break her false teeth.

'Frau Pöhl, listen to me.'

She stared up, her eyes clouded.

'I believe your husband is alive,' he said, hurrying to get it over. 'I believe he might try to contact you ...'

'Not Heinrich,' she said, trying to hold on to her control like a child running its hand along railings. 'If he were alive, he would have contacted me ...'

'Exactly,' said Muntz, improvising wildly. 'Because Heinrich loved you. We all know that your marriage was a love affair for all to see ...'

She smiled, recognizing the pathway to the past. Desperately, Muntz tried to keep her in the present.

'... Which is why he has made no effort to reach you. His love for you is too great for him to do anything that might put you in danger ...'

'Then ...?'

'... But now *he* may be in danger, Frau Pöhl. And faced with that danger, he may turn to the person he loves most of all for help. You.'

'He's here? In Berlin?'

Idiotically, the woman stared around the room, as if she expected the sudden appearance of the husband she hadn't seen for thirty years.

'I don't know,' said Muntz. He was wet with perspiration and his chest burned, as if he had breathed in scalding air. 'He could come here, very soon.'

It was possible to see the effort the woman made. She sniffed noisily, several times, and re-trapped the escaping hair. She scrubbed at her eyes with the damp handkerchief and straightened in her chair, gazing at him.

'I'm ready to do anything you want, Herr Muntz.'

The man smiled, relieved. It was going to be all right, he decided.

'I want you to help Heinrich,' he said, raising his hand as he saw her about to speak.

'He'll need help, a lot of help ...' she broke in.

'... And you know that I and other people are prepared to give it to him,' completed Muntz.

Gerda smiled at him, gratefully. *Such* a good man, she thought.

'You must do two things,' continued the lawyer. 'You must, as I have said, report to me the slightest thing that happens to you that is out of the ordinary. I don't care how trivial or unimportant it seems. Anything. You understand?'

She nodded, dutifully.

'And the moment there is any contact from Heinrich, or anyone saying he represents Heinrich, then you must contact me at once.'

Again she nodded.

'At once, Frau Pöhl. Before going to meet him or anyone at any given spot. Before opening the door of your apartment. I must know, within minutes.'

He held out a sheet of paper he had prepared waiting for her to arrive that morning.

'I shall always be available at one of these numbers. And I want the call at any time of the day or night. Is that clear, Frau Pöhl?'

She moved her head, her face bright with happiness. How good it felt. Alive and vital again. *Doing* something. Being important. And Heinrich was alive! Alive and coming back. She'd protect him. God, how she'd protect him. No man would know such protection.

'Do you understand, Frau Pöhl?'

'Oh yes, Herr Muntz,' she said. She was breathless, as if she had run up stairs. 'Oh yes.'

'Heinrich's life, your life, will depend on how quickly you call me.'

'I know Herr Muntz. You can trust me. You know you can trust me.'

He smiled. She was very simple, he decided.

'I know I can, Frau Pöhl.'

He took out his wallet and extracted 500 marks.

'A gift, Frau Pöhl, from the Organisation. You'll need to buy a new dress maybe. And some food, in case Heinrich arrives suddenly.'

Her eyes flooded again, but this time from gratitude

and she grabbed the hand proffered by the man, lowering her lips to it. Muntz stood over her, wincing with distaste, but allowing the gesture. For the moment, she was very important.

'And take the rest of the day off,' he said, moving his hand behind his back and wiping it against his jacket. '... But remember. Any contact ... anything unusual. Call me immediately.'

Muntz had already finished one schnapps when Frieden arrived at the Am Zoo hotel. Immediately he ordered another, feeling he had earned it.

'Well?' questioned the millionaire. Muntz shrugged, sipping his drink.

'It was dreadful,' he said.

'But she knows what we want ... she agreed?' snapped Frieden, immediately.

'Oh, of course she agreed,' said Muntz, irritably. Contemptuously he added, 'She's a perfect Party member. She's been reborn. She's got a cause again. She'll do exactly as I've told her.'

Frieden smiled, signalling for the menu. He frowned, slightly, when Muntz indicated another drink.

'It was a wise precaution, all those years ago, offering her a job,' said the property-speculator.

Muntz grunted.

'You told her we wanted to help Heinrich?' pressed the millionaire.

Muntz sniggered, slightly drunk. 'Of course,' he said.

'How I'll help him,' mused Frieden. 'I'll help him stand while they put the piano wire around his genitals and steady him as he's lifted up against the beams by the overhead pulley ...'

He caught Muntz's eye and they both laughed, savouring the picture.

'It will be good to kill him,' agreed the lawyer.

'What about the woman?' asked Frieden, suddenly.

'Utterly stupid,' judged Muntz. 'She'll be a nuisance, later.'

'So we'll have to kill her, then?'

'Oh yes. After she's served her purpose.'

Frieden gestured to the hovering waiter, anxious to order. His diet had precluded breakfast. He'd have *Schweinebacken* and then, after the pigs' cheeks, wild boar and dumplings. Then *Harzer* with *Ganseschmalz*. He loved the goose fat with that Harz-mountain cheese.

In the apartment in Seelingstrasse, Uri Perez frowned up at the two men who had spent fifteen minutes giving the detailed report on Gerda Pöhl.

'Different?' he queried. 'How different?'

'She left work after only two hours,' reported the first man. 'She went immediately to one of the stores on the Kurfürstendamm and paid 250 marks for a suit. Then she had lunch, with a half-bottle of wine. And then shopped for over an hour. She bought a whole ham and some *Wurst*. And a bottle of brandy and some wine.'

'French,' enlarged the second man.

'And this morning, Gerda Pöhl, née Köllman, was living as a widow on a restricted income,' reflected Uri. He paused, then added, 'Interesting.'

The stories began the following day in the *Jerusalem Post*, *Ma'ariv* and *Yediot Arathnot*, claiming there had been a response to the £1,000,000 reward. Pressed for comment from all foreign news media, official government spokesmen would neither deny nor confirm the reports. Moshe Dayan stoked the speculation by asserting in the Knesset, as an answer to a tabled question from the Likud, the opposition party, that any public discussion would be premature.

Three days later, when every newspaper in the West had front-paged the speculation, there was another Knesset session when the premier was faced with written demands about the progress of the ransom offer.

He repeated Dayan's assertion that public discussion would be harmful and then made a disclosure that fuelled the interest even further.

The approach had emanated from Berlin, he conceded. Yes, the West German authorities had been informed. The box had not, however, been retrieved. The following day, the Foreign Minister flew to New York to defend his country before the United Nations. The Israeli plane arrived two hours after the Soviet Ilyushin had departed for Moscow returning the Soviet scientists from their conference.

Cigarette constantly alight, Vladimir Kurnov read the *New York Times* report of the second Knesset meeting. By his side, Mavetsky wondered if it were his imagination or whether Kurnov was being unusually brusque to everyone's attempts at conversation.

(5)

Kurnov knew Mavetsky was keeping him waiting to prove his importance. The scientist sat irritably in the rambling anteroom to the minister's Kremlin office, purposely avoiding the ashtray and fouling the floor. Already ten cigarette stubs and their ash lay scattered around his feet. Pig, thought the secretary, across the room. She'd make sure the minister knew of the scientist's stupidity. They were all the same, imagining they were indispensable. He'd learn, one day. They always did.

Kurnov stared sightlessly at the opposite wall, trying to stifle the feeling bubbling inside him. It was ridiculous for the nerves to surface so soon. Nervous men made mistakes. And he couldn't afford mistakes, now least of all. He was, he realized, facing the greatest danger since the collapse of the Third Reich. Perhaps greater. In 1945, he'd made his escape-plans carefully and, even though he had so foolishly panicked, they had proven virtually foolproof. But now he was improvising. A man who regarded preparation and attention to details as important, it offended him to approach anything without a rehearsed scheme that had been examined for every flaw.

In an attempt to control the fear, he tried to rationalize what had happened and chart new escape-routes. There'd been scares before, of course, certainly after the Nuremberg trials and then, much later, when the Israelis had snatched Eichmann. He halted the reassurance, realistically. What had happened after

Nuremberg and Eichmann had never been any danger. To imagine they were was an attempt at self-flattery proving to himself how clever he had been in his precautions all those years ago. This time it was different. The one mistake he had ever made was no longer at the bottom of Lake Toplitz. Just one mistake ... one stupid, infantile error that now he could hardly believe he had been capable of allowing to happen. However had he overlooked that damned German mentality for records and documentation? Everything had been destroyed, he had thought. Everything. And then he had remembered the file in the documentation centre in Berlin, and realized that some nameless clerk throughout the years would have recorded against the name of Heinrich Köllman all the research and experiments that he had done for the Third Reich, together with the personal congratulations from the Führer that had led to all the honours and the favoured treatment.

What a drive it had been on that May morning in 1945 through the Russian bombardment of the capital, he recalled. Like rats, the Germans had been scuttling to escape, running in all directions instead of banding together, as the Führer had demanded. There was no jar in that thought against his own behaviour. It was right for the country's leaders to take precautions for their safety. The people should have obeyed the instructions, regardless of the cost. Twice men had actually tried to stop his car, to steal it. He'd shot them both. He smiled at the memory, then immediately became serious again, reliving that feeling of helplessness as he had stood in the deserted headquarters, scattered with discarded S.S. uniforms and stared at the ransacked cabinets, drawers jerked out like half-pulled teeth, and realized the one file that could mean his destruction was missing.

Too late he had learned of the retreat to Bad Aussee. And that in the bleak, cold lake had been dumped the records containing his fingerprints, the one thing that could positively identify him in the Soviet Union with the personal file, containing the matching prints, that had been created since he had achieved such stature.

Then the mistakes began to multiply.

The Nazis began to pursue him, knowing how much he had put into his own Swiss account, to pay for plastic surgery. The fortune was amassed from his victims in the camps, but they regarded it as theirs. They would have killed him, he had known. Painfully. And so for the first time in his life he had moved without proper consideration. He could have escaped them. He knew that now. But shocked by the collapse of Germany, still in pain from the operation and frightened of becoming a victim of men whose ability to inflict pain he had perfected, he had congratulated himself that his new identity was probably more acceptable anyway to the East than to the West, and fled. Behind the Iron Curtain. He screwed around, gazing from the window, watching the snow building up on the Moscow roofs opposite. That, he decided, greeting the familiar regret, was the worst mistake he had ever made. So it was important not to panic again.

Thank God, he thought, he had left one lifeline for himself in the West. 'Always leave an escape-route.' Who had said that? Kaltenbrunner? — no, not him. The fool actually believed they would regroup in Bad Aussee and fight again. Who then? Bormann. That was it, Martin Bormann, who had always advised so cleverly against personal publicity, using his power without the need for the self-adulation that all the others possessed. A clever man, Martin. What a cruel quirk of fate that he should have died so quickly, in the filth of a railway yard.

How secure was his escape-route? he wondered. It had been thirty years, without any contact. The only man who knew his secret had plenty of reasons for still helping, he reasoned, searching for hope. For thirty years the man had had access to a fortune of over £1,000,000.

Over the years, interest would have increased that amount by at least three times.

What if the man had died? He felt the sweat form in the hollow of his back at the sudden doubt. It could easily have happened, he decided.

Why the hell did those bloody yids need to start probing that lake?

'Ficken,' he said, softly.

'Comrade?'

'Nothing,' replied Kurnov, his Russian fluent. 'Just day-dreaming.'

The buzzer on the desk sounded and she nodded to the scientist.

Mavetsky stood as Kurnov entered, smiling broadly. The minister's policy for survival was to establish apparent friendship with everyone who might matter. Kurnov was such a person, and he troubled the minister. They should have been friends, spending time together socially. But the scientist had consistently rejected the overtures, always erecting a barrier. Others called it arrogance, but Mavetsky was unconvinced.

'Vladimir! Good to see you. Sorry I had to keep you waiting ...'

He paused, selecting a familiar pose.

'... It isn't an easy life, being a minister, you know '

Usually that was greeted with a sympathetic smile, but Kurnov remained impassive. He should have known better, Mavetsky told himself. He nodded towards the inlaid cigarette-box on the desk and Kurnov accepted the invitation, still not speaking.

'I thought America was very useful,' continued the minister, enthusiastically. The openly embraced ideas and opportunities already proven acceptable, was another survival ploy.

'Very,' agreed Kurnov. The meeting would be recorded, he knew. Mavetsky was a cautious man.

'Did you learn much from the Americans of their human stress research?'

Kurnov shook his head. 'We're far more advanced than they are,' he asserted.

Mavetsky sniggered. 'Well, we have, shall we say, better facilities than the Americans for your particular form of research. Our experiments can be more complete.'

Kurnov stared at him, staying silent.

'Have you been down to the camps at Potma recently?' dangerously enlarged Mavetsky, realizing his mistake and needing a comment from the other man. Mavetsky was a fool, decided Kurnov. The minister knew precisely what his movements were, so the question was pointless. It was a juvenile attempt to cover himself on tape.

'The Americans had some interesting theories, though,' he sidestepped.

Mavetsky shrugged. Despite Kurnov's suspicions, there had been no initial malice in the question about the Potma labour-camp. It had occurred to him spontaneously to see how mentally alert Kurnov was, and he had thrown the query out unthinkingly. Which had been stupid. It didn't do to be shown to be a person who discussed such things so easily.

'Will you accept the invitation to be at Houston for the link-up?' asked Kurnov. He knew that would be the point of his summons before the minister.

'I don't know. What do you think?'

'I'd like to go,' said Kurnov, consciously attempting to sound casual. 'The Houston communications are good. Electronically, they've established a good investigation pattern. I shall be able to get instant voiceprints for each day's conversation, to enable immediate testing for any tension. One of their astronauts is a trained doctor. He'll be conducting electroencephalographs and cardiac readings in flight for transmission to Houston ...'

Kurnov cut off, abruptly. He'd already submitted a

48

lengthy memorandum to the minister, containing all the points. There was a danger in over-stressing the advantages.

'You seem very *keen*,' said the minister.

Kurnov felt a lurch. The face stayed expressionless, of course. Often Kurnov had reflected on the advantages of having had such complete plastic surgery. There had been some small nerves carelessly destroyed, which had worried him at first. Even now, he realized, it might create some slight deformity as he got very old, but at the moment he looked far younger than his fifty-nine years, and enjoyed being able to hide any emotion. Long ago he had learned how unsettling people found it.

'I've always been enthusiastic about my work,' he said, easily.

Mavetsky was anxious to recover from the earlier blunder.

'Surely our own communications are equal to those of the Americans?'

'Unquestionably,' agreed Kurnov, anticipating the other man's reaction. 'All the more reason for my going to America. I know exactly the detail that will be available here. But we can't be sure what will go into Houston, unless I'm there, ensuring they can't conceal anything. If I have their complete records to compare against those we take at Baikonur, my part of the research will be guaranteed.'

It was unarguable logic, realized Mavetsky. Kurnov was manipulating him, he decided, angrily.

'They will expect to have someone here, for the same reason,' threw back the minister.

'Undoubtedly,' agreed Kurnov again. 'That's part of the agreement, anyway. But I've met every one of their team. Only two speak Russian and then so badly it is almost laughable. For most of the time in any control centre, they won't understand what is happening.'

Kurnov *had* prepared himself well, conceded Mavetsky. He was a very formidable man.

'One is inclined to forget how fluent you are in so many languages,' said Mavetsky, carelessly.

'One should never overlook something to their advantage,' returned the smoothfaced man and the minister frowned. On a recording, what had been a remark of some sarcasm would appear naïve.

'Obviously you should go then,' said Mavetsky, tightly.

It had been stupid to jump so quickly, realized Kurnov. He was approaching the most difficult part of the interview and now the other man was antagonized. Perhaps one day, he thought, accepting the psychological failing, he'd be able to control the need to prove himself constantly superior to everyone.

'I thought I might be able to encompass several things on one trip,' he said. To attempt a casual tone would only have alerted the other man, so he didn't bother.

Mavetsky looked up, like an animal sniffing the wind to detect danger.

'Like what?' he said, cautiously.

It was time to make concessions, decided Kurnov. He wondered if he could disarm the other man.

'There have been one or two things I've found curious in the last few months, during my visits to Potma,' he said.

Mavetsky just avoided the smile of satisfaction. The tape wouldn't be damaging now.

'Curious?' he probed.

'Just odd, inexplicable behaviour, from men finally realizing their lives have ended, even though their bodies continue to function. I felt it might translate to the effect upon a cosmonaut if his craft malfunctioned and he realized there was no way of rescue, although there was the support system to enable life to continue in space for a period of time.'

How had that idea occurred to him? wondered Kurnov. Suddenly he remembered. That bumptious NASA director had asked him whether Russians could survive with such knowledge. He had assured the man they could, he recalled. He hoped the American hadn't continued the discussion with Mavetsky.

It sounded plausible, determined the minister, but he felt Kurnov was floundering. This recording should be put to one side, with the others selected for easy reference if the need arose.

'I can't quite see ...?' Mavetsky encouraged.

'There's a world-wide conference of prison psychiatrists and doctors, a fortnight before the space launch. We've got accreditation, but the party still isn't finally chosen ...'

'And you want to go?' asked Mavetsky. Why? he wondered.

'It might be interesting,' said Kurnov. 'The public sessions probably will be very dull. They usually are. But the benefits will come from private conversations and contacts.'

The hope was just detectable in the man's voice, thought Mavetsky. He was concentrating fully now. Something was wrong, very wrong. He would have to be careful. There might be difficulty from association.

'Strange you've never thought such conferences worth attending before,' said Mavetsky, gently. It would be wrong to frighten the man too soon.

'I haven't encountered the Potma manifestation before,' replied Kurnov. 'Other countries may have done and conducted some research into it. If they have, I'd like to read their papers.'

He's suspicious, he thought, worriedly. It had been stupid to annoy him earlier. The man's vanity was malleable. It would have been so easy to have flattered him and smothered the doubt he was now feeling.

'I really think there would be benefit from attending,'

he said. He was annoyed at the need to speak again. It put him at a disadvantage.

'I don't *doubt* your sincerity,' assured Mavetsky. Never before had he felt Kurnov to be so obviously discomforted. The minister was enjoying the encounter.

'Where is this conference?' demanded Mavetsky.

Kurnov didn't reply immediately, which was a tactical error. God, how badly he'd handled the entire interview, he thought. He wondered if Mavetsky's suspicions could be dangerous. Probably, he conceded. The man was a survivor. People like him remained because they were able to anticipate difficulties.

'Berlin,' he announced, simply.

Mavetsky stared at him, his face quite blank. He let the silence build up, knowing it would unsettle further the other man. He was reacting as Kurnov would in similar circumstances, Mavetsky decided. Any further discussion would be wrong. Mavetsky knew he had to end the winner.

'Right,' he concluded, dismissively. 'Send me a full note ...'

He hesitated, allowing the doubt, knowing the effect it would have upon Kurnov.

'... You know how it is, this mania for bureaucratic records. We'll discuss it finally next week.'

'I really think ...' the scientist tried to enforce again, with just too much hope. Mavetsky raised his hands, cutting him off, then made an officious point of consulting his appointment-book, as if Kurnov were overstaying his time. He changed the halting gesture into an open-palmed movement of helplessness.

'... Like I said earlier ... I've a busy life ...'

Kurnov rose, anger knotted within him. Bastard, he thought. Like a randy dog sniffing lamp-posts for the scent of a bitch in season, Mavetsky believed he could detect an odour to pursue. Kurnov was sure of it. That persistent bubble of fear rose within him.

'Thank you for sparing me the time, minister,' he said, formally. Humility choked him, like a piece of meat badly chewed.

'Any time. You know that, Vladimir.'

For a long time after Kurnov had left, Mavetsky sat, staring unseeingly ahead. He felt like an algebra student abandoned by a teacher in mid-course: all the signs were available, but he didn't know how to arrange them into a formula that would produce a solution. Assessed against Kurnov's known history, Berlin had to be the key, he decided. On impulse, he summoned the fastidious secretary and demanded Kurnov's file. It was returned within thirty minutes, rimmed with dust from the cabinet in which it had lain for so long. He unclipped the spiral holding the pages into position and spread them over the desk, creating a montage from which he hoped to spot the piece that made it incomplete. Before adopting Russian nationality, he read, Kurnov's name had been Klaus Reinhart. A graduate from the Berlin Medical School in 1938, he had been jailed in 1939 for organizing junior doctors against joining the Nazi party. Freed because of the war, he had been rejected as psychologically unsuitable for medical service on any front, instead serving in four prisoner-of-war camps. There were frequent references to operations he had performed repairing the damage caused by the S.S. butchers to extract information from inmates. And numerous commendations from the Red Cross about his work, often carried out in defiance of official Nazi orders. There was even a copy of an S.S. order committing him to Buchenwald concentration camp for the treatment he had given Russian prisoners. Luckily, the war had ended before that order could be put into effect.

He was, noted the minister, a native of Berlin. So what? That didn't give any clue for wanting to return to the city for the conference. Mavetsky turned the page, studying Kurnov's picture. Odd how little the man had aged, he thought in passing. He flicked without interest through the fingerprint file, then read the impressive list of Kurnov's achievements since his decision to settle in the Soviet Union. The minister pushed the file to one side and swivelled to look out over the capital. It was already quite dark, but the whiteness of the snow reflected what little light was left, giving the buildings an unreal glow. There was no clue in the file, he decided. Kurnov was unquestionably an anti-Nazi, properly recognized as a war hero whose work had subsequently proven invaluable to the Soviet Union, so properly earning all the honours and awards accorded him.

There was still something wrong in today's request. He was convinced of it. He went back to the file, shuffling it like a losing card-sharp desperately trying to locate an ace.

The space programme was classified as top secret, Mavetsky knew. Therefore there would have been a detailed investigation into the man's background before he was allowed to become part of it. Accustomed to bulky, exhaustive character-documentation, the minister was surprised at the brevity of Kurnov's personal records. Several times it was noted that data confirming the information supplied were unavailable because all records had been destroyed by the blitz upon Berlin or were thought to be held by one of the other three occupying powers. Nearly all the information, Mavetsky realized, was that supplied either directly or inadvertently by the man himself. Unusual, decided the minister. Although well aware of the chaos and destruction of those last days in Berlin, he would have expected some corroborative evidence to have been available.

There were ten affidavits, he saw, from Russian prisoners, who had been interviewed in rehabilitation hospitals, attesting to Reinhart's treatment of them, often in open contradiction to the known instructions from superior officers. A brave man, thought the minister. Would Kurnov defy authority? he wondered. Of course he would, he answered himself, immediately. He did it practically all the time. He paused, reconsidering the thought. Although not so certain as the other critics, Mavetsky had always thought the man's defiance based upon arrogance, not principles. He found himself unsure whether Kurnov would flout a directive merely from conscience.

He stared down at the papers strewn over the desk. There was no answer there, he decided.

The pages were numbered and he began collating them in order to replace them upon the spiral. He stopped, staring down at Kurnov's picture. A brave man, he reflected, someone who knowingly faced death in a concentration camp rather than sacrifice the lives under his care. He looked away from the picture, back across the room, remembering the man's remarks about Potma. Kurnov's principles about human suffering had altered dramatically in thirty years, he realized suddenly. What he had not been prepared to accept in the extremity of war he was now able not only to countenance but participate in during peacetime. It was the jarring illogicality from the entire file. He read again the affidavits from the survivors. 'Compassionate,' said one. 'Humane,' asserted another. 'Selfless disregard for personal safety,' listed a third. Never, thought Mavetsky, would he have chosen such words to describe the man who had sat before him an hour earlier. He started again replacing the affidavits, re-sealing the box, then sat back, forming a tower with his fingertips, parading the thoughts before him. An inadequate file, certainly. But not unusual in the circumstances.

A character now that did not reconcile completely with the prisoners' accounts of the man who had treated them over thirty years ago. Too flimsy to permit an official investigation, dismissed the minister.

An abhorrence of human suffering apparently now completely overcome. Coupled to the other disparities, an inexplicable change. By itself? — he considered the question, objectively. Kurnov was undoubtedly imbued with a Russian pride, elevated to a position of honour and stature, well aware his privileges were linked with the continuing progress of Soviet space exploration. Was it surprising, then, that a humble prison-camp doctor had been able to temper his morality? Of course not.

And that's all there was, realized Mavetsky. The only sufferer from any investigation, no matter how circumspect, would be himself, decided the minister. Irritably, he summoned the woman from the outer office and handed her the file.

Remembering the cigarette litter in front of her desk, she said hopefully, 'What shall I do with it?'

Mavetsky looked up.

'Put it back,' he said, simply.

'Downstairs? In records?' she pressed.

'Of course. Where else?' said the minister.

The woman walked from the room, disappointed. Mavetsky watched her leave. It was ridiculous, he thought, angrily. He'd wasted nearly two hours, just because he'd allowed one man's attitude to annoy him into believing an ordinary request had some ulterior reason.

That was dangerous. There were enough real problems, without those of his own creation. Within ten minutes, he had dismissed Kurnov and the request to visit Berlin from his mind.

(6)

It had been a good life, decided Helmut Bock, greeting the recurring thought. Although psychiatry was not the predominant feature of his medical practice, he recognized the nostalgia as a need for constant reassurance. Which was hardly surprising, he consoled himself. Considering the disaster that could have overtaken him, particularly in the latter days with his plastic surgery experimentation at Buchenwald, such a complete escape was little short of a miracle. He smiled to himself, in the half-light of the early-morning. How worried he had been, he remembered, at being adopted so avidly by Heinrich Köllman. It had been obvious by then to anyone with a minimum of intelligence that the war was lost and that survival was the only consideration. So association with Köllman, whose record was worse even than that of Mengele, could have been ranked as suicide. But although inevitable, the collapse of the Third Reich was too far away for him to resist openly the friendship of someone still so powerful, and he had allowed himself to be cultivated, not realizing initially that Köllman was already preparing his escape.

It hadn't taken long, though, thought Bock, a conceited man who over-rated his intelligence. And, once realized, what had been more sensible than modifying the method that Köllman had been perfecting for several years? But he still *had* been lucky, he reflected, honestly.

By his side the woman turned, erupting into a bubbly snore. He looked at her, distastefully, then lowered the covering from her breasts, very carefully, so she would not awaken. They sprouted, firm and unsagging, generous mountains in the moonlight that came in from the uncurtained windows. There was no sexual feeling. It had been a good job, he congratulated himself. Her breasts would remain firm for at least fifteen years. And her stomach and buttocks, too, no matter how careless she was about her diet. She would, he decided, continue to be the sex symbol of the international movie circuit. No wonder she had been so grateful. He smiled at the memory. She stirred and he covered her, gently. If she awoke, she would imagine he wanted sex, and he felt drained by what had happened earlier.

Yes, he decided, regressing again, he had definitely been lucky. He hadn't realized, not until he was operating upon the former S.S. colonel only two rooms away from the recovering Köllman, that the Nazis were pursuing his benefactor for embezzling over £1,000,000 from his concentration-camp victims. How sad it had been, he reflected, giggling, that the colonel had never recovered from his operation, having imparted the information. And how easy it had been to convince the nervous, over-reactive concentration-camp experimenter that the survivors of the S.S. were within days of capturing him.

The light grew stronger, and gently, still anxious to avoid disturbing the woman, he sidled from the bed and stood just inside the penthouse veranda, gazing out over the still-slumbering Berlin.

It had all happened so quickly. In June he had been terrified of capture and arraignment as a war criminal who deserved the death penalty that the others had got at Nuremberg. By September, he was a man with a different identity supplied by Köllman's forger. He had a new face created by the man who had assisted in the operation upon Köllman (and then had to die because of his knowledge). And was also a millionaire with a fortune securely hidden in Switzerland because Köllman had panicked and fled to the East.

Köllman had recovered well from that incredible mistake, decided Bock. A man still very aware of the dangers from the past, the plastic surgeon had followed avidly the details available of Kurnov's success in Russia, even keeping a picture scrapbook of the face he had so carefully sculpted from the model provided. Poor Reinhart. The idiot had still imagined he was to continue helping people when he had arrived at Bock's makeshift clinic. Bock could still recall that last-minute look of shocked realization as they had rendered him unconscious.

What had happened at Lake Toplitz was unsettling, he thought. More and more he had been dwelling in the past, since the news of the assassinations and the missing container had been occupying the newspapers and television screens. The Jewish premier's assertion that someone in Berlin was offering the secrets for sale added to the worry. Did anything incriminating lie in the lake? he wondered. He was sure he was safe, personally. The records officer at Buchenwald had been a heroin addict, and Bock had carefully supplied his need, creating a dependence to ensure that when the collapse came, every single document referring to him had been incinerated in the very ovens that had so recently destroyed other evidence. No, Bock assured himself, confidently, he was quite safe from any investigation. A hunt for the Toplitz documents would get nowhere, anyway, he concluded, attempting to reinforce his confidence. The Jews would never be able to buy the records if they were for sale. The Nazi funds were incredible. He paused at the comforting thought, remembering the bank-statement of the previous week. Poor Köllman, he sympathized, existing in the austerity of the Soviet Union, unaware that his carefully garnered fortune had increased to over £3,000,000 in thirty years.

Bock smiled in self-satisfaction, looking back towards the sleeping actress. He'd had no need to touch the capital for almost twenty-five years, since he'd become recognized as one of the world's leading cosmetic plastic surgeons. Payment in kind was always a bonus, but the patients paid in the ordinary way, as well. God, how they paid. The woman stirred. She'd awaken soon, decided Bock. He went into the bathroom, adjusting the shower control to 'water massage'. She really had been extraordinarily inventive, he decided, feeling the needles of water bite into him, bringing his flesh alive. She'd have to be gone by the weekend, though. There was arriving from Buenos Aires an Argentinian woman with the most spectacular breasts he had ever examined. He couldn't understand why she wanted them reduced. Amazing, he thought, what women were prepared to do to remain beautiful.

'Hello,' she said, looking up at him as he returned to the bedside. 'I thought you had deserted me.'

'What a silly idea,' he said, pulling back the covering. Perhaps another quarter of an inch off her stomach, he speculated, professionally. It was a debatable point. Her husband had seemed satisfied, two days earlier.

She smiled, misinterpreting the examination.

'Are you sure I'm the only one who's undergone plastic surgury?' she said, coquettishly, looking at his nakedness.

Crude cow, he thought, straddling her waist.

'I'd hate you to get a stiff neck,' he said, joining in the charade.

'Never.'

Bock wondered if he could stand her for the remainder of the week. Below him, she groaned. He should definitely have taken that quarter-inch off her waist, he thought.

Three miles away, in the apartment on Seelingstrasse, Mosbacher awakened and lay tense for a moment, in that state of immediate awareness to which he had been trained. Sure of his surroundings, he relaxed, turning to look at the twin-bed four feet from him.

Perez slept fitfully. Several times he whimpered, muttering dissociated words, then relapsed into unsettled sleep again. Would he last? wondered Mosbacher. The strain upon him was tremendous. Superhuman, even, particularly considering his personal history. Should he even now inform Jerusalem of his doubt? he questioned. Immediately he rejected the idea, without deeper consideration. It could serve no purpose. They wouldn't abort the mission merely on his fears. And Perez was too used to convincing them, better able to argue and convince other people. With leading politicians and statesmen, Mosbacher was always uncertain, words clogging in his mouth. Any belated objection he put up would be almost flippantly dismissed, he knew. They were committed. And there was no way for the mission to go on without Perez.

The man sighed softly, so as not to disturb his friend. What a shitty business they were in, he thought. Was it necessary to pursue the Nazis after so long? he wondered, raising again the doubt that had begun the break with Perez. Of course it was, he decided. Too many had survived to hold high office in the new Germany. It was the method of the scheme that offended him.

He looked again at the sleeping figure of Perez. But they should choose with more care, he thought. He tempered the doubt. It was too easy for him, a bachelor whose parents had died in Dachau, a man with no home but an apartment in which he sheltered during the night. Perez was married and, a month before, his wife had had a child that the man had not yet been allowed to see. How simple it would be, if it were possible to select a revenge-unit of unattached, totally committed men whose deaths, if they failed, would be mourned by no one. He should have made the sacrifice, instead of Perez, thought Mosbacher. He smiled at the stupidity.

How could he have done it? Perez was ideal because of his stature and because of that very history which at the same time made him unreliable. There was no way Mosbacher or anyone else could have replaced him. Knowing sleep would not return, he got up from the bed and went to the window, staring out over the city. Directly in line, but not visible, was the penthouse apartment in which Bock was at that moment moaning, half in pleasure, half in discomfort, above the film star.

It really began tomorrow, thought Mosbacher. He corrected himself, looking at his watch. Not tomorrow. Today. How fortunate it had been, he remembered, that Bock chose to sleep with every attractive female patient. She had been a brave Jewess, he decided, to report that tell-tale scar beneath the left arm, indicating the removal of the tattooed S.S. number. The Mossad had spent a lot of money paying for two more women to undergo treatment and seduction to establish the suspicions of the first genuine patient. But never, when they started to intercept his letters through the bribed sorter at Berlin's Central Post Office, had the Mossad imagined they would discover that one of the most renowned plastic surgeons in the world had learned his craft under another name on unanaesthetized patients at Buchenwald. And more important still, they learnt that he had apparent control of Heinrich Köllman's Swiss bank-account, the most decisive clue that the scientist was still alive and in hiding.

Mosbacher went to the table, flicking through the photostat of the account-records that had arrived five days ago *en route* to the surgeon. Over £3,000,000. He wondered how Bock had gained control. It didn't matter. It was certainly enough to buy back embarrassing secrets being held to ransom. The Nazis would have even more, he knew.

He was aware that Perez was awake, watching him.

'It'll be a fine day,' he said, looking out over the city.

'It starts today,' said Perez, dully.

'Yes.'

'Nervous?'

'Yes.'

'Of what — failure? Or getting hurt?'

What answer did the young man want? conjectured Mosbacher. Surely Perez wasn't frightened of being injured. They'd been too well trained for that.

'Both, I suppose,' he replied.

'Do you know what I thought about, yesterday?' asked the younger man.

Mosbacher turned from the window. Perez was lying, hands locked behind his head, gazing at the ceiling.

'No,' he said.

'I was thinking of my son. I looked at the picture that Rachel sent me and I thought that my father must have felt like I did then, when he saw me for the first time. And when he saw my sister. And then I thought of what happened in Buchenwald.'

Let him talk, decided Mosbacher. It was probably useful therapy.

'Can you imagine what it's like, forced to watch children that you've created and the mother who gave birth to them, subjected, day after day, to experiments to establish their degree of physical survival? And your level of mental tolerance?'

He was crying, Mosbacher saw.

'No,' he said. 'I don't think anyone can imagine that.'

'He did it,' said Perez, distantly. 'Köllman did it.'

'I know, Uri,' said Mosbacher, softly. 'They all committed crimes it's difficult to comprehend.'

'We might fail,' said the man, with unexpected pessimism. He turned on his side, so he could look across the room. 'Have you thought about that?'

'Of course,' said Mosbacher.

Neither spoke for several minutes. Then Perez said: 'If we fail ... if there's no reaction, I mean, then I'm going to make them suffer. I'm going to kill every Nazi we can locate ... I'm going to do it, Arron. I'm going to kill them all ...'

He was serious, realized Mosbacher. He would have to act immediately, if things went wrong. An injection would be the best way if he could accomplish it, rendering Uri unconscious until they got him back to Israel. Whatever method he chose, he would have to stop Perez doing something that would get him jailed. Or killed. Uri had suffered enough. And he hadn't seen his son, either.

At least the time-wasting of lunchtime diplomatic receptions could be limited, thought Mavetsky. One could always plead work waiting back at the office and escape after an hour. He accepted the need to attend, of course, now that Russia was pursuing its *détente* with the West, but he always felt vaguely uncomfortable in such crowded conditions. He liked small gatherings, where he was able to observe people, assessing their attitudes and behaviour. At receptions, he always had an unavoidable suspicion that he was being studied and reported upon. Often he looked back with regret to the Stalinist era, when the approval of the outside world was so disdained. Now it seemed the Politburo would hardly move without first considering the reaction of Washington, London or Bonn.

He saw the American ambassador moving towards him and fixed a smile of greeting. Since the space co-operation programme, both sides were going to extreme lengths to prove their friendliness.

'Good party,' opened the American.

'Yes,' agreed Mavetsky.

'I hear you've decided to go to Houston for the launch.'

Mavetsky nodded. 'I thought it would be interesting to view it from the other side,' he said. He took a drink from a passing tray.

'Our people are looking forward to coming here,' assured the American.

Diplomatic small talk was boring, decided Mavetsky.

'There will be a reception for them,' he promised the diplomat. 'We are looking forward to the exchange.'

The American sighed, as bored as the other man.

'The West Germans aren't here,' he said, looking around the room. Since Brandt's policy of *Ostpolitik* had enabled the opening of a West German embassy in Moscow, it occupants had attended every conceivable diplomatic function, anxious to establish contacts.

'No,' agreed Mavetsky, disinterested.

'Wonder if it's anything to do with this Berlin business,' gossiped the other man.

Mavetsky felt like a traveller attracted to a safe path by the summoning of a distant bell.

'What Berlin business?' he asked.

The ambassador looked directly at the minister. Surely he knew about the Israeli announcement.

'The Lake Toplitz affair,' enlarged the ambassador. 'Jerusalem has disclosed an approach from someone purporting to have the missing ammunition box. It could contain enough Nazi records to start a whole new witch-hunt.'

'Yes?' prompted Mavetsky.

'Apparently the contact was made in Berlin,' went on the American. 'Wasn't that ironic?'

The Russian nodded. His stomach felt hollow. Suddenly there was a wave of nausea and he swallowed. Kurnov had hardly talked on the flight home from America, he recalled, hunched over the same page in the *New York Times* recounting the Israeli press conference that had followed the commando raid into Austria.

'I bet there's a few nervous men in Berlin today,' speculated the American.

'Yes,' agreed the minister. 'I'm sure there will be.'

The waiter returned and paused expectantly. Mavetsky replaced his empty glass, but did not take another. He made a show of consulting his watch.

'Forgive me,' he excused himself. 'A busy afternoon ...'

He almost ran into his Kremlin office, startling the secretary who hadn't expected his return for another hour, yelling as he passed for a transcript of the overlooked Israeli announcement and for Kurnov's file. For thirty minutes, he studied the folder he had examined a week earlier and again reached the same conclusion. There was nothing, absolutely nothing, that prompted investigation. He read what had been said in the Jewish parliament, tapping it with his finger, then pushed it away, the conviction growing within him. He had survived Stalin and Khrushchev to reach his present position, he remembered. Several times he had faced purges and on every occasion he had avoided disaster by reacting upon instinct and anticipating any investigation. Had he waited then for positive evidence, as he was doing now like some junior, inexperienced clerk, he would have long ago been incarcerated in a labour camp. The Knesset declaration was the link, he determined. He consulted his desk diary, then double-checked by telephoning the Academy of Science. Kurnov had departed for Berlin an hour before.

Impatiently, Mavetsky jiggled the telephone rest, clearing the line. When the bewildered secretary replied, he demanded an immediate connection to the commanding officer of the Russian contingent forming part of the Four-Power presence in Berlin. As he sat, waiting for the call to arrive, he saw his hands were shaking.

He'd have to be very careful, he decided. If he were wrong, it could result in the purge he had always managed to avoid. The telephone rang, but he hesitated before answering it, staring at the button that would automatically record the conversation. Would it ever be needed, to produce to the Politburo? There was no way of knowing. Determinedly he pressed the record mechanism and picked up the receiver.

(7)

Bock felt very tired. It was fortunate, he thought, there was only one small operation planned for that afternoon. Afterwards he would spend an hour in the sauna, he decided, and then at least another hour on the massage couch. He was too old for such sexual athletics, he thought, ruefully. The door opened and Bock looked up, irritably, at the woman he'd instructed not to disturb him. She was a plump, matronly woman, chosen precisely for her lack of sexual attractiveness. She was, however, a remarkably efficient personal secretary.

'What?' he demanded, rudely.

'There's a telephone call ...' she started, but he cut her off, exasperated.

'In God's name,' he shouted. 'I told you no calls ... no interruptions. Don't you realize I'm unwell?'

She looked at him, unconcerned.

'I told him that,' she replied. 'But he is incredibly persistent. It took him fifteen minutes to persuade the switchboard to put him through to me. He keeps saying that if he's kept from speaking to you, we'll all be dismissed when you eventually discover what we've done.'

'I don't want to know anything about it,' dismissed Bock. 'You handle it.'

He turned away, expecting the woman to leave. Pain swelled in his head and his groin ached. He wondered what excuse he could make that night.

'I said you never took personal calls ... that everything was arranged through junior doctors and assistants ...' continued the woman, remaining where she was.

He swung back, tight-faced with anger.

'... He told me to mention the name Hugo Becker,' the woman hurried on. 'Do we know anyone called Hugo Becker?'

Bock stared at her, slack-mouthed. A numbness spread over him, like one of the anaesthetics that render unconsciousness without the distress of the old-fashioned face-mask. Realizing how he must look to the woman, he brought both hands up, cupping his chin, trying to cover his face. The secretary looked at him, worriedly. She hadn't believed him that morning when he had complained of being ill. He certainly looked it now. It was hardly surprising. He worked so hard.

'I'm sorry,' she said, belatedly, accepting her mistake. 'I'll get rid of him ...'

'No!'

He'd shouted, Bock realized, embarrassed. It had been over thirty years since he had heard the name with which he had been christened.

'No,' he repeated, quieter this time. He breathed deeply, trying to regain control.

'I'll take the call.'

The woman looked at him, uncertainly. 'Are you sure ...?'

'I said I'd take it!' He'd shouted again.

She went from the room, frowning. Within seconds, the light on the telephone console glowed and he reached for the receiver, holding it delicately, as if it might burn. He put it to his ear, but said nothing. There was silence for several seconds and then a voice said, inquiringly, 'Hello?'

It was guttural German, recognized Bock. Bavarian, perhaps.

'Yes,' he said. His own voice was thin and strained.

'Who is this?' demanded the caller.

'Bock,' identified the surgeon. 'Helmut Bock.'

There was a laugh.

'Really?' queried the voice.

'Who are you?' demanded Bock, his voice growing stronger. 'I ...'

'... Be quiet.' said the caller and Bock stopped talking.

'You've feared this call, Dr Becker, haven't you? Ever since 1945, you've been frightened that one day the real identity of the famous Dr Bock would be discovered.'

The surgeon hunched over his desk, feeling numbness edge over him again.

'And now it's happened, Dr Becker. Now it's happened.'

The caller used the name like an obscenity, almost spitting it out.

'I know you're Dr Becker,' insisted the voice. 'I know all about what you did in Buchenwald. And I know something else. I know how close you were to Köllman. Won't that be embarrassing when the details of the Toplitz box get out?'

It *was* a Bavarian accent, decided Bock. He was almost certain of it.

'Tell me who you are,' repeated the surgeon, weakly.

There was another laugh.

'I'm the one who was abandoned, Dr Becker. I'm the one who suffered when the rats ran.'

The surgeon frowned, unable to comprehend what he was being told.

'What do you want?'

'Money, Dr Becker. I want money that's been kept from me for thirty years.'

Köllman? Was it Köllman on the telephone? Hope surged through him. Was that why he had mentioned the name, as a clue?

'Heinrich? Is that you, Heinrich?'

The laugh came again, quite humourless.

'Oh no, Dr Becker. This isn't Köllman. But he's got to come out of hiding, like they all have, hasn't he? We both know that, don't we?'

The surgeon pushed his knuckles into his aching forehead, trying to concentrate upon the thoughts fluttering through his mind like discarded paper blowing in the wind.

'Look. I don't understand ...'

'I don't expect you do,' interrupted the caller. 'It's bound to be a shock, isn't it?'

He'd pay, decided Bock. He had Köllman's money. It would be easy if it were only money. He could pay anything the man wanted.

'Tell me what you want,' he repeated, his mind locked on a single thought.

'Have you realized something?' said the caller, ignoring the question. 'Have you realized what's happened since the yids announced that the Lake Toplitz box was here? Everyone's after it, Dr Becker. Everyone.'

Bock's mouth moved, but the question wouldn't form. He wished the man would stop using his real name.

The voice went on, 'It's going to be an auction. I don't care who gets it. I've contacted the Israeli embassy and got the yids over here in force. The Nazis are after it, ready to pay any money. And you've got to come running, too, haven't you?'

'I ...'

'Shut up, Becker,' said the Bavarian, his voice suddenly harsh. 'I could get you killed. You know that, don't you? And there's only one way you're going to stay alive. And that's by paying to do so. You'd better start raising the money. And quickly ...'

'Let's meet,' urged Bock, quickly. 'We can't talk on the telephone, like this. Tell me how I can meet you ... I can come right away.'

That contemptuous laugh sounded again.

'Oh, you'll come,' said the caller. 'I know you'll come. It'll be fun making you run, Dr Becker ...'

The line went dead. Initially Bock didn't realize that

the receiver had been replaced and then, when it registered, he almost whimpered with frustration. He put down the instrument and sat gazing at it. Oh God, he thought. Oh dear God, please help.

'We've forgotten the doctor,' said Frieden, suddenly. Muntz, sitting opposite the millionaire in the office block in Ludwigsfelderstrasse, jumped at the exclamation. His chest hurt him, very badly. That morning he had started coughing blood again. It was a long time since that had happened. He should get treatment, he knew. Perhaps he would, when this was all over.

'Who?'

'Becker, the plastic surgeon ...' the property man snapped his fingers, impatiently. 'You know ... he calls himself Bock now.'

The lawyer frowned. 'What would he know?'

'Nothing, probably,' agreed Frieden, annoyed at the other man's refusal to accept the point. 'But think it through. It was Bock who performed the operation on Köllman, wasn't it? He treated a lot of important people whose faces might have been embarrassing.'

The fat man fingered his own cheek, remembering. It hadn't been absolutely necessary. But there was a slight risk and he had decided the operation was a sensible precaution. Frieden was seized by the recollection. 'Good God,' he said. 'It was Bock who volunteered the information about Köllman. Don't you remember? It was too late, by several years, to serve any useful purpose. But it was not Bock's fault. He hadn't known we were looking for the man.'

Muntz still looked puzzled.

'Think of it,' encouraged the millionaire. 'That means Bock was the last person in Berlin to have any contact with Köllman.'

'So?'

Frieden looked at Muntz worriedly. The lawyer was

72

obviously very ill, he thought. His mind was refusing to function.

'Think what it means, Manfred,' he coaxed, gently. 'If Köllman comes back to get the records, as we know he must, then who is he going to contact? He won't approach us. He knows what we'd do to him. He won't know where his wife is, but even if he does manage to locate her in some way we haven't considered, we've prepared ourselves ...'

Muntz nodded, with growing awareness.

'... But he's got to have some starting-point. He worked with Bock ... was the man's guardian, almost. It would be natural for him to go to Bock.'

Muntz shrugged, unconvinced.

'But he knows Bock was part of the network ... that he'd have contact with us,' argued the lawyer. 'To approach Bock would be as dangerous as contacting anyone else in the Organisation.'

Frieden considered the objection, then shook his head, rejecting it.

'Bock isn't important in the network any more. Köllman could work that out. He could realize that Bock was useful, once, like the forgers were necessary. But his importance ended within two years of the war when everyone had their new faces. And don't forget their friendship. I know it was a long time ago, but Köllman might try to invoke old associations. That man needs friends more than anything else in the world.'

Muntz gestured, still doubtful.

'For heaven's sake, Manfred,' reinforced Frieden. 'Köllman must start somewhere!'

'It's a possibility that will have to be covered,' admitted the lawyer, coughing into his handkerchief. He looked at it. The bleeding had stopped.

'Can you see Bock?' pleaded the lawyer, 'I feel so bad. I should be in bed.'

It was the strain, decided the millionaire. Muntz was

a weak link in the Organisation now. And they couldn't afford weak links, ever. He would have to summon a meeting soon to discuss a replacement. Poor Manfred.

'Of course,' he agreed.

The call that arrived minutes later completed the plastic surgeon's terror. There had been no contact for over twenty years. That had been the arrangement, for God's sake. Everyone worked to protect each other, but when their particular function was over then the association was forgotten. Hadn't he done his part? In those first years he'd operated practically non-stop. Now this, within three hours of the first call. What did it mean? he wondered. Had they discovered his access to the Zurich bank-account? Frieden had sounded friendly. But then the first approach would be friendly, to avoid alarming him. Before any retribution, he would have to be cajoled along, so they could arrange for him to transfer the fortune to their own accounts. Perhaps it was all an incredible bluff, he considered, suddenly. Had the Nazis been responsible for the first call, to unnerve him, then planned the second approach to take advantage of his fear? It would be a good psychological ploy. It was possible, he conceded. They always had been incredibly devious. The man who'd claimed to have the Toplitz box was unquestionably a German, he decided, remembering the Bavarian intonation. He allowed himself to be reminded of Frieden, exchanged the old code words like children playing a game and agreed to a meeting. It would mean cancelling an operation, he pointed out, sighing. But if it were as essential as the man insisted, then of course he would do it.

He walked aimlessly around the office, awaiting Frieden, considering the escape. He would have to run, he told himself. They obviously knew. He couldn't let them capture him. God, never that. He'd witnessed their treatment of people for lesser crimes than hoarding £3,000,000 which they considered rightfully theirs.

The secretary announced the arrival of the property millionaire, who waddled in almost immediately behind her. He smiled a greeting, then waited until she had left, ensuring the door was securely closed. He came further into the room, then abruptly raised his right arm.

'Sieg Heil,' he said.

Bock wanted to laugh. It was a nervous reaction, he knew, but the little man looked so ridiculous standing there with his arm stuck out before him. Surely they didn't still do such things? Bock struggled for control. He'd have to return the salutation, he decided.

'Sieg Heil.'

Frieden smiled broadly, then extended the hand. Bock hesitated, then took it.

'Good to see you after all these years,' said Frieden.

Bock nodded, settling down behind his desk. He'd chosen it for its imposing size and was glad, at that moment. It seemed to form a barrier between them. He remembered operating upon Frieden, perhaps twenty-eight years before. He'd chiselled the nose, he remembered, and brought up the skin already sagging through over-indulgence. He examined the man intently. Well up to standard, he thought, proudly. It had lasted well. No one, comparing an old picture of the S.S. Standartenführer with the person who sat on the other side of the desk, would have asserted they were the same man.

'You were surprised by my call?'

'Very,' agreed the surgeon.

'Hope you weren't alarmed,' said the property developer.

Fear twisted in Bock's stomach. 'Alarmed?' he queried, pleased at the control over his voice. 'Should I have been?'

'No, of course not,' assured the visitor. 'But we've found that when we contact people after so long, it can sometimes create unnecessary fear.'

Bock smiled. He could be in Switzerland by the evening, he realized. It would be easy to transfer the account the following day and be out of Europe within 24 hours. Where would he go? He'd have to avoid South America, he knew. They were far too well established there. Uruguay was practically a German state. Argentina and Paraguay weren't much better. The United States was the obvious choice. There was a fortune to be made there in cosmetic plastic surgery. But he didn't need a fortune, he reflected suddenly. All he needed was safety. America was the obvious choice.

'You said it was urgent,' he prompted, allowing just a tinge of irritation to register. It was very important not to reveal any fear to a man like Frieden. He would be very susceptible to nuance, guessed Bock.

Frieden quickly reviewed the Toplitz raid, the Jerusalem conference and the Israeli announcement that the box was being held in Berlin. Then he virtually repeated the conversation he had had with Muntz a few hours previously, putting forward the guess that Köllman might contact the surgeon. Bock stared at him, wondering if his feigned surprise seemed genuine to the other man.

'But I don't understand,' said Bock, apparently confused. 'I mean, why should Köllman return for the records?'

Frieden frowned and Bock decided he had almost overplayed his bewilderment.

'Come now, doctor. You were there. You know what he did, as well as I do. He's *got* to come back.'

'Of course,' recovered Bock, hoping Frieden would confuse the attitude as being caused by the reminder of an embarrassment over thirty years ago.

'But I still don't see why Köllman should contact me,' he hurried on.

Was everyone retarded, wondered Frieden, angrily. Subduing the annoyance, he patiently repeated the reasoning he had put to Muntz. Bock sat, shielding part of his face with his hands. It was all right, he thought, the excitement bursting through him. They *didn't* know about Köllman's account. All they wanted was Köllman himself. They thought he still controlled his own money. For a moment, he was safe, decided Bock. Immediately his elation collapsed. There still remained the call from the Bavarian.

'So if Köllman approaches me ... and I can't agree with you that he might ... then you want me to call you immediately?'

Frieden nodded. How, he wondered, had such fools managed to be so highly regarded? He passed over the telephone numbers.

'That's all,' he agreed. 'Just arrange to meet him, get some method of identification and then call me. There will be no need for you to have any other involvement. None. Just leave everything else to us.'

He smiled, and Bock felt cold.

Would Köllman contact him? First the Bavarian. Now Frieden, both asserting that Köllman couldn't stay hidden. And they were right, of course. He was annoyed that it hadn't occurred to him earlier. He wouldn't be able to betray Köllman to them, of course. Within minutes of any Nazi interrogation, Köllman would disclose the secret of that hidden money, and then they would be after him with the same determination.

'Good,' he said, standing abruptly. Frieden accepted the dismissal, rising with him.

'It seems quite simple,' continued the surgeon. 'I'll call you the moment I get any strange approaches.'

'Thank you,' said the Nazi. 'I admit the chances of contact are unlikely. But if it happens, I want to punish the traitor.'

'Naturally,' said Bock. After all these years, he thought, they still retained this laughable Nazi mentality about betrayal. They were like children, he

77

decided, remembering the silly jingle of codes on the telephone. They played stupid games in which people got killed.

'What about the box itself?' questioned Bock, as they moved towards the door. 'Won't that be ... ah, annoying if the Jews get hold of it?'

Frieden stopped, nodding agreement. 'We're very worried,' he admitted.

'What can you do?'

Frieden shrugged. 'Very little. We're just hoping for an approach.'

Bock stared at him, critically. 'But how can that happen? Everyone is underground, living with new identities. How would anyone know who to contact?'

'That's the trouble,' conceded the millionaire. He looked at the surgeon. Why not, he thought. The man was committed. There was no danger in his knowing.

'If the Jews got an approach, it must have been made through their embassy,' he said.

Bock looked at him, waiting.

'We've established a telephone tap,' said Frieden. 'We know of every call that goes into the building, from anywhere in Europe. If the yids had already made a deal with whoever's got the box, there would be a lot more activity ... maybe even an announcement. Indications from the first conference were that all they wanted to do was make public the details, so the proper authorities would have to move. There hasn't been any denunciation. So we don't think any deal has been completed yet.'

Bock nodded, slowly. They were remarkably determined, he thought. But then, they had to be.

'We are assured of knowing if another contact is made. The only thing we can't monitor is the diplomatic radio and their Telex link with Jerusalem. But that doesn't matter. The approaches must come on an outside line, so we're covered.'

'What if the police discover something?'

Frieden grinned, surprised at the other man's naïvety.

'I don't think there is any risk of something going through the police department that we won't hear about,' he said.

Bock smiled back. Their implacable determination made his position very dangerous. He would have to be extremely careful.

From a park bench opposite the clinic, Mosbacher saw Frieden leave and noted the time. A photograph would have been taken by someone closer to the building, he knew, for later identification against the file they held on all the known Nazis. They are gathering like animals bunching together in fright against an unseen danger, he thought, as he looked for a taxi to take him back to Seelingstrasse. They must be very worried. It was a comforting thought.

As Mosbacher's car moved off down Mariendorfer-damm, Vladimir Kurnov was disembarking at Tempel-hof airport from the K.L.M. airliner that had brought him from Moscow.

It was, he thought, a miserable airport. He'd known better railway stations. Far better. He stared around, almost angrily. Had the Führer achieved his ambitions, it would have been different. Speer would have probably designed it, he thought. Then it would have been magnificent, with colonnades and parade areas.

He stood apart from the Soviet party, disdainful of the greeting, staring through the windows towards the city.

Out there, he knew, in the Berlin he had fled thirty years before, were the Israeli secret service, the West German police and the Nazis. All, for varying reasons, would make any sacrifice to know he was in the city.

He was unaware, of course, of the telephone call from Mavetsky, which meant a Russian colonel was at that moment manœuvring an invitation for himself to the official conference reception that evening.

Kurnov shivered, looking at the snow banked up around the arrival building. It was very cold, he thought.

(8)

It was exhilarating to be back, decided Kurnov. He stood in his hotel bedroom, looking out over the Bismarckstrasse, trying to identify landmarks. The majority would be behind the Wall, of course. The Brandenburg gate ... the Reichstag ruins ... the Führer's Bunker, even. He'd heard the East Germans had tried to prevent it becoming a martyr's monument. They'd used hundreds of tons of explosives. And failed to level the ground beneath which it was constructed. He smiled. It was stupid to have tried.

How good it would be to go across into the East, to see it all again. He felt sick, like a teenager excited at the approach of a birthday party. It would be wonderful to go there again, wandering the streets, remembering how it had been. He sighed, staring at the city. Everything was so unexpected, he thought. So bad. The skyscraper blocks, stark and functional, offended him, like rotting teeth in an old man's head. The neon burst and glared around everything like a whore's necklace.

How sad it was. He moved away from the window, not wanting to look upon it any more. It was cheap and tawdry. So different, he reflected, from what the Führer had planned. He remembered the dinner-parties, here in Berlin and then at Berchtesgaden, with the papier mâché models showing the city that was to be built as a monument to the leader's genius. The Führer had been so excited, so vibrant, hurrying from plan to plan, gesturing with a baton to each building, knowing by heart the function of each.

He glanced back to the window. The Führer would

have hated it, Kurnov knew. He shrugged, pushing away the nostalgia. He hadn't come to reminisce. He'd exposed himself, perhaps stupidly, merely to survive.

Where should he start? A stupid question. There was only one way he could begin. The dangers were incredible, he thought, a recurring mental admonition. But then, he'd had no choice, no choice at all. This couldn't be criticized as panic, like the ill-considered flight from Berlin in 1945.

An arrogant man who always sought complete control over everything in which he became involved, it irritated him to be exposed in a situation where he would probably have to accede to demands, rather than make them.

In every move, he would have to be incredibly circumspect. He was well known as Vladimir Kurnov, so any long absence from the conference hall or official function would be noticed. He'd already decided how to get away, but it wasn't a good excuse, so it would have to be used sparingly.

The city would be crawling with Nazis and Jews, seeking the Toplitz evidence. So, he presumed, would the police, irked by the Jerusalem announcement. He wouldn't know what any of them looked like, he accepted. Nor know their names. But then, by the same token, neither would they be able to identify him. There were no pictures, linking the new face with Heinrich Köllman. Thank God. It would be a minor advantage, but he needed every advantage, no matter how small. He would have to tread with the delicacy of a man crossing a lightly frozen stream. If the ice broke suddenly, there would be no way he could avoid drowning. He grimaced at himself in the mirror. Compared to what might happen if he were caught by the Nazis or the Jews, drowning would be an acceptable death. Welcome, even.

What would Bock be like, after all these years? he wondered. Definitely successful, guessed Kurnov. Certainly the listing he had immediately checked in the telephone book, flushing with relief that Bock was still alive, looked impressive, a clinic in the best area, a private address in the most expensive part of town, a veritable alphabet of medical qualifications behind his name. Bock was one of life's survivors whatever the circumstances, he decided, smiling ruefully. Not that such ability mattered. He had been handed £1,000,000 after all, a tax-free, instantly available, untraceable fortune.

Kurnov had often recalled the decision to authorize Bock's drawing facility upon the account, convinced through his fear by the surgeon's argument that if the East proved unacceptable, then he would need someone in a Berlin no longer safe who could handle money for an escape to yet another country. Considered many times in Russia, that decision in 1945 had been madness. Now, he decided, the regret was misplaced. Putting his trust in Bock could have saved his life.

Of course, the Nazis or the Jews could outbid him. He'd realized that, within minutes of seeing the television broadcast in his Houston motel-room and knowing he would have to attempt to recover his dossier. Their resources made what he had to offer look like fairground baubles. But he didn't want the box: just a tiny part of what it contained.

The difficulty was going to be conveying his offer. He smiled. Bock was initially going to be useful. The surgeon would have retained links with the Organisation, he reassured himself, even though his post-war importance had been exhausted. The Nazis had always had an excellent intelligence service. From them, Bock would be able to discover if any contact had been established with whoever held the documents. Bock might stall, initially, at helping, thought Kurnov. But there was nothing the man could do. The blackmail was perfect. Gradually, the smile dried on his face. Bock's usefulness was strictly limited, he thought. The negotiations to retrieve the documents could be entrusted to no one. He shuddered, the physical movement jerking through him at the idea of actually exposing himself to such open identification. There was no other way, he thought, the habitual conceit surfacing. He alone would have the guile and intelligence to bargain, anyway. Certainly it was not something that could be left to Bock.

Which resolved itself into a desperate situation, he accepted, again. Realistically, his chances of getting his personal folder back were minimal. Ridiculous even. The anger built up within him and he clenched his hands until his knuckles hurt. He was running, like a dog responding to a trick. But at least a dog could refuse if it wanted to. Kurnov knew he had to perform.

Another doubt settled, like heavy mist. If the money were gone, there would be no way to avoid exposure, he realized, objectively. And there would be nowhere he could run.

But he wouldn't be captured, he determined. Not by anyone. He knew imprisonment, anywhere, would send him insane. And he was well aware he could stand even less the penalties the Nazis would impose. Kurnov knew completely the degree of his personal cowardice. He tapped the left molar, an unnecessary reassurance. The cyanide was still there, the implant originally put there forty years ago replaced every three years in the secrecy of his Moscow laboratory. Better a little agony than suffering that would go on and on.

He shuddered in the warm hotel-room. It wouldn't be difficult to convince people he was feeling unwell. Bock would regret it if he had spent the money, he mused. Before he died, he would kill the surgeon. Very slowly. No, he corrected, immediately. No, *he* wouldn't kill him. He'd use his own death to disclose Bock's involvement in the hidden bank-account and let the Nazis kill him. They were far more expert. He considered the thought. Perhaps they weren't. It was just that in Berlin they had better facilities.

He pulled the telephone directory towards him again. How easy it would be to telephone. He actually reached out, towards the instrument, impelled by the urge to commence the search immediately. He halted, reluctantly.

Instead, he carefully copied the address upon an envelope resting upon a handkerchief, so there would be no indentation upon the blotter if there were any unexpected investigation of his room. There was no reason why there should be, but on several foreign trips he had had the impression that his room had been visited by other members of the delegation.

Using the same handkerchief pad, he wrote just the number of the Swiss account and the initials 'H.K.V.K.' After so long, he realized, it might baffle the other man, initially. But the surprise would not last long. Bock would know of what had happened at Toplitz and realize the significance of the note. He would even expect some approach, rationalized Kurnov.

The scientist decided against postal delivery. He could take it himself, providing he was alert for personal surveillance. There was, he had convinced himself, no reason why the Russians should watch him too closely.

He smiled again, amused through his apprehension at a sudden doubt. Did he still know Berlin well enough to elude any followers? It would be an interesting challenge. The amusement vanished. Before everything was over, there was every likelihood that that would not be a flippant thought.

He lay outstretched on the bed, unwilling to leave the safety of the locked room, letting his mind drift. He'd been lucky, he reflected, seeking omens. Bock was alive. His whole survival rested on the man and he was alive and easily contactable. Perhaps the luck would continue.

Was Gerda still here? he wondered. That was odd, he decided, seeking a psychological explanation for the memory. Not once, in the thirty years he had been away, had he thought of his wife. It must be the association with Berlin, he thought. What would she look like now? She had never been attractive, with her buck-teeth and baying laugh and the tendency for yellow spots to form in the crack where her nose met her face. But the Führer had disliked his favourites parading their women instead of their wives, and so he had publicly kept with Gerda, tolerating her snobbery and stupidity. And her incredible attitude towards clothes.

He recalled how bad she had been in bed, lying listlessly, her mind probably on yet another dress. The camp girls had been so much better. But then, they had known they would be killed if they didn't satisfy. Perhaps it was unfair to compare Gerda with them. Gerda would never have lasted a day in a camp, he decided, sniggering. She probably wouldn't have got any trade.

He frowned. The tendency to hysteria was worrying. His nerves were tight, he recognized. And things were likely to get worse. He would have to keep very firm control upon himself. Fortunately, he had brought along enough medication to help. Like the ease of laughter, lying there was another indication of his fear. The security he felt, within four walls and behind a locked door, was a womb complex. It was predictable, psychologically.

He forced himself to move, getting up from the bed. In the bathroom he showered and then put on the uncreased suit. The reception was in fifteen minutes, he saw, checking his watch. He'd left it almost too late. He began to hurry, putting his letter to Bock carefully into his inside pocket, then quietly letting himself out of the room, looking both ways along the corridor. Empty. Keeping to the edge, where the thickness of the carpet would shield his footsteps, he went towards the corridor window, away from the elevator. Nervously, he pushed the unmarked door adjoining the window. It moved easily and he let out a tiny sound of relief. It led out on to stairs that went down to the middle landing, serving both his floor and that below as a fire-escape He'd brought tissues from the supply in the bathroom. He padded his fingers to prevent them getting dirty on the little-used handles, then cupped his palms beneath the two arms of cold metal, heaving upwards. The windows remained unmoving. The ever-present bubble of apprehension popped inside him. He felt around the rim, seeking the lock. It had to be manual. A key would destroy the purpose of a window leading out on to a fire-escape. His throat felt dry, as if he had run a long race. He'd been good at sport at school, he remembered, and recognized the feeling. He'd always won. It was important to win, always. Because of the darkness, he couldn't see how the locks operated, and he groped, trying to bring his face closer to the cold glass. They swivelled, he realized. He found the clasps in the top corners. They were stiff. He pushed and one gave suddenly. He felt his nail split off. Perspiration soaked his back and he stopped, panting. He had left the preparations too late, he decided, angrily. Bloody womb complex.

With the locks undone, the window scraped open, squeaking on its sash-cords. He hesitated, head turned up towards the corridor he had just left, listening for the sound of anyone who might have been attracted by the noise. Turning back, he pulled the window higher, staring out into the coldness that burst in, catching his breath. The fire-escape was tacked zig-zag against the wall, like an afterthought. Snow and ice glittered in the reflection from the sodium street lights. It would be dangerous: too risky, considering his age. He shivered, the perspiration drying coldly upon him. Quickly he closed the window almost completely and stood, quite still, on the emergency landing, fighting the fear that flooded through him. It came in waves, like sickness. He swallowed, gripping his hands around the wad of tissues he'd carried from the room. Too dangerous. Too risky. But unavoidable.

Leaving the window slightly open, he went up again, pausing before the door leading back to his floor. Deserted. He smiled. Another omen, he thought, like a child convincing itself an imagined disaster will be averted if it can avoid stepping on the cracks in a pavement. He hurried out, almost running to his door. Inside, he leaned backwards against it, breathing deeply. How nice to be able to stay here for the rest of the night. Read a book. Or watch television. He shook himself, like an animal casting off water, staring down at his suit. It was dirty, dust and cobwebs at the knees and over the front of his jacket. As he brushed himself, he saw the shirt cuffs were filthy. No time to change, he decided. Quickly he ran water over his split nail, but the bleeding refused to stop. He wrapped more tissue around it and looked at himself in the bathroom mirror. The vision was of a frightened man, he thought. He smoothed his hair back into its military cut and dampened his face, trying to stop the sweat that kept bubbling on his forehead. Suddenly, without warning, he whimpered. He clamped his mouth shut, embarrassed, looking around in the empty room. Careful. He needed more resilience than this. He stared directly at the medicine box he had brought with him. The performance had to be staged, but Kurnov was offended at the prospect. It would mean making a spectacle of himself, and deeply ingrained into every aspect of his behaviour was the need to avoid attention. This time it a sigh, not a whimper. It couldn't be avoided, he thought, taking the syringe and ampoule from the box.

The reception was crowded, smothered with cigarette smoke and talk. He winced, then hurried into the room.

Thank God a waiter was near. He took a whisky, needing it. His throat was so dry, it hurt to drink. Perhaps he should have stayed with vodka.

All the delegates had name-tabs on their lapels, but Kurnov's was hardly necessary. Almost immediately he was enveloped in small talk. He responded beyond his usual protective, monosyllabic manner, forcing himself to be noticed. He began sweating at the effort. The conference chairman, Konrad Bahr, hurried forward, hand outstretched, effusive in his greeting.

'So pleased to meet you,' gushed the German, pumping Kurnov's arm. 'We're honoured you are with us.'

Kurnov nodded. 'I wish I had had time to prepare a paper,' he said. He allowed a pause, then added, 'Not that I think I would have been able to deliver it.'

The chairman frowned, taking the bait.

'Why?'

Kurnov touched his stomach, gently. 'I've been dreadfully ill,' he said.

The chairman smiled, dismissively, 'A small upset, I'm sure,' he said, reassuringly. 'It'll go in a few hours, once you've got used to German hospitality.'

Kurnov fixed the doubtful look.

'Please,' continued the conference official. 'There are some other delegates who particularly wish to meet you ...'

He put his arm around Kurnov's shoulders, but the Russian pulled back. The thought of what was to happen brought out fresh dampness on his face.

'A moment,' he apologized. 'I must visit the bathroom first. Just allow me a minute.'

There was a cloakroom alongside the foyer. Kurnov went straight to it, locking himself in a cubicle. He took the apomorphine from his pocket and for a few seconds stared at the drug, conscious of the vomiting it would cause. Hurriedly, he took off his jacket. The excuse had to appear genuine, he convinced himself.

Quickly, he administered the injection, flushed the ampoule and disposable syringe away, then hurried out, aware of its quick reaction. He felt the attack rising within him as he re-entered the reception area. Doctor Bahr turned to greet him again, gesturing for a group of Italian delegates to approach, but the retching overtook Kurnov. He managed to turn, almost reaching the side of the room before the first wave of sickness engulfed him. He stood, supported against the wall by an out-stretched hand, vomiting again and again, conscious of people moving away.

Bahr appeared by his side, his face twisted in disgust.

'My dear doctor,' he said, forcing the solicitude. Clutching a waiter's napkin to his face, Kurnov allowed himself to be guided from the hall. Spasms of sickness jerked through him and perspiration soaked his face and body. His eyes were running, too, so it was difficult to see. Hotel staff met them in the foyer and accompanied Kurnov to his room. Within minutes, the hotel doctor arrived, fussed over him, then insisted he take the concentrated streptomycin, sulphadiazine and sulphadimidine. Within half an hour he was alone, with the assurance he would not be disturbed for the remainder of the evening. For fifteen minutes he lay on the bed, aching from the convulsions, sure of his rate of recovery.

He'd succeeded, he thought. It had been disgusting and embarrassing, but no one would be able to question the reason for his absence over the next couple of days.

He got up from the bed, dressing slowly. How much he wanted to stay in the room! The recurring thought of cowardice. He shrugged it away. He *had* to stop his mind slipping away like this all the time. Reluctantly, breathing heavily, he took his overcoat from the closet, changed his shoes for the heavier, Russian boots more suitable for the conditions outside, then gently opened the door, to check the corridor. There was the low murmur of conversation and he waited for several minutes before accepting it was a radio from behind one of the closed doors. He edged out, tensed for any movement so that he could dodge back. It remained empty. He hurried along, pushing his way from the fire-escape door on to the middle landing, then through the window and out on to the slippery platform. Immediately outside he stopped, gasping. It was bitterly cold, the wind crying like a petulant child through the narrow alley-way. Soon it would snow again, he knew. He held on to the metal rails and felt the cold bite through his gloves. Far below him, the city heaved with life, headlights fireflying along inch-wide roadways, neon jerking and exploding, the bombs of advertising. It was stupid to stand exposed, in such conditions. Gripping the rail, he began slowly to descend the narrow stairway. Ice and snow were wedged into the steps, reducing their width, and several times his foot slipped, so that his shin grated over the metal. He felt blood running into his boot. The strain began almost immediately as a dull ache in his shoulders and legs and got worse while he continued down, and the nagging pain from the left leg, scarred from thigh to groin in an accident in Hamburg when he was eighteen, pulled at him. He had to stop on the first landing. He stood, panting. He was soaked in sweat but had no feeling in his frozen hands or feet. The abused muscles in his arms and legs made his limbs twitch uncontrollably. The scar hadn't troubled him so much for years. He crossed his arms, cupping his elbows, and hugged himself. The pain began to subside. He knew it indicated the muscles were setting and forced himself to reach out and grab the rail to continue down. His breath came out in tiny, white clouds and he was grunting with effort. He slowed on the last landing, trying to reduce the sound. For several minutes, he stood completely unmoving, trying to penetrate the dense blackness of the alley-way below him. No one waiting below could have remained still for so long, certainly not in this cold, he determined. Satisfied he was unobserved, Kurnov finished the descent, hesitating until his eyes had become accustomed to the darkness so he could detect the dustbins and litter over which he might have stumbled, then moved off towards Eckerndorferplatz. He moved awkwardly, his feet shuffling over the ground, cramped by cold and exertion.

Twice he had to stop, gripping his hands tightly by his side, to stifle the sobs of self-pity that welled up.

Inside the hotel, Colonel Pyotr Suvlov, who had succeeded in getting an invitation to the reception, excused himself from the meal, explaining to Bahr he had to return early to the Russian sector. He stood undecided in the hotel foyer for several minutes, then left hurriedly, driving immediately eastwards.

Frieden had sensed the excitement as soon as the consumptive lawyer telephoned. He agreed immediately to the meeting and sat now in the luxury penthouse atop the office block in Ludwigsfelderstrasse, staring out over the park. It was a pity about Muntz, he reflected, in genuine sadness. He had been a loyal man, a true Party member. But he had no choice, Frieden decided. The continued existence and safety of the Organisation demanded that everyone stayed alert, both mentally and physically. Muntz had to be dispensed with because his health had failed. It was like easing the suffering of a favourite animal which had grown too old. If the circumstances were reversed, he would have expected Muntz to behave in exactly the same way with him. Muntz would understand. It was one of the rules by which they survived.

The elderly lawyer came breathlessly into the room. Speech was difficult and Frieden waited patiently for him to recover, pouring his friend a brandy. Muntz sipped it, gratefully, wincing as the liquid reached his raw throat.

'Luck,' he managed, at last. 'We've had some luck.'

From his briefcase he took a tape already mounted on a miniature cassette-player. He placed it on the table between them, adjusted the volume control and then started the machine. Immediately there was the hiss of recording.

'The quality is not very good,' he said, apologetically. The words groaned out, as if his voice were being squeezed through a narrow opening. He began again. 'It was difficult for our man to record without the telephone supervisor spotting it.'

Frieden nodded, gesturing impatiently for the man to stop talking. He didn't want to miss any part of the recording. The tape unwound, crackling, and then the sound started, abruptly, with no preliminaries.

'Israeli embassy, shalom,' said a girl's voice, the university-taught German clipped and precise in the customary greeting. There was a pause. 'Shalom?' prompted the girl again, an edge of irritation in her voice.

'Hello ...' said a man's voice, hesitantly '... I called before ... I spoke to someone in your security section ...'

'Who is this, please?' continued the Jewish girl.

'No name,' said the caller, his confidence growing. 'Just say it's about the box ... about Toplitz ...'

Frieden looked up at the lawyer and smiled, a self-satisfied expression. The girl's reaction was immediate, as if she had been given explicit instructions for such an approach.

'A moment, please,' she said, quickly. Almost immediately a man's voice came on. Again it was was the perfect German of a foreigner well-instructed.

'Hello,' said the Jew. 'Who is this?'

'I called before,' repeated the man.

'We've been waiting for you to contact us again,' said the embassy security-man.

'Said I would,' mumbled the man, with a trace of

93

truculence. 'Just got to wait. That's all. Everyone has to wait on me now.'

'Of course,' soothed the Israeli, quickly. 'We were just ... just concerned. Several weeks have passed, after all. Jerusalem have sent some men here, in anticipation of your contacting us again.'

'They brought the money?' demanded the caller.

A note of caution entered the Israeli's voice.

'I told you on the first call there would be no difficulty about the money. But I've got to have proof that what I'm buying is genuine. Can't we meet?'

The sneer was immediate.

'Oh no. They're after me. I know that. They might even get their chance. Who knows? They might make a better offer than you. It's going to be an auction ... the highest bidder wins.'

'The Nazis would kill you. And you know it,' warned the embassy man, urgently.

'Not if they didn't get all the details. If I had copies made and put in a bank vault, to be produced if anything happened to me, they couldn't kill me, could they?'

Frieden frowned, head close to the recorder, his entire concentration on the voice.

'They'd defeat you,' insisted the Israeli. 'You don't know what they could do ...'

Again the sneer over-rode him. 'Don't tell me what the Nazis can do,' he said. 'I'm an expert.'

'They'll kill you,' asserted the embassy official. 'We are the only people you can trust.'

The disbelieving voice grated on the tape.

'I don't trust anyone,' it said.

'Why don't we meet, so we can talk about the evidence you have,' tried the Israeli again.

There was a pause. The caller's heavy breathing was etched on to the tape.

'Got it all,' he resumed, like a man recounting a

memory. 'The Swiss account of Mengele ... Heinrich Müller. There's all the information about Richard Glücks ... the sterilization experiments of Heinrich Willermann ... the facts about Oscar Dulwanger, who's still drawing on Swiss funds while hiding in Aswan ... Hans Eisele, the Buchenwald doctor ...'

The Israeli over-reaction to the promised evidence sounded in the sharp intake of breath on the tape.

'... and everything about the partnership of Otto Grüber and Heinrich Köllman. I've got it all ... I'll hang every one of them ...'

The Israeli came on, urgently, unable to keep the anxiety from his voice.

'Now listen,' he said. 'Please listen. We've got the money we promised. We will pay it anywhere you want ... in any currency in the world. We will even assign men to protect you. But we've got to have the contents of that box. Let's meet ... just the two of us. Let's arrange a meeting anywhere in Berlin that you decide ... outside of Berlin, if you like ... anywhere ... I'll come anywhere, at any time. Just bring one document, something from the box as proof ...'

'... you might trick ...'

'... There will be no trickery ...' cut off the embassy man, in his eagerness. 'You *know* that we are the only people you can deal with safely. We'll meet any conditions ...'

'I'll see ...' began the caller, dismissively.

'Don't go,' demanded the Jew. 'Don't go without our setting up some form of contact.'

'I'll have to work it out,' said the caller. He spoke confusedly, like an old man. 'I'll call again ...'

'... When? Let's fix a time ...'

'A week. Maybe I'll call again in a week. I'm in contact with someone else. He might have a better offer.'

The line went dead as abruptly as the conversation

had commenced. For several seconds Muntz and Frieden sat looking at the tape scratchily unwinding, then the millionaire reached out and depressed the stop button.

'When was the call made?'

Muntz glanced at his watch.

'Five hours ago,' he said. He was smiling, like a child — who had brought home a good school-report.

'We're getting somewhere, Max,' said the lawyer, hopefully. 'It's a lead.'

His exuberance faded at the look on Frieden's face.

'Isn't it good, Max?' he probed, worriedly. He began to cough.

The fat man shrugged. 'Could be,' he conceded.

'But we know the man's here,' argued the lawyer. 'And we know the evidence he's got ...'

He stopped, halted by the recollection.

'God, Max. That bloody box seems to contain everything. It could destroy us all.'

Frieden nodded, slowly. 'Everyone,' he agreed, reflectively. His voice changed, becoming incisive. 'Pay the telephonist double whatever we agreed ... treble if needs be. We've got to know of the other calls. They'll arrange a meeting soon. Tell him there will be a bonus every time. We can't miss anything.'

Muntz nodded.

'Who's the other person with whom he's negotiating?' questioned the millionaire, distantly.

Muntz waved a hand, vaguely. 'I don't believe it,' he said. 'That's the sort of thing people say to inflate the value of what they're selling.'

'He *knows* what he's selling,' argued Frieden. 'It's impossible to inflate the price of something like that.'

'Who, then?'

Frieden didn't reply immediately.

'Bock?' he wondered, suddenly.

Muntz laughed, ridiculing the idea.

'You said he'd promised to call us immediately, if there were any contact,' pointed out the lawyer. 'Bock's rich, certainly. But he's not as rich as you, even. Where could he put his hands on to the sort of money being discussed here? And *why* should he? He's got every reason to come to us the moment any call is made to him.'

Frieden nodded, convinced. He started the machine, rewinding the tape. Then he began to play the conversation again, stopping after a few minutes.

'Notice anything?' he demanded from the lawyer.

Muntz frowned.

'The man's a German,' enlarged Frieden. He played a further section of the tape and Muntz nodded.

'Bavarian,' he identified. 'The man's got a strong Bavarian accent.'

Kurnov lay on the bed, his body shaken by waves of shivering. The emotion was an amalgam of many things, he accepted, through his distress. Of the numbing cold from the frozen fire-escape; of fear; and of the relief at having regained the room undiscovered. But there had been an excitement, too, he recalled, hugging himself as the shaking subsided, a thrill at walking again through the streets he had once known so well. The bloody West Germans had renamed most of them, but he'd soon realized when he had made mistakes and walked along, ignoring the new street-signs, remembering the old names and the old associations, even able to disregard at times his own immediate danger in the warmth of the nostalgia. Bock had done well, he decided, bringing to mind the sleek, modern clinic, its twin towers rising into the darkness, hurrying white-coated figures of efficiency visible through the windows.

My money built that, Kurnov thought, suddenly. That's mine, all mine. Bock was a thief. He should suffer. He smiled. The man would suffer, decided Kurnov, when he opened that hand-delivered letter inscribed 'personal'.

And then even more, if there were insufficient money to negotiate for what Kurnov wanted.

The shuddering lessened and he stood, examining himself in the full-length mirror. He was sagging with tiredness, red-veined eyes pouched in blackness. The suit that had been crisp and fresh six hours before was sodden high above the knees and hung around his legs in concertina creases, and the jacket was filthy. But he'd made it, he told himself again. The knowledge intoxicated him, pushing away the fatigue. It wasn't going to be easy. But he was capable of doing what was required. He undressed quickly, throwing his clothes in a pile for express cleaning the following morning, then showered for the second time that night, easing the numbing cold from his body by gradually increasing the heat of the water. He knew from the experiments that it would hurt, initially, but that the discomfort would be transitory. They'd screamed and writhed, he recalled. But then, he had tested their reaction with water boiling sufficiently hot to strip the skin.

He slithered almost sexually into bed, huddling the covering around him. Womb complex again, he decided. Suddenly he began to giggle, the amusement almost uncontrollable. He sniggered on for several minutes, then lay on his back, looking up at the ceiling, still smiling. How dumb he had been, he thought. How incredibly, unthinkingly stupid.

He'd just realized where to hide if he were discovered. He was amazed that the way of locating Gerda hadn't occurred to him before.

(9)

The following morning, Bock cancelled indefinitely all further personal operations, giving instructions to both medical and administration staff that he was not to be bothered. There would be talk, he knew. It didn't matter. Survival mattered, that was all. He sat in his office, the door locked, staring down at the letter that had been awaiting him when he arrived at the clinic two hours before. Just the number ... and the initials.

Fear knotted inside him, like a badly eaten meal he couldn't digest. Was it genuine? Was it really from Kurnov? He turned the envelope over. No stamp or postmark. If it were, it meant he was here, in Berlin. What about Frieden? Could it be a trap set by the suspicious, fat Nazi? No, he rejected. No, definitely not from Frieden. He certainly didn't know the number of the Swiss account. Or Köllman's chosen identity.

What about the anonymous caller with the Bavarian accent? Again, no. The Swiss number was not listed on any Nazi records. And 'Vladimir Kurnov' was the name Köllman selected *after* the box had been sunk and he fled to Russia. So it could not be the Bavarian.

Bock shivered, a man suddenly cold. Köllman was back.

The surgeon gazed out over the city, remembering the man. Almost everyone had been frightened of Köllman, thought Bock. It was said even the Führer had been unhappy to have Köllman in his presence for too long, but Bock had always considered that an exaggeration. He'd never been part of that inner group and had no way of knowing what the relationship had been. Certainly Köllman had been invited to Berchtesgaden as well as to Berlin. But always in a crowd, he recalled, as if that confirmed the rumour. Köllman had no friends, decided Bock. Nor had he seemed to need them. Bock halted his thoughts. Not true, he corrected. *He* had been the man's friend, he supposed. That wasn't strictly accurate, either, thought the cosmetic expert. He had believed he was being cultivated for friendship, he recalled, but he couldn't have been more mistaken. Köllman's friendship arose entirely from the use he could get from it when the Third Reich collapsed. Bock laughed aloud, a nudge of hysteria. But *he'd* got the benefit, he gloated. He'd got the Swiss fortune and the life of luxury and Köllman had got thirty years' unnecessary exile in the Soviet Union. The ever-present fear wrapped itself around him, like a damp blanket. Was there any way of Köllman discovering he had been tricked? Unlikely, decided Bock. But then he couldn't be sure. He wasn't sure of anything, any more. Off his office there was an examination room, with almost one whole wall entirely occupied by a medical cabinet. Bock hurried to it, shaking his head in self-apology. It was no good. He couldn't stand any more without help. The hypodermic rattled against the kidney bowl as he prepared the injection, then swabbed his arm. He winced slightly as the needle went in, then began inhaling deeply in anticipation as the 25 ml of Librium entered his bloodstream. There was no danger, he assured himself, professionally, no danger at all. He paused before the array of drugs, staring to his left. The heroin and cocaine phials, encased in their neat cardboard boxes, were stacked in tiny walls. Just like walls, he thought, expanding the metaphor, walls behind which people could hide, safe from everyone. The tension began easing away as the Librium took effect and he looked away from the heroin and cocaine. No, he determined, realistically.

Not again. Never again. Back at his desk, he sat staring down at the single sheet of paper, turning it over seeking clues. None, he realized. Köllman — or Kurnov, thought Bock, deciding to revert to his adoptive Russian name — would have given no clues. Or would he, inadvertently perhaps? Kurnov was in Berlin. It wasn't easy for a Russian to travel, he knew. There had to be permission and travel documents. For someone as well known as Kurnov, it would be even more difficult to move. He could be in East Berlin, reasoned Bock. No, that was wrong. It would be as restrictive behind the Wall as it would be in Moscow. To have personally delivered the letter — and Bock was convinced Kurnov would have entrusted it to no one — would mean crossing the Wall. For Kurnov, so easily recognizable, that would be impossible. And to have applied officially would have made the Soviets or East Germans immediately suspect a defection.

So it couldn't be East Berlin.

Then he was here, in the city. But how? There were Russians in the Control Commission, of course. But what excuse could Kurnov, a scientist specializing in human stress, create for being with the commission?

None.

Bock sat back. He was reasoning well, he thought, gratefully. Each possibility was coming easily to mind, being logically examined and then discarded when flaws were discovered. He wouldn't need anything else. Librium would be sufficient.

Kurnov must be officially in Berlin, in circumstances that allowed him reasonable freedom of movement through the city. The surgeon pulled the medical diary towards him, examining it for a week prior to that day's date. The conference of prison psychiatrists was the only entry. The excuse *had* to be something medical. And the psychiatrists' convention was the only internationally attended event taking place within a period of three weeks. Bock looked away, frowning. Thirty years before, Kurnov could have been the main speaker at such a gathering. But now ...? He looked at the diary again. Foster Dulles Allee. Less than three miles away. He hurried from the office.

The personal secretary looked up, expectantly, for Bock never left during the day without saying where he was going. But today he did.

Which was why the girl was unable to help the insistent Frieden, who telephoned fifteen minutes later, demanding to know the surgeon's whereabouts.

Two thousand miles away in his Kremlin office, Mavetsky read for the third time the overnight report that had come from Suvlov. He threw it down, half-covering Kurnov's file which now permanently occupied his desk drawer.

'... Unkempt ... profusely sweating ... over-compensatory in conversation ...'

Definitely not typical Kurnov behaviour, thought the Russian minister. But then, according to the report, he had been disgustingly ill. But apparently not too ill to descend a frozen fire-escape and make his way to a famous plastic-surgery clinic. So his suspicions were justified.

Mavetsky picked up the man's file. If Vladimir Kurnov were not Klaus Reinhart, the brave opponent of Nazism who had risked death to treat Russian prisoners of war, then who was he? Again he remembered the man's preoccupation with the reports of the Israeli commando raid into Austria. Not a war hero, but a Nazi war criminal. That could be the only interpretation, decided the minister. A man guilty of atrocities had managed to infiltrate the highest echelon of the Soviet space programme. And he was closely associated with him, realized Mavetsky. He looked down at his hands, lying on the desk before him. They were shaking, the Russian saw. There would be scapegoats, determined the minister. The blood-letting would be reminiscent of Stalin, as culprits were rounded up to answer for the embarrassment.

He felt in the drawer, finding the tape that had been recorded just before the man went to Germany. Little use now, he thought. He stood and began pacing his office, head down on his chest. He would be the first victim, decided Mavetsky. He had to be. He'd been seen too often in Kurnov's presence, even recommended the exit visa to Berlin in advance of the Houston visit. Mavetsky was aware of his enemies. How easy it would be for them to show Kurnov to be the minister's protégé.

The decision to check Kurnov in Berlin had been wise, he reflected. There was a tape of the initial conversation with Suvlov, too. It would be irrefutable evidence of his suspicions, a useful defence. He smiled, buoyed by a sudden thought. Why defence? It might, just might, be possible to emerge from the disaster with enhanced stature. He came back to the desk, looking down at the first tape. And that wasn't worthless, either. Far from worthless, in fact. Presented in the proper way, that recording could be damning against the scientist. He ran his hand over the Suvlov report. Good enough, he decided.

Quickly, he booked a call to Suvlov, then summoned his secretary.

'A memorandum,' he ordered. 'To every member of the Politburo ...'

He paused, assembling his thoughts.

'... I request,' he began, 'as a matter of urgency affecting the highest security of the Soviet Union, that an immediate emergency session of the full Politburo ...'

The telephone rang with the Berlin call and the secretary sat back, looking at the minister curiously.

(10)

It was a frightening sensation, seeing him after so long. Bock's entire body was permeated again with the unreal feeling that occurs seconds before an anaesthetic takes effect, when the body appears to float, disconnected from the mind. How little change there was in the man he had last seen thirty years before, scurrying from the back door of what passed then as a surgery, disguised as a laundryman against the Nazis he believed would be watching, basket held high to protect him!

Kurnov's hair had greyed, of course, and receded considerably, but his face was remarkable. It had lined, of course, on the forehead and around the eyes, which were more pouched than he recalled. There was some sagging near the ears, too, he thought, professionally. But then, there had been some damage to the nerves, he remembered. In all, he decided, Kurnov didn't look any more than ten years older than he had that June evening, three decades ago.

Even more than by the minimal facial changes, Bock was arrested by Kurnov's demeanour. It was almost identical to the way he had conducted himself in the camps, Bock remembered, straight-backed, head high at that autocratic angle which had always seemed to overawe. Only the cigarette jarred. Bock did not remember him as a smoker. In fact, he had a faded recollection that Kurnov positively disdained smoking, because the Führer objected. As he watched, almost completely concealed behind one of the pillars in the vestibule leading into the conference hall, Kurnov lit another from the stump of his cigarette.

Bock had decided against attempting to enter the hall. He had no accreditation, and to have attempted to obtain it at such a late stage, even though he probably had the medical qualifications, would have been ridiculous, he determined. The only result would be to attract attention. Instead, he had positioned himself with a perfect view of all the entrances, grateful for the growing flow of people that gave him added concealment. At first, he had been frightened he had made a mistake, waiting, with a growing feeling of foolishness, as the delegations, easily identifiable from their lapel designation, had arrived. He had actually been preparing to leave when he had seen him, a little apart from the rest of the Russian contingent, gazing around in the haughty manner Bock recalled so well. He had always stood apart from a group, remembered the surgeon, constantly disdaining association by close contact. Even from the Führer, the rumours had said, Kurnov had stood back. So, recalled Bock, had Bormann. He wondered if it were for the same reason, the instinctive objection to being photographed. The delegations were jostling the crowded entrance-area, renewing the friendships made at the reception the previous night. Bock started to withdraw behind the pillar, then stopped. Why hide? Kurnov knew who he was and had made contact. Their mutual survival was intertwined. There would have to be a meeting, and Bock wanted desperately to share his burden. The man with the Bavarian accent would call again, inevitably. And Frieden, too, he guessed. Bock smiled, warming to optimism. He had fooled the other man before and sent him into an unnecessary exile. Very soon there would have to be a meeting with the anonymous telephoner. He shuddered at the prospect. How much better it would be if Kurnov made that contact! And how much safer! Purposefully, he pushed away from the concealment of the pillar, moving openly through the crowd, slowly but quite definitely taking a course that would lead him to within feet of the adoptive Russian. As he came closer, Bock again began to revise his earlier impression of the unchanged face of the other man. He *had* aged more than ten years, he corrected. Particularly around the eyes. But then, he decided, that could be sleeplessness. There would have been many nights without sleep in the last few weeks, he estimated. Kurnov continued to survey the crowd, apparently seeing no one. Bock slowed further, moving even nearer, fixing his eyes directly upon the man.

How would Kurnov react? wondered the surgeon, confident he could remain expressionless because the shock of recognition had passed now. Three more steps and he would be past. Bock came almost to a standstill, knowing that to stop completely would attract attention. Already he had intercepted curious glances from people who saw he wore no identification and carried no conference literature.

Then Kurnov saw him. His head was moving in that almost perpetual motion when their eyes met. For seconds, the look held. There was no change of expression from Kurnov, not even recognition. The hesitation was almost undetectable, then the head moved on. Bock continued walking, against the tide of people, out into the grey morning.

Immediately outside he stopped, breathing deeply. Irrationally, he felt relieved. For days he had swirled like a feather in a breeze, from one frightening encounter to another. Now the nervousness began slipping away. Kurnov would manage a meeting, he was positive. He'd be able to talk to the man, to discuss the approaches and the threats. And use him, of course, he thought again, smiling.

He crossed to where the convertible Mercedes 450

S.L. was parked and drove happily back to the clinic.

Perez looked up smiling as Mosbacher entered the Seelingstrasse apartment. The older Jew stared at the man upon whom so much depended. His attitude had improved over the last few days, he thought. The pendulum between euphoria and depression appeared to have stopped swinging so dangerously.

'Bock's made a contact,' he reported, shortly.

Perez stared, expressionless.

'Are you sure?'

Mosbacher nodded. 'I followed him from his apartment to the clinic this morning, then waited. He was inside about an hour, then came dashing out ...'

'... Dashing?' picked up Perez.

He *is* improving, decided Mosbacher. That was an intelligent query.

'Really,' assured Mosbacher. 'He was definitely hurrying.'

'You're not imagining it,' pressed the younger man. 'If we misinterpret any action now, we could blow the whole thing.'

Mosbacher shook his head, adamantly.

'I'm certain,' he insisted. 'He was a man moving without too much thought. And remember the pattern. He *never* goes out in the morning.'

Perez shrugged in uncertain agreement.

'He took off down Dahlemer Weg but pretty soon began dodging through the side-streets until he got to Foster Dulles Allee in the Tiergarten ...'

He paused, expecting reaction, but Perez said nothing.

'He went straight to the medical convention,' completed Mosbacher.

Perez sighed and finally smiled. It was a reluctant expression.

'So he's here,' he said softly. 'The bastard had to break his cover.'

He looked up, having to prove himself against the other man. 'It's working,' he insisted. 'There's been contact.'

'That wasn't my doubt. Nor my objection. You know that,' snapped back Mosbacher, raising his hand, like an after-dinner speaker interrupted before his punch-line.

'He hung around in the vestibule in the Kongress-halle,' he continued, 'watching the delegations arrive. I was only about eight feet from him. I thought he was going to faint when the Russians arrived. He actually swayed ...'

Perez stared at his friend, his eyes wide with emotion.

'Which one is he?' he demanded, his voice dry. 'Which one is Köllman?'

Mosbacher hesitated, then shrugged. 'I don't know,' he admitted.

The tension went out of Perez, like a spring from which pressure is slowly released.

'There are fifteen in the Russian party,' defended Mosbacher. 'About five minutes after they arrived, Bock went near them. There was no personal contact. And nothing was said. Nearly all of them looked at him, at one time or another. But there wasn't the slightest recognition.'

The big man stopped, waiting for approval. Suddenly Perez stood up and walked towards him. He held out both hands, seizing the man who towered over him and pulled him forward in a bear-hug.

'We've got him,' he predicted, excitedly. 'It's *got* to be right.'

Mosbacher sighed. He still thought the operation wrong, even if the eventual conclusion were successful. 'We'll see,' he cautioned.

'It could be within days,' said Perez, distantly. 'The whole thing could be over before the end of the week.'

Mosbacher smiled, exerting the steadying influence.

'Careful now, Uri,' he warned. 'This is only the beginning ... the very beginning. There's still a million things that could go wrong.'

'Nonsense,' dismissed the other man, with optimism Mosbacher had almost forgotten. 'My plans never go wrong ...'

They both remembered Toplitz at the same moment.

'Sorry,' mumbled Perez. 'I didn't mean ...'

'It wasn't your fault,' insisted Mosbacher. 'If they'd followed your orders, it wouldn't have happened.'

Perez looked at him, but didn't say anything.

There was no sound whatsoever in the committee-room in which the other fifteen members of the Soviet Politburo sat, all waiting for Mavetsky to continue.

'... And so,' picked up the minister, 'those are the facts as I know them at the moment. Obviously the man is now constantly under observation. I consider a method has now to be devised to bring him back to Russia without arousing the slightest interest in the West.'

He sat down, damp with apprehension. It had gone well, he thought, without any interruption that would have indicated anyone had isolated a flaw in his argument. They were scared, he knew.

'Before the discussion continues,' said the Party chairman, Valery Shepalin, 'I think it should be made a matter of record that we register our appreciation of the vigilance of Comrade Mavetsky ...'

There was a muttering of assent and Mavetsky nodded his head, modestly. Imperceptibly, he released the pent-up breath. Thank Christ, he thought.

'But I have one slight disagreement,' continued the chairman. Mavetsky's eyes came up, warily.

'I am not sure about immediately withdrawing him,' said Shepalin.

They all waited.

'If this mysterious box does contain all the Nazi

records, then presumably they are sufficient to identify Kurnov for whoever he is?'

Mavetsky gestured. 'I don't have that information,' he apologized.

'Quite,' Shepalin agreed. 'But it's a fair assumption to make?'

Mavetsky nodded.

'Therefore no matter what diplomatic reason we create for withdrawing him from Berlin and the Houston space-shot, it will be criticized as a blatant example of Russia protecting one of its scientists, once the details become public ...?'

Around the table there were movements of agreement. It was subtle reasoning, admitted Mavetsky. Discerning the mood of the committee, the chairman went on, 'And the last accusation that should be levelled against us is protecting a Nazi war criminal.'

He paused, looking around, embracing all with the criticism.

'... It is, after all, going to be embarrassing enough conceding that for so long such a man fooled us and managed to reach such a high position ...'

Everyone avoided the gaze. Scapegoats were being selected, thought Mavetsky. He should cement the advantage so far achieved.

'What do you suggest?' he asked. The question would show he was not frightened of involvement in the purge that was to come. The chairman turned to him and Mavetsky answered the look steadily. Shepalin smiled, slightly.

'There is no possibility of his being able to escape our surveillance?'

'None,' answered the minister, too quickly. He would have to call Suvlov immediately after the meeting to ensure every available man was put on the observation. If necessary, they would infiltrate some from East Germany. He swallowed, worriedly, realizing how easily he had entered the chairman's snare. The assurance that Kurnov was being constantly watched would be recorded against his name. If Shepalin's plan misfired, the blame would be channelled towards him. He sat, tight-faced, his eyes fixed on the man.

'Excellent,' greeted the chairman. 'Then I propose we just let everything continue, without any interruption whatsoever. We will keep the closest watch on every contact and move that Kurnov makes, both in Germany and then in America. If the contents of the box are disclosed, we will immediately arrest him and hand him over to the West Germans or American authorities, together with all the evidence we have collated.'

Mavetsky looked uncertain. 'You mean we would willingly hand over a Russian to be tried in another country?' he asked, allowing the surprise to leak into his voice.

'But that's just the point,' said the chairman, triumphantly. 'He isn't a Russian. He's a naturalized German. The propaganda victory to be gained by arresting him, then handing him over for trial, would be enormous. It would certainly eradicate any criticism of our having harboured the man for all these years.'

Again there were indications of approval along the table.

'The only difficulty', argued Mavetsky, seeing an opening through which to recover, 'is that Kurnov's knowledge is incalculable ...' he paused, wondering whether to mention the camps. He decided against it. '... And not only in matters directly connected to how advanced our space programme has become,' he compromised.

Immediately the attitude in the room shifted in Mavetsky's favour. Shepalin sensed it and looked at the minister, curiously. A challenge? Perhaps he should be more careful.

'Of course,' he agreed, easily. 'I said merely that he

should be made available to the authorities, not that he should survive ...'

Mavetsky frowned, realizing he had lost.

'... I feel that Kurnov should perish within twenty-four hours of entering captivity. There are many delayed-action poisons suitable for the purpose ... the K.G.B.'s Department V will provide them at a moment's notice.'

He paused, enjoying the meeting.

'... And then imagine the propaganda! An accused Nazi war criminal able to commit suicide, most likely in a German jail, rather than face trial for which the Soviet Union made him available. Even better, if it were to happen in America.'

His eyes swept the room.

'Oh yes,' predicted the chairman, confidently. 'The only people to emerge from this with any credit will be the Soviet Union.'

Frau Pöhl gazed at the food in the ancient, gas-operated refrigerator. It had been almost a week since her conversation with Herr Muntz and gradually the euphoria had evaporated. She had expected almost immediate contact from Heinrich, jumping at every sound outside the apartment, staring for hours down into the street outside, examining everyone. But he hadn't come. Now she felt cheated, like a child who knows there's a party in progress to which it hasn't been invited.

She closed the refrigerator door, shaking her head. When he came, he might be hungry. Herr Muntz had said he was in trouble. Perhaps he wouldn't have eaten for days. She walked to the bedroom, looking at the new suit hanging unworn in the wardrobe. She moved her hand over the material caressingly, feeling the stiffness of the new fibres. She hoped she would have some warning. She wanted so much to impress her husband when he finally came home. She would need at least an hour to prepare. She took the suit from the closet and brushed it, needlessly, then carefully replaced it, a strip of plastic wedged over the shoulders as a protection against the dust.

Should she break her ritual and miss her visit the following day to Heini's grave? She pondered the decision, walking slowly back into the kitchen. How awful, not to be here when he arrived, she thought. But she so enjoyed her Saturday visits. They were her only association with the past in which she desperately wanted to live. It would only take an hour, she reasoned, provided she cut out the coffee and cake on the Kurfürstendamm that was her other Saturday-morning luxury.

She looked back at the refrigerator. He wouldn't mind, she told herself. Quickly, the decision made, she cut two pieces very thinly off the ham she had bought for Heinrich's return, laid them on the pumpernickel and began eating, happily.

She'd take a chance the following morning, too, she decided.

(11)

Kurnov sat in a place of honour at the top table, his mind closed to the babble of the banquet going on around him, allowing only that amount of concentration necessary to give the briefest response when people spoke to him, constantly referring to his illness and asking for their understanding. There was movement behind him as a waiter appeared with cigars and liqueurs and Kurnov turned away, accepting the drink but refusing the cigar. He preferred cigarettes. The speeches began, long platitudes of greeting, and assertions of the importance of inter-country co-operation. How little they knew, reflected Kurnov, reviewing the day's discussion, about the psychiatric damage that could be caused to a person forced to accept a lifetime's incarceration in the sort of prisons to which he was accustomed. He smiled to himself. Every ridiculous theory would change if they visited Potma or Siberia.

Kurnov discarded thoughts of the convention, which irritated him, concentrating on what faced him, wondering how easy it would be to get away that night. Throughout the day he had maintained the pretence of ill-health and obtained sympathy from everyone. Certainly, the reflection that had looked back at him in the washroom mirror during the lunchtime adjournment had supported the lie. His resilience had a time-limit, he accepted. His nerves would not stand the sustained tension to which he was being subjected. He sighed, dismissing the reservation. It had to be concluded in five days, anyway. The conference ended then, closing the excuse for remaining in the city.

Distantly he heard a reference to honoured guests and realized people were looking at him, expecting reaction to the toast. He smiled, bleakly.

What would Bock have done after establishing contact? Very little, he guessed. There was nothing he could do, after all. Except await an approach. The surgeon would not come again to the conference, decided Kurnov. He'd taken quite a risk at exposing himself that morning. So the next move had to be his. Where would Bock anticipate it? At the clinic? Or at the apartment? It had to be his home, Kurnov decided. Just as Bock would not risk appearing a second time at the Kongresshalle, so he could not expose himself by going for the second night in succession to the clinic. Bock would realize that, guessed Kurnov, and know where to wait.

Around him people began applauding and Kurnov automatically joined in. He realized everyone was standing, indicating the end of the meal, and he rose with them.

Coach-tours of the city had been organized, with visits to several nightclubs, he knew. His excuse of continued ill-health was readily accepted by Bahr, unwilling to have a repetition of the previous night's sickness in another public place.

At the exit from the dining-room, tour organizers began mustering the coach parties and Kurnov stood, watching them depart, accepting with wan smiles their freshly expressed sympathy.

Kurnov baulked at descending the fire-escape again. During the day he had located the ground-floor corridor at the end of which an emergency door opened directly on to the alley-way into which the iron stairway led. After lunch, he had made a point of strolling from the conference to the hotel and had carefully left his overcoat in the unattended cloakroom on the ground floor for collection that night. He meandered around the foyer, allowing the delegates time to clear the hotel, then gave himself more time by taking one brandy at the bar. After fifteen minutes, he started walking as if towards the lift, but continued straight past. The topcoat was where he had left it during the day. He carried it from the cloakroom, glancing along the corridor. There was still time to return to the lift and make the difficult descent if he were spotted. The passageway was empty. Quickly he went to the end of the corridor, pushed the locking bar and went out into the alley.

Colonel Suvlov, a slightly built, nondescript man who merged well with the walls against which he usually stood, watched the entire charade, then walked back to the hotel bar for another cognac, grateful he wasn't one of the six men positioned outside in sub-zero temperatures.

'I'm apprehensive about Bock,' said Frieden.

Muntz looked up. God, how tired he felt, thought the lawyer. He wanted to go to bed and never get up again.

'Why?'

'That's the stupidity of it,' replied the Nazi millionaire. 'I don't have a reason. It's just a feeling.'

Muntz shrugged, unwilling to continue such an aimless argument. The tension was pressing upon the other man's nerves, he decided.

'He *was* Köllman's last contact,' continued Frieden, trying to convince himself.

Muntz took the handkerchief from his mouth. He was bleeding again.

'Obviously it's impossible to establish another telephone tap, like we have at the embassy,' admitted Frieden. 'That would increase greatly the risk of exposure and ruin the whole thing. But why don't we watch him for a few days?'

The lawyer looked at him, wearily.

'If you like,' he said, without enthusiasm. It hardly seemed to matter.

'Just for a few days,' emphasized Frieden, as if the decision needed justifying. He picked up the telephone and began dialling the man who would do it.

'You never know what you might discover,' said the millionaire, but the lawyer had stopped listening.

The car still retained some of the warmth that had built up from the heater during the ride from Seelingstrasse. Mosbacher lowered his head inside the collar of his overcoat, burying his hands in the pockets, preparing for a long wait in Severingstrasse. But he'd only been there forty minutes before he detected the figure approaching the apartment-block. He strained for better identification, cursing the need to park the vehicle so far from the building. It could mean nothing, of course: dozens of people lived in Bock's apartment-block. He stared fixedly at the telephone identification-system for Bock's apartment, which he had marked earlier that day. He started forward, hands gripping the driving wheel, as the figure paused briefly before the intercom, apparently spoke, and was admitted within seconds. It had definitely been Bock's flat. He was certain of it. Perhaps Perez's optimism was justified, he thought.

(12)

The two men stood warily on opposite sides of the penthouse lounge, Kurnov just inside the door, Bock in front of the veranda window. Neither wanted to speak first. The only sound was the muted noise from the city outside. He was a frightening man, decided Bock, looking at the scientist. Kurnov still had the unsettling ability to remain utterly still, staring wide-eyed, hypnotically almost, at whoever interested him. Bock remembered the effect, even upon brave men. Some had tried to answer that look, unflinching, with the final desperate awareness that there was no longer any hope and that they had nothing to fear by a last-minute show of defiance. Always their determination had collapsed under that unremitting gaze.

He's scared, judged Kurnov. Good. That would make the encounter easier. A frightened man was always the most malleable. How many years ago had it been when he formulated that basic philosophy? Too many to remember. It was important to maintain the man's fear, so Bock would have to break the silence, decided the scientist. He stared steadily, waiting. Inevitably, the surgeon averted his eyes, walking forward.

'Hello, Heinrich,' greeted Bock, softly.

'That's a name from another time,' threw back Kurnov, immediately knowing the correction would jar. 'Let's use our current names, shall we?'

Bock hesitated, hand half-raised. Would the man insist on the ridiculous Nazi salute, like Frieden? he wondered.

'Of course. I'm sorry,' he agreed, instantly. Nervously, he extended his hand.

'You've hardly changed, Helmut,' said the scientist, smiling. Apparent friendship would create false confidence.

Bock shook the hand, effusively, cupping the man's elbow in his left hand and leading him further into the room.

'Neither have you. I did a good job,' he said. There was the slightest edge of uncertainty in the laugh, a man wondering if he were going too far.

Kurnov did not smile, allowing the other man to think he was offended. He looked around the apartment, with its magnificent views over Berlin, then came back to the surgeon. Making the criticism just discernible in his voice, he said; 'It seems you've done a great many "good jobs".'

Bock shrugged, uneasily.

'I've been lucky,' he admitted. 'Other people's vanity pays well.'

He gestured to a seat, then indicated drinks laid out on a small table.

'Brandy,' selected Kurnov, lighting a cigarette. He watched quizzically at the amount Bock splashed into the glass, half filling it. The fool imagines he can get me drunk he thought. Bock took the same, then settled into a facing chair, holding the glass before him in both hands, so that his face was half hidden. He needed a barricade behind which to hide, judged Kurnov.

The anaesthetic-like numbness he had felt seeing Kurnov that morning swept over Bock. He wouldn't be able to manipulate Kurnov as easily as he had before, guessed the surgeon. Admittedly the man must have been desperate to come to Berlin, but he was still more controlled than he had been in 1945.

'You've prospered,' said the surgeon, positively. 'In a

119

country where personality cults are frowned upon, you're quite an exception.'

Kurnov slipped his drink, fixing his unblinking stare, letting silence frost the room.

'Small talk is a little out of place, isn't it?' he challenged, finally. It was time to harry the other man.

'... Well, ...' began Bock, but Kurnov over-rode him, deliberately.

'... I know I'm the last person in the world you want to see, Helmut. There's no need to maintain a pretence ...'

'That's not true,' tried Bock, flustered.

Kurnov took another drink, satisfied. It had really been quite easy, he thought. He imagined the other man would have developed more confidence after so many years of success. But then, Bock had always been a coward. What was it Yevtushenko had written? '... Cowards have small possibilities ...' Very appropriate in Bock's case.

'I'm here because I've got to be,' said Kurnov, flatly. 'We both know why. The risks I've taken, in the society where I exist, are terrifying ...'

He was setting out on a charted course, saying nothing the other man did not know. The apparent confession would allow Bock to believe in some slight superiority, a crutch that could easily be kicked away.

'I haven't time for chit-chat ...' he paused, preparing the threat. '... And neither have you, have you, Helmut? You're in as much danger, from the same people, as I am. Even more, perhaps.'

Bock sought an answer, moving a hand helplessly as if he could seize the words.

'Is it safe, Helmut, the money I left you? It would be very unfortunate for us both if it were all gone, wouldn't it ...?'

Bock started at the menace in the other man's voice, drawing back as if Kurnov had spat in his face.

'Surely you don't think I would have …?'

'Of course I do,' cut off Kurnov, again. 'Why shouldn't you have spent it? You didn't expect to see me again. Ever.'

'Wait,' said Bock, urgently. The ever-moving hand flapped as if he were pushing away an over-boisterous puppy. He hurried into a room behind Kurnov, who sat examining his drink, never once turning to see what the other man was doing. There was the sound of drawers being opened, then the scrape of what could have been a key in a lock. Bock hurried back into the room, wordlessly offering the bank-statements. There was a thick bundle, all carefully clipped together, dating back over thirty years. Kurnov glanced at them, almost as if he were disinterested, easily concealing the warmth of relief. It was all there, he saw. More than he had expected, even, unaware of how the interest would have accrued. The fool seemed to have kept every pfennig, like the coward he was.

'You're a good friend, Helmut,' conceded Kurnov and the other man flushed at the praise. 'I'm sorry I ever doubted you,' Kurnov added.

He humped his shoulders, indicating helplessness. 'It's just that I'm frightened … I never expected all this to happen. There are few people to whom I can turn for help.'

None, assessed Bock, looking down at the man. Was he really frightened? It was impossible to gauge anything from that blank face. It never had been possible, even before the operation.

'It's desperate,' warned Bock, hoping to instil into the other man the fear he felt. Kurnov remained unmoved. 'Desperate,' emphasized the surgeon.

'I want to know everything,' said Kurnov, calmly.

Hurriedly, but omitting nothing, Bock recounted the telephone call from the Bavarian, then told of Frieden's visit, searching Kurnov's face for reaction. What was

121

he, for God's sake, some kind of robot? he wondered, unconsciously settling upon Damerov's nickname.

Kurnov sat nodding, like a man hearing a record with which he was already familiar. His disguised reaction was mixed. Good. And bad, he decided. He hadn't expected direct contact would have been made with Bock. He felt the vague stirrings of unease. The Nazi interest was worrying, he thought. Most of them were ridiculous figures now, old men clinging to memories and mentally moving toy armies into position to win a long-forgotten war. But they retained the capacity to hate those who had offended. And the ability to punish.

'So the Nazis still want me,' mused the Russian, reflectively.

Hoping confirmation would endorse the reasoning he had put forward thirty years before and perhaps create some gratitude, Bock said quickly, 'Oh, yes. Even more so. You wouldn't believe how much they want you.'

Kurnov wondered why Bock had over-stressed himself. Was there some reason of which he wasn't sure for the man's nervousness? He smiled, not allowing the man comfort. There was still some resistance to be broken down.

'If they knew, they'd want you just as much, wouldn't they Helmut?'

The surgeon nodded, a gesture of hopelessness. He felt exhausted, like a man not properly recovered from a serious illness. He wondered if he could excuse himself to go to the bathroom. He badly needed another Librium injection.

'Do you believe the man with the Bavarian accent?' demanded Kurnov.

Bock looked at him, uncomprehendingly.

'I'm unsure about it,' continued Kurnov, tilting the balance so that Bock's uncertainty would be constantly agitated.

'I don't know,' shrugged Bock, discomforted, as had been intended. 'I suppose it's odd. But then, how else could he have made contact?'

The Russian nodded, as if in reluctant agreement.

'I suppose the bloody yids are here, sniffing like dogs around a dustbin?'

Again Bock gestured helplessly. 'How would I know?' he said. 'I expect they are.'

For several minutes, Kurnov was silent. Then he said, definitely. 'They're the danger, the Jews. Or the authorities.'

'Everyone is a danger,' corrected Bock, unhappily.

'True,' conceded Kurnov. 'But it's official action that could cause me most difficulty.'

'The Nazis would just kill you,' jabbed Bock, sarcastically, still anxious for some response from the other man. Kurnov had said 'me', not 'us', he noticed.

Kurnov smiled at the reminder.

'They've got to catch me first,' he pointed out. 'And they've no idea where to look ...'

He stopped, fixing Bock with that unsettling stare.

'... You're the only one who can expose me, Helmut,' he said, 'And if I die, you die.'

Bock stood up, refilling his glass. He held out his hand for Kurnov's brandy glass, but the Russian shook his head.

'I know,' said Bock, a man accepting defeat.

Kurnov sat back, happily. Bock was quickly becoming cowed. Soon he would do what he was told, without argument. Kurnov still experienced something approaching a sexual feeling at breaking another man.

'We've got to get to this Bavarian first,' announced Kurnov.

Bock laughed, a jeering sound. 'How, for Christ's sake? Don't you think that hadn't occurred to me?'

'That sort of remark doesn't help,' rebuked Kurnov. Once a man came near to being beaten, he had to be allowed no opportunity to recover. Under proper conditions, it took only days of constant, relentless pressure to create a complete slave-mentality.

Bock stared at him, clinging to the defiance.

'All right. How do we do it?' he demanded. 'It's a voice on the telephone ... someone who's called just once ...'

'... And will call again,' predicted Kurnov.

'What if he doesn't?' questioned the surgeon, isolating the Russian's fear.

That was the one unpredictable thing. Kurnov moved his tongue over the tooth in which the cyanide was embedded.

'He'll call,' he repeated. He paused. It was the time for commitment. 'And you are going to have to arrange a meeting ... between him and me ...'

'You ...?' queried Bock, amazed. It had not occurred to the surgeon how any exchange would be negotiated, but he had never imagined Kurnov would become personally involved.

'Do you think I could trust anyone else?' demanded Kurnov, arrogantly. Momentarily, the attitude faltered. 'There isn't anyone else,' he added, sadly.

'And if he doesn't call again,' persisted Bock.

'Then,' said Kurnov. 'It's as you say. Very desperate.'

The Russian picked up the Swiss account, finding the statements that had arrived a few days before.

'Over three million,' he mused, tapping the paper with his finger. 'That's a lot of money.'

Bock sat waiting. Kurnov looked up.

'You're sure that's all he wanted? Just money?'

Bock nodded, immediately. 'Positive,' he said. 'That's all he kept on about, money that he said rightfully belonged to him. He said he was holding an auction, selling to the highest bidder.'

Kurnov frowned, trying to analyse the remark. It made little sense, he decided. The only inference was that the caller was a disgruntled German who felt he had been cheated. Whom had he ever known closely enough to have felt personally robbed? No one. No, that was not strictly true. Grüber perhaps. But Grüber was dead. Bock had been the man who had conducted the inquiries, although for reasons other than worrying about the fellow-scientist's safety, while he recovered from the plastic surgery.

'You never heard anything to suppose that Grüber survived the Russian attack?' he asked, abruptly.

Bock looked at him, baffled.

'Who?' he asked, stupidly.

'Grüber, for Christ's sake,' shouted Kurnov, pressing the man.

'I'm sorry,' stumbled Bock. 'No, of course not. Why should I have done?'

'Because he is the only person who might have had reasons to complain, like the Bavarian. He would have known of the fortune I was collecting, too. And he came from Munich.'

Bock made a dismissive gesture. 'He's dead,' he insisted, definitely.

'And why you?' Kurnov asked, speaking his thoughts aloud. 'Of all people, why did the Bavarian choose to contact you?'

'I wish to God I knew,' replied Bock, sincerely.

Kurnov stood up and began pacing the room, trying to resolve the doubt. Why would the blackmailer assume Bock had money? He gazed around the penthouse. An obvious answer was the luxury in which Bock lived. There was no secret about the extravagance and a lifestyle associated with film stars and the famous. It was part of the public relations, in fact. But that could not be the only incentive. He was sure that whatever had been recovered from the Austrian lake would have contained no details of the Swiss account. But there were other pointers, he realized. If the Bavarian were a

125

disgruntled Nazi, then it was likely he knew of Bock's immediate post-war treatment to all the men who had wanted new faces. And guessed that Bock might have retained ties that would have made a lot of money available. That was it. The approach hadn't been connected with him; it had been a way of getting to other Nazis.

'Could the box contain any details about you?'

Bock played with his glass, considering the question. The heroin addict had handed over all his personal records, he knew. He'd even insisted on going through the filing cabinet himself.

'I don't think so,' he said. 'I took every precaution.'

Kurnov sighed, irritably.

'Didn't I?' he demanded, rhetorically. 'What about centralized records, in Berlin? How else could the Bavarian have known of the details he mentioned in his telephone call?'

Again there was the movement of helplessness from the surgeon. What a fool, decided Kurnov, angrily.

'There must have been *some* record,' insisted Kurnov. 'How else would people have known where to come for new faces?'

Bock considered the question. Then he said. 'Word of mouth. There was never anything written. Frieden assured me of that, years ago. He came to me because he knew of the work in the camp. And he just recommended people when they sought help from him.'

'Rubbish,' rejected Kurnov. 'Somewhere, probably in Frieden's safe, there will be details of everything you've even done for the Organisation, just as in some Berlin office there would have been records of your work at the camp. In Frieden's case, it would have been kept for blackmail purposes. Never forget, the Nazis were efficient, above all else.'

Bock shuffled, uncomfortably. He would *have* to take another injection soon. Kurnov looked away. There was no point in furthering Bock's fear at the moment. He wanted the man manageable, not apathetic.

'We're going to make a deal, when the man calls again,' said Kurnov.

'*If* he calls again,' cautioned Bock.

Kurnov ignored the interruption. 'He's got a black-mailer's dream and he knows it ...' He waved the bank-statement. '... All we've got to do is capitalize on his greed.'

'I don't understand.'

Kurnov closed his eyes, wearily. 'According to what's been printed,' he explained, 'the box contained details of nearly every wanted Nazi. The Jews have already said they're prepared to pay a million ...'

He paused. Bock watched him attentively, head to one side.

'... But that's for everything. We will pay a million. But just for the folder that contains the material about me and the folder about you ...'

Bock smiled. He recalled his relief of that morning. He knew Kurnov would have it worked out.

'... And he'll still have everything else to sell. If he deals with us first, he'll double what he stands to get ...'

He hesitated, looking at the statement again.

'... And if he baulks at one million for just two folders, then we'll offer him two million ...'

He threw the statement down.

'... In fact,' he said, 'he can have it all.'

He looked up at the surgeon. 'I want several bank drafts, starting with a million ...'

'There's no way ...'

'You've got bank-authorization documents,' broke in Kurnov. Bock nodded agreement.

'That'll enable a withdrawal,' Kurnov said. He nodded his head back towards the study. 'Tonight,' he insisted. 'I want it tonight.'

The surgeon hurried away and Kurnov sipped his

drink. The bank-drafts would be an embarrassment if they were found in his possession, he thought. Still, his stature was such that a search was unlikely.

'We've no guarantee there's going to be another call,' said Bock, reiterating the doubt as he returned, holding out the written authorizations.

'There will be,' said Kurnov, taking the papers. 'Look at it psychologically. From the Jews, he knows he can get a million, probably more. But he still calls you. For all we know, he might have contacted other people, trying to get through to the Nazis as well. What does that indicate?'

Bock looked at him blankly.

'Remember his expression ... "the money that was rightfully his" ... and his Bavarian accent. He's a German, a Nazi most probably. And although he's prepared to screw everybody, he's still got an inbuilt reluctance to deal with the Jews.'

'That's a wild assessment,' said Bock.

'No, it's not. It's an intelligent analysis of what we know so far.'

Still Bock looked doubtful.

'Look at another indicator,' pressed Kurnov. 'There would be no point in telephoning just once. He probably assesses you as a link with a lot of Nazis, because of the work you did just after the war. And thinks you have access to a great deal of money. So even if the Jews came up with a fortune, he'd still come back to you, just to see if you'd top it. There's never been a shortage of money in the Party.'

'I hope you're right,' said the surgeon, unconvinced.

'So do I,' muttered Kurnov, fervently.

(13)

Because it was Saturday, with the conference suspended, tours were organized throughout the morning. Kurnov allowed himself to be carried in the crowd towards the waiting coaches, but carefully avoided contact with everyone around him. His fame within Russia assured his superiority and no one challenged his insistence upon a seat by himself, at the rear of the bus.

The first stop was at Berlin's famous zoo, for which Kurnov was grateful. Slowly, he allowed himself to drop further and further behind the main party, anxious to avoid being trapped by his own companions. Twice the party slowed, to permit him to catch up. Each time he feigned interest in the animals and mumbled a vague apology befitting a man still feeling unwell. The main thoroughfare was intersected by minor paths. He maintained the slow progress, apparently intent upon bordering cages, again preparing the shrugging apology, but no move came from the party ahead. Suddenly he darted sideways, hurrying into an even narrower walk and heading for the exit out on to Budapesterstrasse. He had to fight against running, still tensed against a yell of challenge that would destroy everything. He dodged traffic to cross the busy main road, then cut down Wickmannstrasse, walking close against the tall buildings, seeking their concealment.

He turned right, into Landgrafenstrasse, looking at his watch. Nine forty-five. Tempelhof was at least thirty minutes away. It took nearly ten minutes to find a taxi and he was perspiring with nervous annoyance as he settled back, snapping out the address in Hermann-strasse. As the noisy, diesel-driven Mercedes edged through the morning traffic, he forced himself to relax, seeking old landmarks, needing the comfort of nostalgia. This was the greatest risk he had taken, he realized, bringing his thoughts back inside the vehicle. Several times back there in the zoo he'd seen the frowns of bewilderment from Russians unable to reconcile his behaviour with whatever illness he was suffering. So far, his luck had held. Amazingly so. But it couldn't last, he accepted, realistically. Now he had vanished, in broad daylight. Which amounted to near-insanity. Would the excuse that he had become lost in the labyrinth of path-ways be as acceptable as the illness? Hardly, he decided. There was bound to be a report made to Moscow, he thought; his conduct was almost infantile. But it had to be. Again the helplessness of his position washed over him and he grimaced, to himself, then shrugged, in resignation. He was like a puppy chasing a leaf in the wind, he thought, running without direction. He hesitated, correcting the simile. More like the leaf, he decided, thrown whichever way people decided to blow.

It had been madness to take this chance, he suddenly thought, angrily. He did not know if Gerda were still alive. Or if she retained the habits of thirty years ago. He stopped, re-considering. If she were alive, he thought, then she would have retained the habit. Dull, boring Gerda had always been a woman of rigid, unchanging routine. Only in clothes was there constant change. It was an odd psychiatric paradox that hadn't occurred to him before.

He paid the taxi, looking nervously around, then went through the main gate of St Thomas Kirchhof. Immediately inside the cemetery he stopped, trying to recall the location of Heini's grave. Had he ever visited it? He must have done, he supposed, when the boy was buried. He couldn't remember. Methodically, he began searching for the tombstone, moving along the winding pathways. Overhead, the jets roared in arrival and departure. He wondered how many nervous flyers were made more frightened, with a flight-path immediately over a cemetery. Occasionally he glanced up, envious of the freedom of those cocooned passengers, going anywhere they wanted. He would sacrifice the £3,000,000, he thought, for just one such ticket.

All around him the graves were assembled in their orderly rows, the headpieces heavy with Germanic stonemasonry. He couldn't recall ordering a gravestone for his son. Gerda would have done it, he decided. It was the sort of thing she would have enjoyed doing, studying the designs and involving herself with sympathetic officials who would have fawned upon her, conscious of his position. She would have ordered several black suits and dresses, he was sure.

He had almost passed the stone, black with neglect and tilted sideways from some long-ago accident, before he realized it was the one he was seeking. Weeds straggled over the mound and leaves from a nearby tree were banked against one side.

' "Heini Köllman," ' he read, ' "Born July, 1926, died May, 1943." '

How abrupt, he thought sadly, that a person's life should be dismissed so briefly. A statistic, nothing more. He had slowed, under the pretence of examining another grave, trying to recall his son's image. He could not remember him, he realized. He had a vague recollection of a thin, intense boy, rolling the cant phrases of National Socialism in his mouth like a schoolboy tasting sweets. Heini had had fair hair, he determined. Or was it? He couldn't be sure. It was like trying to identify a casual acquaintance through a fog. He broke away from the past abruptly, remembering why he was there.

And then he saw her. She was lingering over another mound, two graves away, disguising her pilgrimage.

Every Saturday for over thirty years, he reflected, in amazement. How many people must have guessed in that time? As he watched, she looked up, towards Heini's resting place, and smiled. She was an old, grey-haired woman, he saw, with varicose legs bulging the heavy, darned stockings, which puckered around her ankles, when she stooped beside the adjoining abandoned burial-place. Her straggling hair had fallen from its retaining band, half covering her face. Her shabbiness shocked him. Gerda, who had changed at least three times a day when his position in the inner caucus of the Party had made unlimited funds available, wore a suit shining with use and the shoes, half-on, half-off her feet as she squatted, were trodden down at the heel. A slut, he thought. A fading, ageing slut. How ugly she was. To imagine, he thought, that he'd actually married the clumsy woman getting to her feet fifteen yards away. And gone to bed with her. Touched her even. And made love, albeit more from duty than from desire.

He shivered, like someone coming into close contact with a person suffering an incurable illness. Horrible, he thought.

She began walking away, and he turned to avoid her, but as she went by their arms actually brushed. She glanced an unseeing apology, hurrying on. He allowed her to get about twenty-five yards ahead before turning, to follow. She walked jerkily, as if she suffered from rheumatism. It was her thigh, or maybe her back, he thought, professionally. She had tried to simulate a model's walk, he recalled, all those years ago. And had succeeded, he remembered. Yes, she had once had quite a graceful carriage.

He was worried about her realizing the man near the grave was in the same bus-queue, but she seemed oblivious to her surroundings, glancing constantly at her watch as if she feared being late for an appointment. He sat six rows behind, eyes fixed intently on the back of her head as the vehicle wound its way back through Charlottenburg *en route* to the city centre. She got up in Westfälischestrasse and he hurriedly glanced away, stupidly fearing identification. Quickly, just before the bus moved off, he followed. She was some way ahead in the Saturday-morning flurry of shoppers, but he had little difficulty in keeping her in view. She was obviously in a hurry, he decided. Several times she consulted her watch, bustling up Paulsbornerstrasse into Brandenburgische and then turning almost immediately into Duisburgerstrasse. He had moved closer, fearing he might lose her as she twisted through the streets, and was only feet away when she turned into the building where apartments had been constructed over shops. He was at the entrance when the concierge looked up and greeted her.

'Guten Morgen, Frau Pöhl.'

He moved on, smiling. His luck was holding, he decided, desperate for omens.

Frau Pöhl? He wondered where she had got that name. Wasn't there some member of her family named Pöhl? He couldn't remember.

He looked around, anxious for a taxi. How, he wondered again, as the vehicle moved off towards the hotel, would his story of becoming hopelessly lost be accepted?

Five miles away, Suvlov replaced the telephone, considering the result of that morning's surveillance. He shook his head, sadly. Kurnov must be insanely desperate, he decided, to behave as he was doing. Who, he wondered, was the old lady whom he had so clumsily followed?

In the Seelingstrasse apartment, the two Jewish agents gave a detailed report of their observation of the man whom Mosbacher had identified from their file pictures as the person he had seen leaving Bock's flat the previous evening. Perez fingered the thick file that had been amassed over the last thirty years on the wife of Heinrich Köllman.

'Frau Pöhl?' he mused. 'Well, we wanted confirmation. I never guessed he would provide it for us so positively.'

'He's running scared,' said Mosbacher, unknowingly echoing the thoughts of the Russian secret policeman.

'Not yet he isn't,' argued Perez. 'He's not as scared as he's going to be.'

He looked up, inviting the argument from the fat man facing him.

'If it works,' said Mosbacher definitely, 'then one day you'll hate yourself.'

'Bullshit,' rejected Perez.

There was nothing, thought Mosbacher sadly, that could save their friendship. Whatever the outcome of this operation, their association would never be the same again.

(14)

There were many related telephone calls in Berlin that day.

The first, by carefully rehearsed design, was to the apprehensive Bock. He feared the call, of course, staring at the strident telephone like a small animal gazing hypnotized at the snake whose bite it knows will kill. And with that same inevitability, facing danger instead of running from it, he reached out, picking up the instrument.

Immediately he heard the accent, the fear cut through his drug-induced shield and, dry-mouthed, he mumbled single-word responses to the instructions, twitching at the other man's harshness. The man had Nazi training, he decided. All the intonations were there, so similar to Buchenwald.

Like water bursting a blocked stream, his anxiety flooded over immediately he telephoned Kurnov, who had arrived back at the hotel thirty minutes earlier to find his explanation of getting lost easily accepted by the other Russians.

Kurnov sighed at the babble, closing his eyes. Bock was becoming an encumbrance, he thought. And a danger. He could never leave Berlin with the man alive. He paused, considering the decision. He'd killed before, countless times. But it was always quite automatic, dispatching people with the lack of feeling of a scientist killing animals upon which he had experimented and written opinions, and for which he had no further use. With Bock he would be for the first time killing someone he knew, albeit distantly. He wondered if it would make any difference. He smiled into the chatter coming through the receiver, personally embarrassed at the reservation. A ridiculous thought, he decided. Of course it would make no difference, no difference at all.

The Bavarian had been curt, Bock reported. The surgeon was speaking in spurts, as the recollections came to him, with the anxiousness of a pupil wishing to recount verbatim the lessons from a teacher he wished to impress. The Bavarian had appeared even more confident than before, laughing almost as if he had expected the suggestion when the surgeon had put forward the idea of purchasing only two folders, leaving the rest to be sold to the highest bidder.

'Did he agree?' snapped Kurnov, urgently.

For several seconds there was no reply, as if Bock were unsure of the answer.

'Did he?' demanded the Russian, shouting.

'Yes,' replied Bock, simply, at last. Then he added, 'He said "What else could you do?"'

Kurnov considered the reply, the familiar feeling of helplessness coming again. A leaf blown in any direction, he decided again. The Bavarian knew the value of what he held, and was aware they would do anything to recover it.

'He said "us"?' queried Kurnov.

'Yes,' reported Bock. 'The moment I identified the files, he started laughing.'

'What did he say?'

'He said, "So Heinrich had to come running",' replied the surgeon.

Kurnov stared down at the telephone number the Bavarian had given and which he had written, under Bock's dictation, upon the bedside pad. He checked his watch. Three minutes before he had to make the call.

'So he mentioned my name?' said Kurnov.

Again Bock hesitated before replying. Then he said,

'Of course. Once I'd mentioned the files, it was a fairly obvious inference, wasn't it?'

Kurnov slumped, weighed by fatigue and the inability to run the negotiations as he would have liked. If only that gibbering fool at the other end of the telephone could be trusted. But he couldn't, certainly not with anything upon which his life depended. So Bock was useless. He paused, halted by the word. Bock *had* exhausted his use, he thought. In a few minutes, he would be taking over the discussions with the Bavarian. Carefully hidden in his briefcase were the bank withdrawal-forms that Bock had already signed. So when should the man die? Tonight? Kurnov shook his head in the empty room. It was ridiculous to eliminate his only contact in Berlin before he held the file in his hand. But he must deal with him immediately afterwards, he thought. Bock's collapse was far too dangerous to be allowed one minute beyond what was absolutely necessary.

It was almost time to make the telephone call.

'Stay in your apartment tonight,' ordered Kurnov. 'This has got to be finished. Soon. I might need help.'

'Of course,' concurred Bock, immediately. It would be wonderful, he thought, to complete everything, so that he could go back as he was before. He replaced the receiver and headed for the bathroom. It was only temporary support, he reassured himself. Once this was over, he would stop again. It wasn't difficult. He'd done it before, for God's sake. His hands shook as he prepared the injection.

On the far side of the city, Kurnov took off his wrist-watch and placed it on the bedside table, so he could watch the sweep of the second hand wiping away the time. He was very frightened, Kurnov realized. Because it had been far easier to move unrestricted around Berlin than he had expected, he had gained confidence, he knew. But equally, he accepted, it was a brittle sureness, easily shattered.

The second hand moved quickly past the six and sped up the watchface, and the hour hand moved almost imperceptibly to one o'clock. Somewhere outside the hotel-room, a distant clock struck agreement.

The breath jerked from him, in stages, and he pulled himself upright, nervously. He recognized the symptoms, the abandonment of hope he had seen so often in his experiments. Not yet, he determined. He was a long way from capitulation. He'd win. He knew he'd win. He always had. There was no reason why there should be a reversal now. He twitched, disconcerted, recognizing the shallowness of his confidence.

Swallowing, the Russian picked up the receiver, obtained an outside line and dialled, holding the instrument away, as if there might have been an electrical shock from it. The receiver at the other end was lifted after the second ring and a voice came almost cheerfully on the line. The Bavarian accent was very pronounced, he thought.

'Guten Abend, Herr Doktor Köllman,' greeted the man.

Kurnov gasped, immediately regretting the reaction, knowing the other man would have detected it.

'Come now, doctor. Or shall I call you Heinrich? Yes, I'll call you Heinrich. Come now, Heinrich, let's not have any theatricality ...'

'How do you ...?'

'... Know that the infamous Dr Köllman would be the person on the telephone? Because it had to be, hadn't it? Remember what I've got from the lake. I've always known what you did, Heinrich. Now I've got proof. I've got the secret you hoped would never come out. So I knew you'd have to come and get it back, if you were alive, no matter where you were hiding ... and then, Bock mentioned the files he wanted to buy. So I knew you'd arrived. Just simple deduction.'

'No matter where you were hiding,' picked up

Kurnov. Did that mean the man at the other end didn't know his new identity? An ephemeral hope. But hope, nevertheless. Bock was right; it was unquestionably a Bavarian accent. Kurnov wished he had had the forethought to have a glass of water on the tiny bedside table, coughing through his blocked throat.

'Who are you?' demanded the Russian.

It was a jeering laugh. 'You'll be surprised, Heinrich. So surprised. I can hardly wait to see the look on your face ...'

'You mean ... I know you ...?'

Again the laugh. 'Oh yes, Heinrich. You know me. That's what is making this all the more enjoyable for me.'

Kurnov squeezed his eyes shut, forcing himself to think. Who? It had to be possible to guess. But there was no one, no one at all. Only Grüber. And Grüber was dead. Yet it was obviously someone who knew him. And knew him well. But there was nobody that close. There never had been.

'Bock's broken, isn't he?' said the other man, defining Kurnov's earlier thoughts. This time the Russian avoided any obvious reaction. But only just.

'He's very dangerous to you, Heinrich,' continued the Bavarian. 'You'll have to dispose of him soon, for your own protection. You've decided to kill him, of course, haven't you?'

Kurnov's mouth moved, forming the words, but no sound emanated. He recognized the method: had used it even, to break a person. A cardinal principle was to anticipate the thought in the victim's mind, as it occurred, so that he became disorientated and muddled, feeling the interrogator could reach in to control his reasoning. But it was necessary to have studied the victim first, for the psychology to succeed.

'Come now,' went on the Bavarian, the lilt in his voice hinting his elation at his control of the conversation. 'There's no need to be shy with me, Heinrich. I know you. So I know just what you will have been planning over the last twenty-four hours. Bock's probably necessary as a contact. But that is over now. Remember what you always said, Heinrich — "Stay alive. Whatever happens, stay alive." That was your credo, wasn't it? Bock's endangering your chances.'

Who? searched Kurnov, desperately. Whose knowledge was complete enough to recall remarks he'd made over thirty years ago? In every sentence there was a clue and still he was unable to identify the man. He stared at his hand, vibrating on the table. His nerves were being destroyed, he realized. He would have to conclude everything soon, otherwise he would be reduced to a mumbling apology of a man. Like Bock.

'You must tell me ...' he started, but immediately the German talked him down, enjoying his superiority. Another psychological trick, identified Kurnov. Bully an uncertain man, to keep him jumping.

'I haven't got to do anything for you,' insisted the voice, with sudden vehemence. 'Nothing. Just as you did nothing for me.'

Another clue, snatched Kurnov, desperately. It was someone he'd offended, in the past.

'Look,' tried Kurnov, urgently, gesturing with his free hand. 'I don't know who you are. But you're obviously someone from the Party ... someone I've hurt, unknowingly. I don't know how ... unless you tell me. Or why. But I'm sorry. I'm prepared to make any apology. And to pay ... to pay very well for what came from that damned lake. There's no point in this baiting, no point at all ...'

He stopped, abruptly. It was working, he thought, worriedly, analysing what he had just said. He was capitulating, offering concessions unthinkingly ... just like his own victims had, over and over again, when he had practised the same approach.

'It's not nice, is it, Heinrich?' teased the voice, and Kurnov gripped his hands, tightly clamping his mouth together to prevent the exasperation escaping in a sound. He was doing it again! Always the other man was ahead, anticipating the thoughts. It was almost as if the two had worked together, in the early days. Another clue?

'... This must be one of the first times in your life that you've lost control and had to beg ... to plead with someone,' the torment went on.

The sentence broke away into a sniggering, unsympathetic laugh.

'... Think, Heinrich. How many times have you heard such pleas from people who've known you're going to experiment upon them until they die? It's not nice, is it, Heinrich, being brought to this level?'

Kurnov breathed in, deeply, fighting for control. The bastard, making him grovel. How wonderful it would be, he thought, to make the man suffer.

'What do you want?' he asked. The desperation leaked into his voice and stupidly he snapped his mouth shut. He had to conceal any weakness, he knew. It was part of the psychology, identifying his own gradual collapse. He sighed, reluctantly. It was pointless, he thought. The man seemed to know his weaknesses before he revealed them. He straightened in the chair, angrily. That was *exactly* the mental attitude the other man was trying to engender, he knew.

'Want?' echoed the Bavarian. 'What do I want? Oh, many things, Heinrich, many things. Money, of course. A lot of money. And I shall get that. I shall get it from you and Bock very easily. And from the yids, too. Those bastards can suffer ... because they were born to suffer. They're good at it, aren't they. You proved that, years ago.'

Kurnov seized the word, 'yids'. A Nazi. The man had to be a committed Nazi whom he had once known, intimately. But he had known no one that well. By careful design. His very survival had been built upon a platform of remaining aloof.

'... But satisfaction, too,' continued the man. 'Satisfaction most of all. You're going to crawl to me, Heinrich. You're going to repeat, again and again, how sorry you are for what you did ...'

'What the hell did I do ...?' yelled Kurnov, uncontrolled. The man was right, Kurnov accepted. It *was* one of the first times he'd had to beg. And it was bad. Very bad.

The laughter jarred down the telephone, stretching Kurnov's annoyance.

'Come now, Heinrich. There's no point in losing your temper. I'm holding all the bargaining points ... don't forget that ...'

Was it a trap, a Nazi ploy to punish him after all these years? The fear came at him, suddenly. No, he dismissed, immediately. It wasn't a plot. The Nazis weren't like that. They'd snatch him and torture him for what he had done. But such a psychological approach was beyond them. Always they had veered towards thuggery. And if they'd had the evidence they wouldn't be proclaiming it around Berlin.

'I'll need to be sure ...' he began, but again, confident of himself, the Bavarian cut in. It was a practised persistence, accepted Kurnov, rehearsed to unsettle him.

'Of what, Heinrich? That this isn't some elaborate Nazi plot to trap you after all these years ...?'

Oh God, thought Kurnov. Every time he was being anticipated. He mumbled, sentences not forming.

'... Got to be sure ...' he managed.

'I really don't see you can be,' said the other man, lightly. 'I don't give a fuck for the Nazis ... they're like children with an old game ... something played years ago and outgrown. But there's no way I can convince you of that. Or want to, particularly. It's simply a matter for you. I've got the dossiers. If you're uncertain, then don't buy. Leave it to the yids.'

'I can't do that,' blurted Kurnov.

'I know you can't,' came back the other man. He giggled. '... You wouldn't believe the pleasure I get from the power, Heinrich. I'm aware it's not like that you've known, conscious that whole camps of men, women and children have quivered and tried to run away as you've entered. But it isn't bad. It brought you running. And reduced Bock to a nervous breakdown. The yids are running around, beside themselves with anxiety. And I expect the Organisation der Ehemaligen S.S. Angehörgen have committed themselves totally to recovering evidence that they think could hang them all.'

How much he needed a drink, thought Kurnov. He felt like a man abandoned in a desert.

'What do you want me to do?' he asked. The words rasped from him, the defeat obvious.

'Oh, Heinrich,' jibed the Bavarian. 'I expected you to last out much longer. After all, no one should know better than you how to resist psychological pressure. But now you've given in. What a disappointment!'

'What do you want?' the Russian repeated, dully.

He would defeat the man, he decided, suddenly. He'd allow himself to be led along, like a bull with a ring through its nose, but he would beat him, in the end. He bit against the knuckle he pressed into his mouth, reinforcing the vow with pain. God, how he'd make the bastard suffer.

'A meeting, I think, Heinrich,' said the Bavarian, picking up the question. 'A meeting, so I can get the pleasure of seeing you physically squirm.'

Kurnov's anger evaporated like mist in a summer sun.

'A meeting? Certainly,' he responded, ignoring the laughter with which the eagerness was greeted.

'Somewhere open, I think, don't you, Heinrich? Some-where like the Grunewald Park?'

Kurnov winced. It was miles on the other side of the city.

'Have you a pen, Heinrich?' prodded the Bavarian. 'You'd better write it down. You don't want to get the directions wrong, do you?'

'I'm ready,' recited Kurnov.

'Good. Go along the Autobahn, until you see the sign for the Teltower Weg. Go down that filter road until it's intersected by the Verbindung. The first road leads down to the Sportsplatz. Wait at that junction, Heinrich. Just wait and I'll come when I'm ready ...'

'Wait,' said Kurnov, desperately. 'It's difficult for me ... I can't wait indefinitely ...'

'You can, Heinrich,' jeered the man. 'You can wait just as long as I determined you should. You've no control, you know. None at all ...'

'Please ...' started Kurnov again, but then stopped as the receiver was replaced.

Kurnov sat on the bedside, unable to move. He shuddered violently, frustration bunched inside him. Quickly he walked to the bathroom, gulping water, finally immersing his face in the shallow bowl. He stared up at himself in the mirror. In just a week, he saw, he'd become an old man. The strain and fear was marked into his face as if Bock had incised it there all those years ago, with his scalpel. Without any sound he began crying, watching the tears form their own path down his face. Please God, he prayed. Help me. Please.

The second call from the Bavarian was much shorter and more businesslike. The same Israeli took it, noting the instructions immediately and without challenge, running from the embassy to get to the stipulated meeting-place. The phone-box was on Hüfner Weg, near the park.

As the Bavarian had promised, the stopping-place was identifiable from the box-number.

The topsheet from a file upon Richard Glücks, water-stained, was stuck lightly in the page where the Israeli embassy number was listed. As he snatched the page out, the Israeli tore the reference to Glücks. He quickly checked nothing of importance was left, apart from the name that he didn't want, then hurried away from the box, hesitating momentarily outside to ensure he was not observed.

Even though Muntz argued they would probably be too late, Frieden insisted upon driving to the telephone-box four hours later when they got the recording of the intercepted message.

The portly Nazi stumped from the telephone-box, driving his fist into the side of the car in frustration.

'It's happened,' he said, definitely. 'As the man promised in the call, he left something as proof of what the box contains.'

He waved the directory in Muntz's face, so the ailing lawyer could see that the page listing the Israeli embassy had been ripped out. Still adhering was the water-stained strip that had come away when the security man had pulled at the page.

'He itemized the page it would be on,' reminded Frieden.

Muntz looked at him, wearily. How pointless it all seemed, he thought. Frieden answered the look.

'We can't miss them again,' he said, definitely. 'Tell the telephonist we must be called, immediately another meeting is arranged, so that we can get there at the same time as the yids. I don't care if it costs the man his job. The Organisation will pay him for life, just for that one piece of information.'

'How do we know it isn't too late?' queried Muntz. 'Perhaps the Jews have bought everything already.'

Frieden shook his head, angrily. The lawyer's mind

was seizing up with his illness, he decided.

'We know from the blasted tape,' he insisted. 'They had no idea we would intercept that conversation. So what would be the point of stage-managing what happened tonight? None at all. The final hand-over will be in a house or an apartment. It has to be. They're hardly going to exchange an ammunition box for a million pounds in the middle of a public park, are they?'

Muntz nodded reluctant agreement.

'I'm very frightened, Max,' said the lawyer, unexpectedly. 'I've a feeling we're going to be beaten.'

The millionaire stared at the other man, the anger returning at the easy capitulation. It was difficult to argue, however. Because Frieden was experiencing the same doubts.

These were increased four hours later by the announcement in Jerusalem that there had been further Israeli contact with the man purporting to hold the Toplitz box.

'We are confident of a major development within days,' asserted Moshe Dayan. 'We have information already about Richard Glücks.'

The Politburo listened patiently to Mavetsky's report. Towards the end, Shepalin began nodding, but the minister was unsure what the gesture meant. Mavetsky paused, looking back to the last page of Suvlov's report, picking up the sentence.

'... And certainly from the oddness of his behaviour, disregarding the caution that any normal Russian would show during a foreign visit, it would seem that Kurnov's control is fast slipping away,' he read aloud. 'The thought that he might be under surveillance does not appear to have occurred to him.'

The minister looked up.

'I think,' he said to the assembled government, feeling it wise to voice the fear, 'we should be careful of that development. I am concerned at the continued freedom we are allowing the man, matched against this reported deterioration ...'

Shepalin smiled at the anxiety.

'... But we have your assurance that he's adequately guarded,' the chairman prodded gently. 'And don't forget that West Berlin is an encircled city. There's nowhere he can go, is there?'

Mavetsky abandoned the argument, sitting down. The protest had been registered, which was sufficient for the moment, he decided. He'd definitely infiltrate more men over the Wall, he thought.

At that moment, in West Berlin, Kurnov was returning to the hotel after spending four hours waiting, as instructed, at the junction in Grunewald Park. He slumped in his room, head hanging forward on his chest, his mind fumbling to understand what was happening.

The man was playing with him, he knew, like an angler tiring the fish that had seized the hook but could not be immediately taken from the water. He straightened at last, trying to breathe in courage. He'd refuse any demand when the man made contact again, he determined. He *wouldn't* be jerked and made to dance, like a marionette, with no control over himself. Worriedly, he began reviewing his behaviour over the last few hours. Control *was* being taken away, he realized. He was behaving like one of Pavlov's dogs, obediently performing to any command.

Certainly the man possessed something he had to have, to ensure his continued survival. But Kurnov had money, and that gave him some lever. Next time he'd definitely resist!

Then the telephone sounded stridently and Kurnov jumped at the noise, looking fearfully towards it, knowing before he replied he would do exactly as he was told. Pavlov's dogs had reacted to bells, he remembered, picking up the instrument.

(15)

'Cold wait?' jeered the Bavarian, as soon as Kurnov identified himself. The Russian's mouth twitched, forming the obscenity. Then he pulled back, knowing the man wanted just such a response. He had to fight, to pull himself from the apathy being woven over him by the other man.

'Why?' demanded Kurnov, tightly.

'Well done, Heinrich! That shows better control,' praised the German, mockingly.

Here it comes again, thought the scientist; the constant anticipation.

'Why?' threw back his tormentor. 'Several reasons, of course. I had to be sure you'd be alone. That was the most important. I couldn't imagine how it would have been possible, but you might have got some helpers in the city ... people who would help even you for sufficient payment. So I had to make sure I wouldn't be creating a trap for myself by meeting you ...'

'... You mean you watched me? All the time I was there, you were watching me ...?'

Kurnov felt chilled. Another manifestation, he realized. The experiments always shivered under attack, feeling physical coldness.

'Oh yes,' said the Bavarian. 'Do you know what? I actually pretended to fix you in the sights of an imaginary rifle. I pulled the trigger, three times. You died today, Heinrich. Three times. Twice in the heart and once through the head. It would have been so easy, to kill you ... it almost seemed a wasted opportunity ...'

148

The nerves blocked in Kurnov's left arm, so the limb jerked convulsively. He strained, trying to control it, but the vibrations continued, making the flesh jump visibly beneath his shirt. His injured leg ached, too, very badly.

'That's a frightening thought, isn't it, Heinrich?' pressed the other man, presciently. 'Doesn't it make you feel cold to know that you were exposed so long? Just imagine the number of people who would have squeezed that trigger, with you in their sights.'

'What other reasons were there?' said Kurnov. He pushed the words out through a tight mouth. There was a way to combat the other man, he knew. Seize the conversation and insist upon conducting it, refusing to be sidetracked or unsettled by the constant goading. It was an old ploy, gaining control and then phrasing every conversation in questions, forcing the person to be constantly responding, exposing himself, so abdicating even further control.

'Second time tonight you've been clever,' praised the caller, ahead of him again. 'I wonder which one of us will win, Heinrich?'

Kurnov pressed his eyes closed, squashing the anger. I will win, he promised himself, vehemently. I'll win and see you in hell.

'What other reasons?' he insisted, doggedly, sticking to his defence.

The Bavarian laughed.

'As part of the experiment, of course. They're your own rules, Heinrich ... make an arrangement linked to a promise that is very important to the recipient, then immediately break it. That was it, wasn't it ...?'

That formula again. Always end with a query. Kurnov opened his eyes, staring distantly down at the carpet. Thirty-two years ago at least, he decided. The experiments on disorientation at Buchenwald. Had this man taken part in them? Obviously. The best clue so far.

Who had been in the camp with him? Mentally, he started parading names, but immediately the caller punctured the thoughts.

'It was my *proof*, you idiot,' he said. The mockery was gone now, replaced by a voice of quiet anger. 'Don't you remember how carefully you annotated those experiments? I've got all the details here, before me. Everything I've done and said in the last two calls was based upon your ideas, Heinrich. I dictated your notes back to you. And you behaved exactly as you predicted a victim would. Aren't you annoyed, not recognizing the pattern?'

Kurnov felt weak, as if a hypodermic had been plunged into the vein and gradually siphoned off the blood. How obvious. Yet he'd missed it, seeking substance from shadows. He felt suddenly irritated, hot with annoyance. For years … all his life almost … his vocation had been to test people to the very limit of their endurance. Some of the results had been incredible. Men he would have guessed would have broken in hours sustained every pressure, disdaining fear, contemptuous always of threats. And others, often physically strong, had collapsed in minutes. Sometimes, in reflective conceit, he had wondered about his reaction to such stress and always aligned himself with those who resisted the torture. He remembered the arrogant reaction to just such a question from the American director of NASA, a few weeks before. But it was not so, he realized. He had crumbled, like a cardboard house in a gale. The Bavarian was right. It was all there, he remembered, carefully detailed, every case-history recorded. It wasn't until two years after those experiments that he had fully realized the danger of so carefully listing everything. He had had no idea the clerks in Berlin would have been so meticulous. He hoped their deaths had been painful.

'Convinced, Heinrich?' demanded the Bavarian.

Kurnov nodded in the empty room, stupidly, then

150

realized he couldn't be seen. 'Oh yes,' he blurted. 'Yes, I'm convinced.'

'Good,' continued the other man, briskly. 'Have you heard the announcement, by the way?'

'What announcement?'

'I made contact with the yids this afternoon. Gave them something from Glücks's file ... they've already disclosed it, in Jerusalem ...'

God, let it end soon, thought Kurnov. His tongue strayed to the molar housing the cyanide. So easy, he thought. A few seconds of agony, then oblivion. He moved his tongue away, shaking his head. It had been another experiment, as successful as all the rest. The will to live was the strongest desire, he'd recorded, after watching the wretches in the camps, waiting for the men and women reduced to the level of animals to take the offer of self-destruction. Always, he recalled, they had discarded the opportunity, as he was doing now.

'... So we'd better hurry, hadn't we?' prompted the German.

'Yes,' acquiesced Kurnov, obediently. How well the man had studied his papers.

'Like I said, Heinrich, I watched you all the time this afternoon. So I know there's no one with you waiting to trap me ...'

Suddenly the course changed, as the experiments dictated it should.

'... So we'll meet tonight.'

Instinctively, Kurnov looked at his watch. Six-thirty.

'I've been taking too many chances,' he said, attempting to gather some control from the new approach. 'There's an official dinner tonight. I shall have to attend ...'

'Of course,' agreed the Bavarian, easily.

Damn, thought Kurnov. He'd missed it again. The momentary change of attitude was the continuing, unremitting process of disorientation.

Casually, the German went on: 'We can't have our meeting ruined by anyone wondering where you are, can we ...?'

The man paused, 'Listen carefully, Heinrich. Don't leave the hotel until nine-thirty. Two blocks from the hotel, there's a taxi rank. Get a cab from there ...'

'... But they'll see me ...'

'... Not if you're careful. There'll be quite a crowd of people going in and out, so you'll be able to mingle. All you'll need is about ten yards' head-start.'

Kurnov nodded, dully assimilating the instructions. He felt like a man deprived of sleep, numbed with fatigue.

'I'm going to give you an address, Heinrich,' said the caller. The voice changed, commandingly. 'Write it down. Memorize it. And then destroy the paper. Don't carry it with you.'

'All right,' agreed Kurnov.

'No,' insisted the Bavarian. 'Repeat that you'll destroy the paper.'

'I'll destroy the paper,' promised Kurnov.

'And bring the money,' ordered the man. 'You must bring the money. If you haven't got it, Heinrich, I'll throw you to the wolves.'

'I've got it,' said Kurnov, quickly. 'It's a draft, drawn against a Swiss bank.'

'No tricks,' warned the other man. 'Remember. No tricks.'

'No,' undertook Kurnov, cowed. 'I promise.'

There was a pause, as if the man at the other end were making a final decision. Then he said, 'In Buckow, fairly near the Wall, there's a large street. It's called Salmbacherstrasse. Halfway along, there's a shopping area, with two towers. Enter the first of these tower sections. But ignore the lift. It's a basement apartment, number three ...'

Again the hesitation.

'... I'll be there, Heinrich. But I'll watch for anyone other than yourself. If there's any one with you, the apartment will be empty when you arrive. I can easily escape, no matter how well you might think you can cover the place. If you try to be smart, the yids will have everything ... and I mean *everything* ... by this time tomorrow ...'

'I'll be alone,' undertook Kurnov, anxiously. 'I'll ...'

He stopped talking, realizing the instrument was dead. Without any indication, the other man had put the telephone down. Following the rules: always treat the victim contemptuously, destroying his self-respect.

Sighing, Kurnov opened his briefcase and extracted from the tiny space behind the lining the bank-drafts he had hidden there. He gazed down at the amounts. All that money, he thought. It seemed so useless. How empty a rich man must feel being told he has cancer, knowing his wealth can't help him, reflected Kurnov. At least the money was saving his life. He hoped.

It was physically disgusting, thought Frieden, watching the excited man gasp into his handkerchief. Five minutes earlier, Muntz had burst into his apartment after a near-hysterical telephone call, but was still unable to speak. The exertion had exhausted the elderly lawyer, reducing him to paroxysms of coughing that racked his body. Distastefully, the property millionaire offered the man brandy, placing the glass on the table in front of him to avoid contact. He was diseased, thought Frieden. For their hands to touch might infect him.

Muntz ignored the liquor, rocking in the chair, waiting for the attack to pass. Finally, through watery eyes, he looked up at the millionaire.

'We've got it,' he announced. The words came out with effort, destroying the triumph.

Frieden waited, expectantly. So the Bavarian was trapped. With the Jews, he guessed. Good. To kill Jews would be a bonus. He smiled, like a man about to see a favourite play, anticipating the performance. He was going to move, he thought, to go into action again. Just like the old days. It was an odd sensation, he decided, like the tingling one experienced from knocking one's elbow. He'd always had it, being briefed for an assignment during those truly wonderful years of his life.

Breathing easier now, Muntz gulped at the drink Frieden had put before him. He drank too quickly and it engendered another bout of coughing. Frieden frowned, annoyed.

The lawyer groped in his pocket, sensing the feeling.

'Here,' he wheezed, pushing over the piece of paper upon which an address was scrawled. The erratic, uneven writing indicated the depth of the man's illness.

'Only an hour ago,' tried Muntz. 'The call was made to the Israeli embassy only an hour ago ...'

He looked at his watch.

'... And the meeting isn't planned for another three hours.'

Frieden stared down at the paper, smiling emptily. So it *was* the Jews: they had their bonus.

Ignoring the other man, allowing him to recover, he moved to the telephone and for twenty minutes was engaged in a series of brief, demanding calls, snapping orders that were accepted without challenge. Finished, he looked at the address again, mentally reviewing the arrangements he had just made, seeking flaws. Finding none, he turned back to Muntz. The coughing had stopped, but the old man was slumped in the chair as if in pain. Frieden poured two more brandies, then raised his glass, in a toast.

'We've got it, Manfred,' he predicted. 'I've called everyone in the Organisation. We'll blitzkrieg the building ... no one will escape alive ... we'll recover everything.'

Just like the old days. Again, the recurring nostalgia. Wonderful, decided Frieden.

'... So much for your prediction that we were beaten this time,' he said, allowing the sneer as a rebuke to the other man.

Muntz brought the handkerchief to his face, uncaring.

A puff of wind would blow him away, thought Frieden. Muntz was an assortment of bones, just held together by skin. He would have to be disposed of soon, decided the millionaire. Certainly before the end of the week. Every day that passed created an unnecessary danger. Manfred Muntz had performed his last duty to the Party. It would be a good funeral, decided Frieden, objectively. Muntz would be properly honoured.

'There'll be killing tonight, Max,' said Muntz, suddenly.

Frieden nodded.

'I can't come with you,' said the lawyer, definitely. 'I'm exhausted ... I wouldn't be any good ... I'd hinder, in fact ... all I want to do is rest.'

For a moment, Frieden paused. The lawyer was right. An outburst of coughing at the wrong moment would ruin everything. Anyway, what good would he be in a fight?

'Of course,' he agreed, soothingly. 'You've done your share, Manfred. More than your share, in fact. The Party and the Organisation are grateful to you.'

Muntz finished his brandy and rose, unsteadily. At the door he paused, turning.

'Max.'

'What?'

'Call me when it's over. I want to know how it went.'

'Of course.'

'And Max.'

'What?'

'Good luck.'

Frieden grinned. 'We've already had it,' he said, con-fidently. 'We're going to survive. Again.'

(16)

Like the others that had preceded it, the official dinner was a series of tiresome conversations, culminating in a series of boring speeches. It would be an interesting experiment when he got back to Russia, thought Kurnov, to test a man to the limit of boredom. He paused at the thought, irritated. It would, in fact, be particularly applicable in space science. It annoyed him not to have thought of it before.

He nodded and mimed the pleasantries, like a mummer in a medieval court, occasionally feeling for reassurance to the bank-drafts. They were folded in his trouser pocket and rarely did his hand stray away. He smiled, despite the apprehension, at the sudden thought. What would the Russian reaction be, he hypothesized, if he were genuinely taken ill and discovered to have bank-orders for £3,000,000 in his pocket?

Finally the speeches ended and gratefully he stood, watching Bahr approach.

'I hope you're better, Dr Kurnov.'

The Russian nodded, smiling in feigned gratitude at the inquiry.

'Not completely,' he qualified. 'But recovering. I regret not being able to take a fuller part in the convention.'

The German shrugged, philosophically. 'It couldn't be helped,' he said, falling into step as Kurnov moved towards the restaurant door. 'We're grateful you honoured us with your presence.'

'Perhaps', Kurnov threw out, generously, 'I shall be able to come next year.'

Bahr nodded at the prospect and Kurnov seized what had been a casual remark. What irony, he decided, to return next year to Berlin, after the agony of this visit. He would do it, he determined, suddenly. He would come back again and savour every moment of their ridiculous, self-congratulatory convention. He'd even prepare a paper, he thought, a thesis on the ultimate stress upon a man faced with a lifetime's deprivation of freedom. Oh yes, he thought. That would make an excellent subject. In the foyer, he shook hands and turned into the lift. He'd recovered his topcoat within minutes and was out of his room so quickly that he actually passed some of the Russian party in the corridor as he returned to the elevator. They looked at him, inquiringly.

'A breath of air,' he said, quickly, hurrying on, anxious to catch the lift still standing at the floor. As he entered, immediately pressing the descent button, he heard a shout behind him. He allowed himself just sufficient pause before turning, seeing two Russians approaching as the doors closed, cutting them off. There was another lift, he knew, so he had only a few minutes. He thrust through the doors immediately they opened on the ground floor, burying himself in the crush of people, and was actually walking through the exit into the street before Suvlov saw him.

The Russian colonel burst forward, trying to shoulder his way through the crowd. The watchers might be off-guard with so many delegates emerging. And Kurnov had already been seen going up in the lift. The scientist was almost a block away when Suvlov reached the pavement. A controlled man, he looked casually around, then smiled, seeing two men assigned to foot-surveillance had recognized Kurnov and were moving into a shadowing pattern, one following behind, the second almost parallel on the opposite side of the street, shielded by the stream of vehicles. A third man would join them, once he had seen the other two move off, and within five minutes they would be practising the classic triangle-surveillance, which was virtually undetectable as they alternated positions both in front, alongside and behind the victim.

Almost imperceptibly, he raised his hand and an un-marked Volkswagen pulled alongside.

'Leaving openly, tonight,' he said to the driver, as he got in. The man grunted. He had spent the previous three nights hunched in the car, stiff with cold.

'This has to be the meeting,' guessed Suvlov. 'The conference ends tomorrow.'

The driver moved off, glad of the traffic that made anything more than a walking pace impossible. The triangle was in position now, Suvlov saw. He settled back in the seat, relaxed. Kurnov was an important man, he thought. And he was going to be the person directly responsible for trapping him. Promotion was an obvious possibility.

Ahead, Kurnov passed an intersecting street, remaining on the main road. The man following behind paused, obedient to his training, allowing the man parallel to cross the road to be replaced in that position by the third man, then move over to bring up the rear. Traffic was heavy and the man who was to follow had difficulty in crossing. Kurnov increased his lead.

'Quickly,' warned Suvlov, but the driver had anticipated the danger, trying to ease out of the wedge of traffic and reduce the gap. A horn blared and another vehicle flashed its lights, warningly.

'Keep going,' insisted Suvlov, as the driver hesitated. The tiny Volkswagen kept on, but the Mercedes behind came up, blocking the manoeuvre.

The man who had been following originally saw the difficulty and stopped, on a traffic island in the middle of the road. He stayed there, uncertain, knowing that to go back would break the pattern. Finally he continued on, keeping to routine.

'Fool,' yelled Suvlov, unheard.

The replacement finally got into position, but the triangle was uneven and stretched out. Suvlov sighed. It would only take minutes for them to tighten up.

Then Kurnov turned left at the next side street. The sudden move completely broke the planned surveillance. The following Russian was still too far behind and the two others were further apart than they should have been and on the wrong side of a busy road which it was impossible to cross immediately.

'Get after him,' screamed Suvlov, frightened by the effect of Kurnov's move. The driver jerked out, forcing the Mercedes moving parallel to swerve over the central reservation. There was a blare of protest from several car-horns and as the Volkswagen drew out it clipped the bumper of a Rekord in front, collapsing it against the boot. The car jerked to a halt, but the Volkswagen accelerated, the back wheels slipping on the ice. The car was bathed in a glare of yellow lights from offended motorists and the Rekord jerked off in pursuit.

The Russian behind Kurnov had run to the corner and was turning into the side street as the Volkswagen pulled around the corner. Fifty yards ahead, Kurnov was getting into a taxi, following his instructions, appearing almost comatose. As the car pulled away, the second cab in the rank moved out, too, awkwardly, almost blocking the road.

'Around him,' yelled Suvlov, realizing what was happening.

The Volkswagen lurched on to the pavement, around the taxi, into which the Rekord and the Mercedes which had involved themselves in the protest chase collided in a concertina crash. Twenty yards ahead, the first taxi was turning right, with Kurnov quite unaware of what was going on behind him.

'We've still got him,' shouted Suvlov, hopefully, then immediately bit back the words. Slowly, from the left, a huge furniture pantechnicon moved into view, going in the same direction as Kurnov's taxi. Its enormous bulk completely filled the road ahead and instinctively the Russian driver braked, which was fortunate because when it absolutely blocked the road it stopped, making an impassable barrier. Suvlov leapt from the slithering Volkswagen and hauled himself up level with the lorry-cab. It was empty, the key missing from the ignition. He threw open the door, groping beneath the dashboard, sure of what he would find. Ripped-out wiring hung uselessly in his hand. He turned, shouting at his driver to reverse, then stopped at the sight of the police car coming towards him, urged on by a clutch of offended motorists whose cars were spreadeagled in a crumpled block in the street. He began looking for the driver of the second taxi, then shook his head, annoyed at his own stupidity. Of course the man wouldn't still be there, he realized.

Frieden invited reaction from the fifteen men seated around him in the lounge of the Ludwigsfelderstrasse apartment. No one spoke.

They were a good unit, thought the millionaire, gratefully. But then they always had been. The Organisation had sound judgment in choosing a group of S.S. men who had been through the war as a trained team. For over thirty years, he thought, the men grouped in the room with him had protected the surviving Nazis against almost every investigation. They were old men now, Frieden saw, sadly, with fat bellies and receding hairlines. They'd probably be slower than they had been thirty years ago. That was only to be expected. But tonight it wouldn't matter, he consoled himself, happily. Tonight it was an ambush, and they were more than efficient enough for that.

'No questions, then?' he demanded.

'We've to *kill* them?' queried a man near the veranda window. Frieden looked towards the questioner, smiling in recognition. Schmidt, he saw. A good man. A former sergeant who'd once carved tiny notches in the handle of his machine-pistol, like an American cowboy, recording the number of Jews he'd shot.

'All except the Bavarian,' he confirmed. He nodded towards the middle of the room, where Lugers and Mausers were piled. They would be heavily oiled, Frieden realized too late. He hoped the furniture hadn't been marked by the weapons.

'Everything is silenced,' he said, aware everyone must have already seen the extended barrels of the pistols. 'It must be quick, though. They might be armed. It'll be the noise of their weapons that will attract attention. I want enough time to search the room thoroughly to ensure I've got everything ... we can't have a repetition of the Toplitz mistake ... I want the Bavarian alive in case he's taken any precaution against being tricked ...'

He gestured vaguely, indicating the cellars far below where the guardians of Lake Toplitz had been tortured and killed.

'... I don't suppose it will take more than an hour or two down there to learn all we want to know and get everything back,' he said.

Schmidt grinned, echoing Frieden's earlier thoughts.

'Just like the old days,' said the ex-sergeant, enjoying the nostalgia.

'Yes,' agreed Frieden. 'Let's ensure we're still as good.'

He looked at his watch, then indicated the guns.

'It's time to be going,' he said, eagerly.

For at least five minutes after the Berlin report, Mavetsky sat unmoving in his office, searching for an escape. Not only had Kurnov vanished, but there was a full-scale diplomatic incident, as well. He dug his nails into the palms of his hands, as if the pain would make him think more clearly. Finally, he reached for the intercom that would connect him with the Party Secretary. He winced at Shepalin's voice.

'What is it?' demanded Shepalin, when Mavetsky identified himself.

'He got away,' said Mavetsky.

(1 7)

Kurnov paid the taxi in Töpchiner Weg, walking slowly down Delmersteig to the address the Bavarian had given three hours before. He halted at the junction, feeling the nervousness pull at him. It was close now, he thought. Too close. He couldn't recall being so frightened of anything before. He fought back the urge to turn and run, rationalizing the sensation, professionally: fear of the unknown. The most basic fear of all.

He remembered his promise to make the man he was to meet suffer for the torment. That was stupid vindictiveness, he decided, like a schoolboy whistling in the dark to retain his courage. He was in no position to punish anyone, whatever the humiliation. He could only pay the blackmail. And hope. Did anyone ever stop, once they had begun paying a blackmailer? What if the man had taken copies, to sell elsewhere? Or offer as fresh threats, even? Kurnov groaned, aloud, at the frustration, choked at his helplessness.

He walked away from the corner, moving down Salmbacherstrasse. The twin towers were marked out blackly against the night sky fifty yards ahead, on the opposite side of the road. Almost level, he moved into a shop doorway, the determination leaking from him. He was shaking and it was a positive effort of will to force one leg before the other. He breathed deeply, trying to calm himself. It was stupid, he thought. Certainly not the way to go into negotiations with a man as confident as the Bavarian. Gradually the shaking subsided and he sighed, relieved. Only one hour. Perhaps two, he reassured himself. Then it would all be over. By midnight he'd be back in the hotel, destroying forever the last shred of evidence endangering him.

It took fifteen minutes before he could bring himself to move again. He pushed away from the doorway, crossing the road, his footsteps echoing behind him. He looked around, expecting the few other pedestrians to be attracted by the noise. Careful, he told himself, immediately. That was a banal impression, prompted by apprehension.

The apartment entrance lay back off a small courtyard, merely an opening in the wall, with no concierge or nightwatchman. An apartment block of anonymous people in which everyone minded their own business, ignoring their neighbours, he decided. He went inside, stopping again. The lobby was floored with concrete and dirty, littered with long-discarded cigarette-butts, paper and leaves. Above, he heard the murmur of activity from the flats, like the humming of a bee-hive. Somewhere a radio blared pop music and a voice sounded loudly in an unintelligible argument. The smell of cooking permeated everywhere.

Number three, he remembered. In the basement. There were stairs leading down, at the back of the lobby. He pressed the light-switch that should have provided timed illumination. It clicked, but no bulb went on. He pressed again. Still nothing. The light had been destroyed, obviously. Which made it ridiculous to descend. What choice did he have? He started groping downwards, edging one foot exploratively ahead of the other, both hands gripping the iron railing. Halfway down there was a small landing and the stairs twisted, so that he lost even the dim light from the lobby. He scuffed on, counting the steps. Six ... seven ... eight. He moved his foot out, but there was no drop. He blinked, trying to adjust to the deep blackness. It was impossible to see the door, so he ran his fingers along the wall, jumping when his hand went into the depression and encountered the wooden frame. He moved back, seeking the edge for a bell, but couldn't locate it. He stayed there, like a lost child at a school outing. Finally, abruptly, he reached out, rapping the door. The noise bounced in the tiny space and involuntarily he jumped. There was no sound from behind the door. He let the silence stretch out, then knocked again, seized with the stupid comfort that if there were no one there, he could go back to the hotel. He pricked his own hope, anxious to stifle the illogical reasoning. There was no retreat now. He sighed again, the sound very near a sob. Surely the swine wasn't conducting another experiment, like that afternoon in the park?

He was reaching out for the third time when the light came on, brilliantly. He winced, trying to shield his eyes. The switch would have been inside the apartment, he realized. The light was unnaturally bright. In the middle of the door he could just detect a Judas hole, through which the occupant could see all callers. Under this illumination, nothing in the tiny approach area could have been concealed. He heard a noise from inside the apartment; it sounded like a laugh. The latch clicked, but the door opened only slightly.

'Come in,' said the voice he had learned to recognize.

There was another reason for the brightness of the light, he realized as he stumbled forward. After the darkness of the descent, its suddenness was blinding. Now the inside of the apartment was dark again, completing the disorientation. He edged forward, able only to distinguish outlines, his eyes refusing detail. He heard the door close and the burglar chains clatter into place and stood apprehensively just inside the entrance. He had no sensation of anyone near him. Then, frighteningly, he was aware of a man's presence and pulled back, the sound of surprise bursting from him. His response was met with a jeering laugh.

'Come further in, Heinrich,' said the man. 'Come right in and see where you are. You were promised a surprise, remember?'

Kurnov had his hands to his eyes, pressing against them. Again the thought of his hopelessness came to him, but he managed to control the shiver.

Gradually his obscured vision cleared and he began examining the room, his face opening in growing amazement until he reached the man. Kurnov sagged, visibly, unable to comprehend what he saw. All control completely gone, he snatched out, supporting himself against the high back of a chair in the middle of the room.

The man, who was sitting behind a carved, ornate desk too heavy for the room, sniggered in delight at the reaction.

'Told you that you'd be surprised, Heinrich,' he said.

The small apartment, little more than one room with tiny alcoves leading off, was a complete shrine to Nazism. Behind the man the red Nazi flag, the swastika stridently black in the middle, dominated the whole wall, forming the backcloth for a huge picture of Adolf Hitler. Walls either side were cluttered with pictures of the Führer, showing him with every Nazi leader, and there were plaster casts of the Nazi motif. Able to see perfectly now in the subdued lighting, Kurnov recognized an S.S. dagger, the death's-head emblem easily visible, lying on the desk, in front of which stood the high-backed chair upon which he was resting. It was heavy, as ornately carved as the desk. There was a bust of Hitler alongside the dagger. And a Luger, easily within reach of the man.

As he looked up from the desk, the man stood up. He was wearing full S.S. uniform, Kurnov saw, his belt and boots brilliantly polished.

Hesitantly, then with determination, Dr Otto Grüber, with whom Kurnov had conducted human experimentation at Dachau, Bergen-Belsen and Buchenwald throughout the Second World War, extended his right arm, turned halfway round with something approaching doglike obedience to the huge photograph on the wall and said, 'Heil Hitler.'

Kurnov stared at the man, unable to move. His mind was frozen, like those of the men upon whom he had experimented. It was impossible to encompass the scene. Or accept what he was seeing.

'Heil Hitler,' repeated Grüber, insistently.

Relief suddenly flooded over Kurnov, almost painfully, like the immediate coldness of the ice water after a sauna. He was going to survive. The realization exploded in his mind. It was going to be all right. He was going to get out of everything without any difficulty: probably without paying the money, even. Staring at the old, demented man standing before him like an actor in a comedy theatre, Kurnov felt the confidence burn through him. He had been tricked by a crumpled, senile old man who dressed up in a funny uniform and made obeisance to a man dead for thirty years as if he were still alive. He stifled the anger at his own stupidity. Recrimination could come later. Momentarily he allowed himself the pleasure of vindictiveness: he'd be able to keep his vow after all. God, how he would make Grüber suffer for what he had done. But he would have to be careful, he thought, looking back to the gun now held quite steadily in the man's left hand. He was dealing with a sick mind. He would have to take things very slowly. Very slowly indeed. The wrong move, the merest thoughtless mistake, and everything would be ruined.

He extended his arm, feeling embarrassed.

'Heil Hitler,' he said.

Grüber smiled happily, as if Kurnov had uttered the correct password. The man's mind was on the switchback of insanity, guessed Kurnov. Everything Nazi was obviously the key. He reflected upon the man's reaction to the salute. It would be important to pander to his nostalgia, he decided. For several minutes, the scientist remained looking at the old man who had been his assistant for so long. How obvious it was, he thought, in hindsight. All the clues had been there, as obvious as an umbrella on a summer's day. It was not surprising he hadn't decided upon Grüber, though, after all the inquiries he had had made. He'd aged, of course, but the features were unmistakably the same, those heavy bulldog jowls and puckered, sensual mouth. And the eye, that awful deformity that Grüber liked to parade for some bizarre reason of inverted vanity. Grüber's left eye was dead, a greying, opaque pupil in horrifying contrast to the other, which was intensely black. The injury gave him a staring, demonic look. How much he had enjoyed frightening their victims, even before any operations, recalled Kurnov. An early indication, he reflected, of the mental breakdown from which the man was now so demonstrably suffering. The lopsided stare was fixed upon him now, the face twisted in a self-congratulatory smile. Grüber was very dangerous, decided Kurnov again. But manageable, certainly to a man of his training. He answered the old Nazi's smirk. Oh yes, definitely controllable by an expert.

'Otto!' he exclaimed, smiling further, extending his hand and moving forward. Immediately the other man's hand came up, the Luger aimed at Kurnov's stomach. Grüber had moved surprisingly quickly, thought Kurnov, stopping immediately. An error. *He'd* moved too sharply.

'Back,' shouted Grüber, the fear tingeing his voice. 'Get back.'

Kurnov frowned, detecting the break in his voice. He's scared, decided the adoptive Russian. That was good. He'd have to avoid any sudden movement, he realized. Everything would have to be very gradual.

'Otto! What is it?' he protested, the pained expression sounding quite normal.

'I've got no cause to receive you like a friend,' threw back Grüber. 'You abandoned me. You ran away from Buchenwald, never telling me you were going. No one got out, after you. The road was closed, almost immediately afterwards, as Berlin became surrounded. The Russians were everywhere. Thank God it was some days before they got to Buchenwald. At least we had some time to hide.'

He paused, as if trying to remember something. Suddenly he smiled. 'So now you've got to pay,' he said.

Everything had been rehearsed in that sick mind, Kurnov thought. Grüber jerked the gun towards the chair, which Kurnov saw had been carefully positioned a good six feet from the desk, so that no unexpected move could be launched from it. As he sat down, Kurnov realized that the wall behind him was draped with another Nazi flag and two further pictures of Hitler. There were two more busts, as well, on tiny plinths on either side of the room. It was pitiful, he thought, recognizing the mental condition of regression.

'Otto,' started Kurnov, gently, 'I tried to find you. I really did. But Berlin fell, as you say. I was trapped. There was no way I could get back to Arfurt ...'

'You abandoned me,' insisted Grüber, distantly.

'I *didn't*,' argued Kurnov. 'The collapse was too quick. You know how it happened. I tried to get help through to you. But I couldn't find you ...'

Grüber sniggered, offered the opportunity to boast.

'I was too clever for them,' he said. 'They never guessed who I was ...'

He *had* wanted to locate his assistant, remembered Kurnov, although not for the reasons with which he was trying to convince the other man. Like the records he had fled to Berlin to retrieve, Grüber had been a possible source of identification. Kurnov had lost count of the number of times he'd cursed himself for not killing the man before leaving the concentration camp. He had insisted Bock try every means through the clandestine Organisation to discover Grüber's fate, even while he had lain in the clinic, recovering from the operation. The Organisation had been unable to find any trace of Grüber and so they presumed he had been killed by the advancing Russians. But the uncertainty had irked, certainly in the early days. After he had arrived in Moscow, Kurnov had had fresh, discreet inquiries made, but Grüber had vanished.

'But I almost died,' whined Grüber, his voice weakened by the recollection. 'It took me six months to get through the Russians and reach Berlin ...'

Kurnov sat patiently. Let him talk, he decided. For three decades the man had stored resentment. The therapy was long overdue.

'... By then,' took up the old man, 'everyone had gone under ground. I tried to reach the Organisation, but all the contacts had disappeared. No one wanted to know anyone as positively identified with the camps as I had been ...'

It was to be expected, thought Kurnov, in the confusion that existed immediately after the war. All the Nazis had escaped or adopted their new hidden identities within six months. Grüber would have been a dangerous embarrassment.

Grüber jerked towards his dead eye.

'Thank God I'd copied your example and always avoided photographs. But my eye made me an easy target ... the yids at the camp gave a very detailed description of me. Even now, I've got to wear a patch. Several times they came this close to catching me ...'

He made a tiny gap between his thumb and forefinger, chuckling.

'... And that's going to be the greatest pleasure of all,' he mused. 'I'm going to make them beg and pay the earth for the box, Heinrich. Can you imagine that? They're going to have to pay someone who's at the top of their wanted list.'

Knowing he would need response, Kurnov laughed, too effusively. Grüber grinned, happy at the reaction. Should he raise the purchase of his personal file? wondered Kurnov. He remembered Grüber's nervousness at the proffered handshake. He'd reject any verbal suddenness, too, decided the scientist. It would be better to wait.

'That's wonderfully ironic,' he encouraged. 'Remember the old motto — "always make the yids pay" ...'

He stretched out, pointing to Hitler's picture, anticipating gestures would have to be exaggerated to penetrate the fogged intellect. 'The Führer would have appreciated that.'

The old man turned, his shoulders drooping with sadness as he looked up at the picture. He came back, swallowing, and it seemed impossible for him to talk immediately. It had been wise avoiding premature demands for the file, decided Kurnov. Grüber had a lot left to say.

'Remember how it was, Heinrich?' reflected the old man, wistfully. 'The honour ... the way we were treated ... the importance to the Fatherland of the experiments ...'

The memories had to be drained from Grüber's mind by reminiscence, thought Kurnov. And he would help. People always responded if the person to whom they were talking appeared to be confiding, Kurnov knew. It was basic psychology that trust had to be created this way between a doctor and patient. He hesitated for a moment, then thrust the doubt aside. Why not? Grüber had worked with him. He would be saying nothing the old man didn't already know. It would establish a bond between them in Grüber's crippled mind. He'd always been a dutiful, subservient assistant. Before the evening was over, he would become so again, a completely malleable man.

'They were great days,' he agreed, recognizing he was half enjoying the nostalgia, too. 'The Führer was a great man ... so enthusiastic about the work ...'

He paused, casually moving his hand towards his jacket pocket. It was important to get Grüber used to movement. The other man made no move for the Luger, as Kurnov took out the cigarette, inserted it in the holder and began smoking, gratefully.

'... He knew the importance of the studies,' continued Kurnov, wanting to embrace Grüber in the praise. 'Another three years and we would have perfected the germ experiments that would have rid Europe of every Jew, gypsy and black ... changed the setbacks of the war, even ...'

'... So near ...' sighed Grüber.

'... The benefits of our experiments to mankind would have been enormous, too,' added Kurnov, his voice strengthening with the indignation of a committed man denied the completion of his life's work. It *had* been close. Often, in Russia, he had daydreamed of the role that would have been his in Germany had the outcome of the war been different.

A cunning look flickered over Grüber's face.

'Other things went unrecognized, too, didn't they, Heinrich? And that was fortunate.'

Kurnov hesitated, guessing the way Grüber's mind was slipping. It would bring them to the evidence he wanted, he decided. He sat, waiting.

'I didn't *know* you'd gone to Russia,' confessed Grüber. 'There were the odd stories, like there were about Bormann and Mengele. But I was never sure. I only approached Bock because I thought he would have contact with some Nazis to make them sweat. I threw out your name, like bait ... I decided to gamble, knowing what I held would make it suicide for you to stay in

Moscow ... and I knew you had money, after all ...'

He *would* have known about the Swiss account, accepted Kurnov. Or guessed about it, certainly. He had been too close to miss the collections and the ransoms. It had been another reason for wanting to find him in those last days. It was important, thought Kurnov, that his former assistant shouldn't get too confident. There was an easy method of control, he decided. He gestured towards Hitler's picture.

'It was the Führer's own instructions that the freezing experiments should be conducted not only on Jews, but on the Russian prisoners as well,' he defended. 'We had to know whether someone born into the Russian environment had an inherent ability better to resist cold.'

'True,' agreed Grüber, quickly, as if he wished to appease Kurnov's irritability. 'I'm not questioning what was done ... just remarking about your luck. Weren't you worried that they'd find out in Moscow? Imagine what would have happened to you!'

Kurnov smiled at the hint of admiration in the old man's voice. There was still respect, he judged. That was important. Gradually the conversation was moving in the right direction. He'd end the victor, Kurnov knew.

'I hate to think what they would have done to me if they knew I had frozen four hundred Russians to death,' he agreed. 'But I took as many precautions as I could. My Russian file shows me to be Reinhart ... Remember that fool, who spent all his time trying to help everybody ...?'

Grüber burst in, a mocking laugh. Kurnov joined him, over-effusive again, judging the reaction like a man tuning a musical instrument.

'... I know,' he agreed. 'Ironic, isn't it?'

He paused, reviewing the old Nazi's question.

'They wouldn't imprison me,' he said, distantly. 'The Russians would shoot me, if they knew. They'd stage a huge public trial, then shoot me. The Russians are odd people ... often very stupid. They've created a gigantic myth about their heroic Red Army during the last war, when it was nothing more than a rag-taggle collection of peasants. They won on the same principle that the Chinese would win a war today ... they've just got more people to sacrifice as cannon fodder until the other side becomes exhausted. But for them to discover I'm the person responsible for Russian deaths in a concentration camp ... deaths of members of their wonderful Red Army ... would drive the fools insane ...'

He stopped, to light another cigarette from the stump of the first. He was going too far, he thought suddenly. The admissions should be confined to what Grüber knew. It had been stupid to talk so openly about Russian reaction. It was time for more movement.

Casually, he got up, stretching, wandering to the side of the room to examine one of the busts. He turned. Grüber was frowning, as if the action were confusing him. Not giving him time to think, Kurnov hurried on.

'But you were right. I had to come out of the Soviet Union to get the file. You found the one thing that made me destroy a cover it's taken half a lifetime to build up ...'

He moved over to the Hitler picture, near the door. It was time to start the pressure, very lightly.

'What does it say, this file about me ...?'

Grüber laughed, happy at his power.

'Everything, Heinrich. Every experiment that was ever conducted ... letters of commendation from the Führer ... descriptions of you as the doctor of a new race of super-men ... demands for more prisoners, to speed up the work being done ...'

Kurnov swallowed, nervously. Damn the Nazi aptitude for keeping records. He was half turned, towards the pictures, and knew the gesture of uncertainty would be missed by Grüber. He'd been right in coming out of Russia, to reclaim it, decided Kurnov. It would have certainly meant his destruction. He turned back into the room.

'How was it that you got hold of the box?' he probed, gently.

Grüber played with the gun, smiling at the question.

'My luck,' he said, simply. 'After years of almost starving ... my luck finally changed ...'

The mind was unlocked, realized Kurnov. There would be little need to prompt him.

'Only one man bothered about me, ever,' complained Grüber. 'If it hadn't been for him, I'd have died ... the rest of the family treated me like a maniac ... somebody to be given money to go away, so I would not embarrass them ...'

Kurnov sat, waiting patiently.

'Remember Fritz Grüber?' demanded the old man. 'My cousin ... the one in the camp ...'

Kurnov frowned. There *had* been a relation, Kurnov recalled. Grüber had brought him into the laboratory in the very last year of the war, as soon as the boy had left university ... a spotty, callow youth, who never said anything.

'It was the raid on the lake,' began Grüber again, obtusely. 'Fritz is one of the forestry workers employed by the Austrian government to patrol the lake. It was he who found the bodies, early after the morning of the ambush. He's a quick boy ... always was ...'

He stopped, deflected by another recollection.

'... He's as nostalgic as me about the old days,' said Grüber. 'He likes coming to this room and putting on the uniform. We sing the Hörst Wessel song and listen to the recorded speeches of the Führer ...'

He had to be steered back, Kurnov knew.

'What did he do?' he prodded.

'He didn't panic, like the other idiot who eventually raised the alarm,' said Grüber, almost belligerently, like someone giving a character reference. 'He guessed what had gone on. So he searched. The box was in just three feet of water ...'

Grüber gazed maniacally through his one eye.

'There was almost half a million in gold in that box, as well as the files. It took him nearly a month to ferry all the stuff to me here. I couldn't believe my luck ...'

Kurnov walked casually back to the chair.

'And then you began negotiations?' he encouraged.

Grüber's face began working, the triumphant smile that had constantly lurked near his mouth disappearing.

'No, Heinrich,' he corrected, his voice grating out. 'Not negotiations ... demands. After thirty years of hiding in slums, constantly frightened of discovery, knowing that around me are Nazis living in luxury, I decided to make insane demands and see they were met by everyone. I'm going to expose every Nazi still alive ...'

'... Except me,' broke in Kurnov, eager to prevent the rising hysteria.

'... That's right, Heinrich. Except you. I've got something different decided for you ...'

Kurnov began reaching for the bank-draft, but the gun came up, unwaveringly. Kurnov stopped.

'It's the money,' he explained, gently. 'Just the payment you want.'

'I want more than payment, Heinrich. Something much better than money.'

Kurnov waited, uneasily. The man's sanity was slipping, fast.

'I hate you, Heinrich,' announced Grüber. 'I *know* you left me to die. I know you're lying when you say you tried to locate and help me. You were always the same, interested only in yourself ...'

'... No, believe me ...'

'Shut up,' yelled Grüber, enjoying the role of bully. Kurnov snapped his mouth closed.

'I decided on a very special retribution for you,' Grüber continued. 'I remembered your arrogance ... your incredible disregard for everyone ... You're going to beg, Heinrich. You're going to go down on your knees, just like the Jews used to do, pleading with you to be spared. You won't like that, will you, Heinrich? You've never begged in your life, before.'

Grüber jerked the gun, like a blackboard pointer.

'Go on, Heinrich,' he ordered. 'We don't even talk about money until you've gone down on your knees and told me how sorry you are.'

He'd kill him, decided Kurnov, calmly. Once he'd got every file, he'd strangle the man. It wouldn't be difficult, he thought. Grüber was obviously physically weak. The files were a worry, though.

Kurnov suddenly realized he hadn't seen any sign of them. As if aware of his thoughts, Grüber reached into a drawer, taking out the red-bound documents. The edges were blackened, the water-stain running unevenly around the edge. Even from where he was sitting, Kurnov could see the name 'Heinrich Köllman' embossed deeply into the cover.

'There it is, Heinrich,' said the Nazi. 'This is what you want. Now beg for it.'

Kurnov sat, staring at it. Two steps, he thought. Just two steps and he could reach out to snatch it away.

'I'm waiting,' goaded Grüber. 'I'm waiting for your apology.'

There was no point in arguing with a sick mind, Kurnov knew. He'd managed almost to get control, like trying to tickle a trout from the side of the river bank. But always it slipped away from him. Now Grüber's insanity was unarguable, his mind locked by the imagined deprivation of three decades upon the humiliation of the man he believed responsible. He could only comply, remaining tense for the indications that the spasm was passing. Reluctantly, Kurnov got up from the chair, moving slightly back into the room. He stood there, the anger flooding through him. Grüber was right. He'd never begged to anyone.

'Down you go, Heinrich.'

Slowly, using the chair again as a support, Kurnov lowered himself to one knee.

'Both knees,' insisted Grüber, 'And your hands together, as if you were praying, like the yids used to.'

Kurnov knelt completely, his hands gripped in front, knowing he had to adopt the posture the man had carried for so long in his mind.

'Now say "Please forgive me for abandoning the S.S. code of loyalty and leaving fellow Nazis to die ..."'

Softly Kurnov began intoning the stupid diatribe.

'Louder!' shouted Grüber.

Kurnov halted, then started again, his voice higher.

'"... And I solemnly swear my regret ...",' took up Grüber, waiting for Kurnov to follow.

'..."and reiterate my oath of allegiance to the glorious Führer and the Nazi party."'

Kurnov finished and remained kneeling. Grüber's madness was far more severe than he had first estimated. His knees began to ache and his thigh hurt, but he knew he would have to wait until given permission to stand. Grüber had been too long deprived to miss a second of his retribution. The insanity was matched with cunning, thought Kurnov, crouched with his head slightly bowed. To catch the old man off-guard he would have to increase the movement towards the desk.

Grüber seemed reluctant to abandon the spectacle. But finally, after several minutes, he said, 'You can get up now, Heinrich.'

Kurnov rose, easing gratefully into the chair.

'That's how I've been, since the war ended ... since you abandoned me,' said Grüber. 'Constantly on my knees, just to live. Not nice, is it, Heinrich?'

'No,' said Kurnov, honestly. For the moment, he would

179

have to agree with everything. But it would soon change. Grüber had rehearsed the humiliating charade a dozen times, guessed Kurnov. But the apology would have been the highlight of the manic depression. As if in confirmation of the scientist's diagnosis, Grüber sat gazing at him, as if he expected Kurnov to say something. Time for a little more pressure, thought Kurnov.

'I've apologized,' he reminded. Perhaps it was a good idea still to exaggerate. 'And I meant it. I'm sorry for everything I did to harm you ... and the Party ...'

This time the gun wasn't raised as he took the money-draft from his pocket. His voice took on the coaxing tone one used upon a stubborn child. 'And here's the money. You're going to give me the files, aren't you? You know the ones. Those that identify me ... the one you showed me a few moments ago, identifying me with the Russian experiments. And those involving Bock. That's all I want.'

Grüber seemed to be receding in the chair opposite, exhausted by what had happened. He had been fuelled too long by the need for revenge, assessed Kurnov. Now it had happened. Now he had seen the man his twisted mind hated grovelling before him, and there was nothing left to sustain him. Grüber suddenly pulled himself up, as if determined to regain control. It wouldn't be long now, judged Kurnov. Another thirty minutes ... perhaps less. To recover his lapse, Grüber reached forward, taking a cigarette from an engraved box on the desk. Almost as an afterthought, he pushed it towards Kurnov. Recognizing the first chance to get nearer the desk, Kurnov accepted. Grüber snapped at the lighter, needing several attempts to light it, and then had to use both hands to hold it steady for Kurnov's cigarette.

Kurnov smiled his thanks, pulling the smoke into his lungs. It burned and he coughed slightly and then realized the sensation was not that of a different tobacco, but something else. His last moment of consciousness was as Grüber laughed aloud, an animal-like shout of triumph.

Frieden sat awkwardly in the Volkswagen, unused to small cars. But the discomfort was necessary. It was important not to attract attention. And a man sitting in a Mercedes or a Rolls might have been remembered later. Nobody would recall a parked Volkswagen in West Berlin. Ahead he saw a second Volkswagen pull into the street and stop. The former Standartenführer twisted in his seat. At the other end, he could detect the cigarette-glow from inside a Ford. Good men, both of them, he thought. Once the Jew from the embassy had entered the street, they would stay with their vehicles, not sealing the thoroughfare, but alert for police cars or anything else that might impede the ambush. Frieden began to look along the street, isolating the loitering pedestrians who would form the squad the moment he gave the signal. They'd be enjoying it, he knew, welcoming the adrenalin driving through their bodies at the prospect of action after so long. Frieden wondered how many men would be in the apartment that had to be reached through the tiny courtyard opposite. Probably only two, he decided. Pity. Perhaps, he thought optimistically, the Israeli would ignore the instructions and arrive with accomplices. Frieden hoped so.

He brought the watch up close to his face. Eleven, the Bavarian had stipulated. It was seven minutes before the hour. Frieden felt the first twitch of nervousness, but was unconcerned by it. Anyone who didn't feel frightened before an action was a fool.

Lights glared in his interior mirror, the first indication of the arriving Jew. Frieden looked away, trying to huddle inside the parked car as the other vehicle approached from behind. The man drove slowly down the road, obviously seeking the address. He was late in identifying it, swinging over abruptly against the pavement. He had to reverse, then go forward again to park properly. Frieden smiled; the man drove a Volkswagen, too, without any C.D. insignia. How careful they were all being! For a few seconds, the Israeli sat unmoving. He'd be scared, decided Frieden. He searched for any companions, but the car was empty. The guards at either end of the street would watch for any followers.

Slowly the embassy man got from his car, hauling the heavy briefcase from the passenger seat. That money would come in useful for Organisation funds, thought Frieden, smiling again. And it would pay for a celebration party, too. It was gestures like that which bound soldiers to their officers. Yes, there would definitely be a party. They would have every reason to celebrate.

The Jew hesitated at the opening into the darkened courtyard, confirming the number, then entered. Frieden waited for just three minutes, keeping strictly to the plan that had been formulated in his apartment. Then he got out of the vehicle, pausing for the action to be a signal. Immediately the squad formed along the street. Six got out of three separate cars in which they would later escape. Seven moved from shop doorways, and from apparently aimless promenading. Frieden reached the entrance to the courtyard first and stared in, seeking the light. The entrance was in complete darkness. He looked back. The road was utterly deserted. The Bavarian had chosen well.

'Now,' he whispered, and moved into the courtyard with the men following tightly behind. Their eyes grew used to the darkness. It was a cobbled area, dotted with dustbins and backyard debris of the flat-dwellers who lived around it. There were inner balconies, so none of the apartments directly overlooked the middle area. Ahead, the apartment entrance was a rectangle of dull light. Frieden went towards it.

The pudgy Nazi died first, the silenced bullet hitting

him with a dull slap directly in the middle of the forehead, throwing him back into the men behind. Immediately the other hidden guns began firing and, because each one was silenced, the Nazi squad stumbled in momentary confusion, imagining their own men were shooting, but unable to identify the target.

It was a perfectly co-ordinated ambush, fire coming from the four corners of the courtyard into the tightly grouped squad. Only two shots were fired by the Nazis, and there was insufficient sound even to penetrate the set-back apartments.

Out in the street, both watchers stood casually against their vehicles, unaware of what had happened fifty yards away. Both scarcely glanced at the pedestrians approaching until they were almost upon them, and then it was too late. Both died instantly and were caught by their assassins and eased back into their cars. Within three minutes, both looked like men asleep.

It took just seven minutes to kill the fifteen Nazis, but it was a further five before the assassins walked calmly from the courtyard, hesitated at the entrance and then dispersed along Rathenowerstrasse, three streets away from the other Buckow apartment that Kurnov had entered three hours earlier.

Four miles away, Muntz stirred painfully, unable to sleep. It would be morning before he learned he was the sole survivor of the Organisation der Ehemaligen S.S. Angehörgen.

Suvlov had been flown to Moscow immediately he had been released, after intense diplomatic protest, by the West German authorities. It had been ridiculous to attempt sleep on the military plane and now he stood, cowed before the full Praesidium of the Soviet Union, feeling the fatigue press down upon him. It was still only 6 a.m. and everyone showed signs of having been hurried from their beds. They had insisted he review the entire history of his surveillance, even though he had submitted reports that they had before them. When he had omitted a fact, either Mavetsky or Shepalin had jumped, anxious nothing should be missed.

The account over, he waited before them, recognizing the questioning that had already been put as the avoidance of responsibility by everyone else involved. He'd be sent to a prison camp, he accepted. He *hoped* that would be the punishment. He couldn't face the incarceration in a psychiatric hospital, like Grigorenko. Thank God psychiatric imprisonment was confined to political dissidents. He shifted, suddenly frightened. Kurnov was obviously a political matter. Surely his mistakes didn't come under the same category?

'So he had help?' pressed Shepalin, at last.

Suvlov stiffened to even more rigid attention.

'Undoubtedly, in my opinion. The following car was perfectly positioned to slow any surveillance vehicle, and the furniture lorry was carefully in place to block the road.'

'Why hadn't you anticipated such planning?' demanded the chairman.

It was the weakness of his account, accepted Suvlov, reducing him to incompetence.

'There had been no indication that he had assistance ... He had wandered about Berlin almost like a man who was lost ...'

'You knew he had *some* contact,' insisted Mavetsky, fluttering the report in which the meeting with Bock was recorded.

Suvlov nodded, dismally.

'The man recognized the surveillance and employed a reasonably simple manœuvre to avoid it continuing,' bulldozed Mavetsky, deciding to sacrifice the colonel. 'And beat you completely.'

Suvlov remained silent. Bastard, he thought.

Shepalin waved him dismissively to a chair, looking

at the men gathered around him. Slowly, the chairman began reviewing the affair.

'The conference that he tricked us into being allowed to attend ...', he paused, looking at Mavetsky, letting the criticism settle, '... concludes tomorrow. I feel what happened tonight was the culmination of what he's been doing for the past week ... tonight he was making the final contact with his Nazi friends ...'

He waited for reaction. No one spoke.

'If he knew he was being watched ... and every indication is that he did, from what happened, then he has no intention of returning to the Soviet Union ...'

'... So ...' tried Mavetsky, anticipating the chairman's idea. Shepalin waved him to silence.

'... The Soviet Union must act immediately,' continued the chairman. 'We don't know what has happened in Berlin, but it can only mean difficulties for us. I propose we immediately announce the defection of Vladimir Kurnov ...'

He stopped, enjoying the looks registered on the faces along the table.

'... And include in the announcement that, according to our inquiries, the man is a former Nazi, wanted by the authorities ...'

He sat, waiting. The tired men considered the proposition, one by one nodding acceptance.

'Any contrary thoughts?' invited Shepalin.

'No,' said Mavetsky, speaking for all of them.

'Then let's hope we can get the announcement out in time,' said the chairman.

The declaration of the Israeli government was very short. Following the world outcry at their intrusion into Austria and their apparent willingness to pay a ransom — a practice they had always criticized in aircraft terrorism — they had decided to conclude the matter of the Toplitz evidence in a fashion befitting a civilized state.

All contacts that had been made with the person claiming to have the contents of the Lake Toplitz box had therefore been communicated to the West German authorities. Israel was withdrawing from any negotiations, confident the Germans would successfully pursue all inquiries and bring to trial anyone thought guilty of any crime. The Israeli government regretted any offence it had caused to any other country by its action, but trusted the announcement indicated their future intention to abide by international law.

(18)

The effect of the inhaled anaesthetic welled up within him and Kurnov retched, helplessly. Immediately he felt the coldness of a surgical kidney-bowl pressed against his cheek. He coughed, choking almost, but managed to stop himself vomiting.

'I think he'll be all right,' said a voice, and the bowl was withdrawn.

Kurnov tried to move and found he couldn't. His arms were clamped to the chair, pulled tightly by his side. Whatever tied him was looped beneath the seat, he thought. His legs were manacled, too, allowing almost no movement. But neither restriction was as bad as the pain in his neck. His head was being held rigidly and forced upwards. He realized there was a securing band around his throat.

'Why not open your eyes, now that you've tested everything?' invited Grüber.

Hesitantly, Kurnov blinked into the room, the nausea returning. But it was fear now, he knew, not anaesthetic.

Grüber was perched on the edge of the desk, one leg swinging easily in front of him. He was out of S.S. uniform now, casual in shirt and slacks. Something else was different, thought Kurnov. He squeezed his eyes shut, then opened them, trying to clear his vision, but couldn't isolate what it was.

'Feeling better now, Heinrich?'

For the first time, Kurnov experienced the numbness in his face. The moment he moved his tongue to explore the cause, he knew why he had been rendered

187

unconscious. Grüber saw the probing and smiled.

'We had to do it, Heinrich,' he said, conversationally. 'An old S.S. man like yourself, with the facilities you've had constantly available, would obviously have maintained the cyanide implant. And we couldn't have you escaping us, after all this trouble, could we?'

Kurnov's tongue came away from the empty socket. He was going to be killed, he thought, calmly. He would have expected the realization to have frightened him more. Perhaps it would, later.

'But you must admit we were very humane about it,' went on Grüber. 'No one ever bothered about the niceties of anaesthetic or novocain, extracting teeth in the camps, did they?'

'What ...?' tried Kurnov. The anaesthetic had dried his mouth and his voice was very weak.

'You've been trapped, Heinrich,' said Grüber, simply. 'You've been brought from the safety of the Soviet Union and put into a situation from which there's absolutely no escape. You're as helpless now as all those Jews you tormented.'

Belatedly, Kurnov realized the difference in the man facing him. The eye was no longer dead. Grüber was looking steadily at him, both eyes focusing upon his face. Kurnov looked away, his mind slipping.

'Confusing, isn't it, Heinrich? Don't you remember those experiments you conducted at Dachau, working with Mengele, trying to assess how long a person's sanity would last under sustained, unremitting pressure that apparently had no correlation? That's what's happened to you, Heinrich. I've been particularly careful about that. Every psychological pressure that has been applied upon you is one that you've worked upon.'

'You're Jewish,' accused Kurnov. He desperately wanted a drink.

'That's right,' agreed the man, facing him. 'My name is Uri Perez ...'

He paused, his voice becoming almost toneless. '... And until the age of eleven,' he went on, 'I was an inmate of Buchenwald ...'

Kurnov wondered if there would be torture before they killed him. The frequent fear returned. He'd collapse immediately there was any physical pain. He stared up at the man with Grüber's face. Perez saw the look and fingered the folds of skin irritably, as if trying to pull them away.

'It's very good, isn't it?' he asked. 'Much better than that plastic surgeon of yours could have done. It took a long time to get right. And it was very painful. But I've got this face engraved on my memory, so I knew it was right ... that it would deceive you completely. The eye was an advantage, of course. No two people could have possibly looked like Grüber, could they? ... I knew the sight of his face would throw you completely off-balance. Any doubt you might have had would have disappeared at seeing Grüber ... and I knew you'd over-compensate, imagining you had an old imbecile to placate .. ' He paused. 'Imagine, Heinrich. You've actually knelt before a Jew, to beg forgiveness ...'

He reached behind him, picking up a small piece of plastic. 'The eye was easy,' he said, tossing the object in his hand. 'A contact lens.'

Again the tonelessness came into his voice.

'Remember how good an assistant he was, Heinrich? Remember how dutifully he obeyed your instructions? I saw him freeze my mother and sister to death. It took a long time ... nearly all morning, in fact. You wouldn't recall it, of course. It was just part of the experiment ... there were dozens of others. I had to watch. So did my father. But you'll know about the double experiments, of course. You devised them, after all. The relatives had to observe what was happening to see how long they could stand it. My father went insane. A lot of them did, didn't they? Grüber was particularly interested in how unmoved I appeared to be ... personally tested me for a long time, imagining he had encountered a mental condition he hadn't known before. That's how I came to have the face imprinted in my memory ... Every day, for nearly a month, he spent several hours with me ... he and that relation of his, Fritz ... and they talked. That's how I know so much about what you were doing ... There isn't a word I've forgotten, after all these years ...'

Again he tugged at the skin of his face.

'... Can you imagine how determined we were to get you?' he said. 'I actually agreed to have grafted on to my body the face of a man I hate only slightly less than you ... a face it's going to take six months to have removed ... just to catch you ...'

He moved off the desk, standing over him. 'And it's been easy, incredibly easy. Because you were so arrogant. I never guessed you'd have such an inflated idea of your own mental strength, making you so easy to control ... like a well-trained animal ...'

He laughed and went back to the desk. Kurnov's head began moving, from side to side, and a series of moans broke through his lips. From far away, he heard Perez's voice continue, but recognized he wasn't addressing him. It was as if he were lecturing a class.

'... This is important,' he heard Perez say. 'This is the moment of complete realization ... the acceptance of defeat. It's impossible to guarantee, but the collapse can't be far away now ...'

Kurnov stifled the sound he discovered was coming from him, blinking up at the man.

'... Ah, notice that,' went on Perez. 'He's fighting against it ...'

The Israeli came back to Kurnov. 'That was very good, Heinrich,' he praised. 'You've drawn back, haven't you?'

'You're going to kill me,' challenged Kurnov.

Perez smiled. 'In a way,' he agreed.

'I don't understand.'

'There's so much you don't understand, isn't there, Heinrich? You still don't know what's really happened, do you?'

'Please don't hurt,' pleaded Kurnov.

'Notice the sudden relapse,' said Perez. He'd turned his head slightly, Kurnov saw. He strained against the neckband, but could see nothing.

'It's a shame, really,' came back Perez. 'That the whole operation that has so enmeshed you will never be known ... It's my plan, you see. I'd quite like to be known as the originator of it.'

Kurnov tried to block the man's voice from his mind, staring over his shoulder at Hitler's picture. How easy it was to hear again in his mind the vibrancy of the Führer's voice ... remember the dynamism he instilled in everyone by his leadership. The adulation at the 1936 Olympic Games had been wonderful to witness. Later, he recollected, he had cried at the Nuremberg rallies. Why had he had to die in the Bunker, like a squalid gangster?

Again the lecturing voice intruded. '... Regression into the past,' he heard Perez dictate. 'The need to go back to hide with known memories ...'

With difficulty, Kurnov came back to the Israeli. It was much better, thinking of the past.

'It was all staged for you, Heinrich. Everything ... the raid on the lake ... the Jerusalem announcements ... all those bizarre telephone calls ...'

Again a stop. The hesitations were carefully staged, guessed Kurnov, to enable every point to be assimilated, and hurry his confusion.

'... We were worried about those calls. Everyone said you'd become suspicious because of them. It was the most artificial part of the whole operation. I argued that I would already have made sufficient inroads into your mind by that time so that you wouldn't be panicked by them ...'

Kurnov felt his concentration wavering. It would be the anaesthetic, he thought. He *wouldn't* let the man beat him.

'The capture of Heinrich Köllman is to be Israel's final coup ... that and the destruction of as many Nazis as we could kill in the process,' enlarged Perez. 'We could easily get the small fry, of course. But that wouldn't have been spectacular enough. We knew you were in the Soviet Union, although we didn't know the name you'd adopted. Or that you'd become so important. All that has been a bonus ...'

Kurnov's head began to loll. He pulled himself up, fixing his eye just below the man's mouth. They wouldn't see him collapse. Even in the end, he'd prove a Nazi was stronger than a Jew.

'I never guessed, as I watched you and Mengele and Grüber grope into the psychiatry of deprivation, that I'd one day become a psychiatrist ... and be able to practise upon you the very science you were trying to perfect. I've used your entire capture as a thesis, Heinrich. I'm going to lecture in psychiatry now and I'll use the whole experiment to teach my pupils ... I've even taken recordings as we've been speaking, so that nothing will be missed.'

Perez laughed. 'That's the beautiful irony, isn't it, Heinrich? Your capture and complete defeat being used to train people you once used as guinea pigs.'

The explanation was definitely part of the assault upon his senses, Kurnov decided, calculated to encourage self-anger at his own stupidity.

'It was my ability as a psychiatrist which initially led to my being entrusted with the job of getting you out of the Soviet Union. That's why I chose the phoney raid upon Lake Toplitz ...'

He hesitated.

'... That went so badly wrong ... The only thing that didn't work out as I planned ...'

Kurnov had seized a word, like a drowning man grabbing a lifebelt.

'Phoney?' he asked.

Perez laughed again.

'Oh yes, Heinrich. Phoney. All I did was work upon your fear ... I manipulated you entirely, through fear ...'

Kurnov shook his head, unable to comprehend. He wasn't meant to, of course. Not yet. He had to be teased sufficiently to the brink of collapse.

'We had plenty of accounts from the Jews who survived Buchenwald and Auschwitz of the experiments upon the Russians ... I saw them myself. But we had no documentary, irrefutable proof. And the relationship between the Soviet Union and Israel isn't one where they would accept sworn evidence from Jewish ex-prisoners. And we didn't know your adoptive name, either. So I had to do two things: discover the name, and create the evidence. That's why I mounted the dive in Toplitz. All I wanted was some Nazi debris ... anything would have done, for us to produce at a Jerusalem press conference ...'

The acceptance of what he was being told began to settle, and Kurnov slumped in the chair, held there only by the bonds that secured him. For the second time in his life he had panicked, he realized.

There had been no need to come out of the Soviet Union. Had he stayed, behind the barrier he had created for himself in Russia, he would have been safe for the rest of his life.

'You mean ...?' he groped, needing the confirmation.

'Yes, Heinrich,' said Perez. 'There is no fourth box from Toplitz. There never has been. We had no proof at all that you were Heinrich Köllman until your carefully recorded confession here tonight. Our only lead was knowing that the surgeon, Bock, controlled the money you'd hidden away from the Nazis. Because he never used it, we guessed you were still alive. And that, as far as we could establish, you were somewhere in Russia. That became my strongest lever. I knew if you thought we had evidence of the Russian atrocities you'd have to come out from wherever you were hiding. Apart from the obvious communication problems, you couldn't ask the Nazis to recover it for you. Because they wanted you as much as we did. And it would have been equally impossible to get an undetected message to the surgeon from Russia. I *knew* you'd have to expose yourself ... nobody could have been entrusted with recovering something as important as this ... that's why I knew you'd need to take over from Bock. *No one* could get involved but you, could they?'

Perez stopped, looking down.

'The deaths of the commando squad were my only mistake,' he reiterated. 'If they hadn't been assassinated, the whole project would have gone off perfectly.'

The recrimination he had been fighting against engulfed Kurnov. He twitched against the manacles holding him and slowly tears began to run down his face. There was no sound as he cried.

'If their deaths served any purpose,' continued Perez, reflectively, 'it was to focus world attention far better than we had hoped upon the raid. And the box which Shapiro recovered was seen as absolute proof of our story. All we had to do then was talk about the fourth box we believed contained your records, create a story based here in Berlin, and wait for you to capture yourself.'

There was no way he could have known, Kurnov tried to reassure himself, wanting to control the tears. He couldn't break down in front of them and give them the satisfaction of knowing they'd broken him. He'd made a mistake, certainly. But there was no way he could have avoided it.

'It had to be Berlin, of course,' said Perez, shifting on the desk. 'That was most important. Everything had to be connected with memories that would fill your mind and unsettle you. In any other environment, you might have developed doubts and pulled back. But I knew Berlin would smother your mind, like a blanket. All we had to do was pressure Bock, knowing he would be the only man you could approach. And watch for you to get here.'

He smiled across the narrow gap between them. He was very excited by what he had done, Kurnov knew.

'And you came, just like I said you would. Nobody else thought I could manipulate a man's mind as I have manipulated yours. Do you know, Heinrich, there has scarcely been a moment since this began that I couldn't have guessed exactly what you were thinking? I anticipated everything ... the trauma of returning to Berlin ... the fear of knowing that everyone would be looking for you ... the apprehension that the Russians might discover what you were doing ... the memories ... everything ...'

'What are you going to do?' asked Kurnov. If they intended killing him, they would have done it immediately. They wouldn't have waited this long to torture him, either. The detailed account that Perez was giving wasn't the boasting of a man who had succeeded in springing a perfect trap. So what was the purpose?

'That's always the greatest fear, isn't it, Heinrich? Not knowing. It's quite easy to send a man insane, just from apprehension, once fear has been instilled in him, isn't it?'

Kurnov stared up, waiting. Was that it? Were they trying to crush his mind? He snatched at the flicker of hope. He'd be able to resist, he decided. He'd be able to anticipate the pressures and easily counteract them.

'It's very clever,' said Perez, without any conceit. 'You see, Heinrich, Israel knows that the world is irritated by her ... that it would lose more than it gained by another Eichmann trial ... you're the last spectacular *coup*, but even that is only for our own satisfaction. No one else will know we're involved ...'

He glanced at his watch.

'... Only two hours ago, Jerusalem announced an abject apology for intruding into Austria and said all inquiries about what was alleged to have been recovered from the lake would be handed over to the appropriate authorities ...'

Kurnov felt his mind wavering again and tried desperately to understand what Perez was saying.

'You're in a whirlpool, Heinrich. And there's no possible way you can stop yourself being sucked down.'

'For God's sake ...' pleaded Kurnov, confused.

'Listen carefully,' insisted Perez. 'Listen to what's going to happen to you ...'

Kurnov snapped up, eyes fixed on Perez's face and then regretted the gesture. It had been part of the psychiatry, he realized, and was carefully prepared to determine the degree of mental erosion.

'Like I said, I knew you'd have to come out of hiding. Although we didn't know your identity, we had some clear indications that you had achieved a position of some authority, so there'd be no difficulty in your getting exit permission. I also knew that the Organisation der Ehemaligen S.S. Angehörgen would be desperate to get the evidence, too. Not because it involved you, although that was sufficient reason, but because we were careful to announce it contained evidence against nearly every surviving Nazi ...'

He paused, to make a point.

'It was quite easy to test how close the Nazis were. It was obvious that with the facilities they command, they would put an intercept on the Israeli embassy telephone. We experimented. We staged a fictitious meeting between someone from the embassy and the person supposed to have the box. Within two hours, they turned up. So we knew we had them, just like we had you.'

'I don't understand ... I still don't understand,' protested Kurnov.

'Last night we baited the real trap,' said Perez. 'And they all walked into it, all fifteen of them ...'

He coughed, tired by the explanation.

'... They're dead,' he went on. 'We've destroyed the Organisation der Ehemaligen S.S. Angehörgen in Berlin ... there'll never be another moment when the Nazis in Egypt and South America can feel completely secure, knowing that they have a control set-up here.'

'Why are you telling me all this?'

'Oh, it's very important to you, Heinrich,' assured Perez. He stood, moving closer to the tethered man. Kurnov pulled away, expecting to be hit, but then realized Perez was holding up something for him to see. Oh God, he thought, how completely they'd trapped him. There were over a dozen photographs, perfectly taken through an infra-red filter with a fast film. Print followed print, each more damning than that which preceded it. There was Kurnov giving the Nazi salute ... standing admiringly before the picture of Hitler and the Nazi flag ... even kneeling in a position that looked like homage before one of the busts at the side of the room.

Happy at Kurnov's reaction, Perez pulled back, edging on to the desk again.

'How about this?' he commanded. Kurnov's voice filled the room, the tape recording perfect.

'... The Führer was a great man ... Another three years and we would have perfected the germ experiments that would have rid Europe of every Jew, gypsy and black ... It was the Führer's own instructions that the freezing experiments should be conducted not only on Jews, but on the Russian prisoners as well ... The Russians would shoot me, if they knew ... For them to discover I'm the person responsible for Russian deaths in a concentration camp ... would drive the fools insane ...'

Perez stopped the machine.

'I never guessed you would offer so much for the tape recording, while you believed all the time that you were manipulating the mind of a deranged Nazi,' admitted Perez.

'There's a movie film, of course,' added the Israeli. 'We've several copies of everything. But one is in a brief-case that the West German police recovered two hours ago lying beside the body of a very famous man in West Berlin. He's known now as Frieden, but it won't take long to establish that he was a former Standartenführer for the area that covered Buchenwald. He's one of the Nazis we killed. But ballistics examination of the bodies will show the bullets all came from guns still in their hands or around their bodies ... with their fingerprints on them ... a classic case of Nazis falling out over something very important ...'

He paused.

'... And you will be that very important reason, Heinrich. That will be the only conclusion the police will be able to draw. Another gun was taken from the scene. That's got your fingerprints on it, which we carefully took when you were unconscious ...'

Kurnov's head began to move again, unable to accept what was being explained to him.

'Think how the police will reconstruct it all, Heinrich. Fifteen men, who will be proven within twenty-four hours all to have been Nazis, all dead after what looks like an internal fight. Inside a basement flat in the apartment-block they uncovered a room, decorated exactly like this, a shrine to Nazism. And inside the briefcase by the body of the obvious leader, there is a record of you bargaining for the evidence that the world has been assured was uncovered from Toplitz ... plus the confession of why you had to leave Russia to retrieve it. There's only one possible reconstruction, isn't there?'

He paused, as if he expected Kurnov to give it. Kurnov just moaned.

'The only assumption can be that, with a group of Nazis still loyal, you went tonight to collect the evidence from another group ... After the bargaining, there was a fight ... a fight from which you and perhaps others escaped ... presumably with the evidence you'd come to collect, apparently unaware of the recordings Frieden intended to use for blackmail ...'

'Stop,' shouted Kurnov, hysteria very close now. 'I don't want to hear any more. It's madness ... madness ...'

'No, it's not,' rejected Perez. 'It's perfectly simple. And there's even better to come ...'

Kurnov stared, dully.

'This was as far as we had planned it,' he conceded. 'We wanted to create the situation where the West German police, with fingerprints proving you were Heinrich Köllman and a full tape-recorded confession of war crimes, would be hunting you in West Berlin for involvement in murder. But now the Russians have made it even better. They've been aware of what you've been doing here. We know that: I was quite surprised you missed the surveillance. We even had to block them following you tonight. It seems they've drawn the same conclusion as that which we've tried to implant in the minds of the police. Four hours ago, they announced you'd defected. And that you were a Nazi, undoubtedly contacting old associates. What better confirmation will the authorities want?'

Kurnov was soaked in perspiration The sour smell of his own body came up at him, disgustingly. At least he wasn't going to be tortured, physically, he thought.

199

They were merely going to hand him over to the authorities. Somehow, it seemed almost an anti-climax. Inexplicably, he felt suddenly happy. He tried to control the emotion, recognizing the ski-slope of hysteria.

'So there you are, Heinrich,' finished Perez. 'You're completely exposed ... fingerprints, that confirm you are Heinrich Köllman, on a gun that killed at least two people tonight ... an admitted slaughterer of Jews and Russians ... wanted by West Berlin and Moscow ...'

Kurnov dragged his face up to the other man, realizing he had not finished.

'And now we're going to let you go,' announced Perez, simply.

Kurnov searched, unable to form the words. Again the head shook.

'Yes, Heinrich,' pressed the psychiatrist, 'I intend you to suffer. Don't you remember what one of your early experiments showed? That the human acceptance of knowing there is nothing a man can do to avoid disaster is one of the most horrifying of mental pressures? That's what it was like at the camps, Heinrich. That was the most insidious torture of all, knowing that there was nothing, absolutely nothing, that anybody could do to avoid whatever fate you decided for them. And that's what's going to happen to you. You're as imprisoned as if you were an inmate of Dachau or Buchenwald. There's no way you can get out of this encircled city. The West Germans are looking for you ... the Russians want you ... probably a few surviving Nazis, too, if they can group themselves again. All of them, chasing you ...'

Perez nodded, and Kurnov felt the manacles being removed.

'So now you can run, Heinrich. You can run, to try to hide, like the Jews did when you came into the camps, looking for a fresh consignment of guinea pigs. There won't be a moment when you can relax, Heinrich. The pictures taken here tonight will be released, showing your new face. Which is hardly necessary; Russia has made photographs available. They'll be in *Bild Zeitung* and *B-Z* and *Die Welt* and every other newspaper circulating in the city. There'll be massive coverage on both A R D channels, so anyone who has a television set will recognize you. By tonight, there won't be anybody in West Berlin who doesn't know what your face looks like. Imagine that, Heinrich! You'll be just like the Jews ... hunted wherever you go ...'

Kurnov slipped off the chair, kneeling in the room for the second time.

'No,' he pleaded. 'Please God, no.'

He reached out, imploringly, and Perez stared down at him.

'I had one doubt, about the entire operation,' said the Israeli. 'I never thought, once I'd captured you, that I'd be able to hold back from hurting you, physically. But I can. I can because I know exactly what I'm going to do and I know it's causing more pain than any physical torture would.'

He nodded, and Kurnov felt himself jerked up. 'You've still got all your Russian documents in your pockets,' said Perez, evenly. 'And I've left you with two marks. That's a personal gesture. That's exactly what I had, when I came out of Buchenwald ...'

He waved the bank-drafts that Kurnov had handed over, hours before.

'And thanks for the £3,000,000,' he said 'Such a present to yids from a Nazi like you!'

He turned away, exhausted.

'Put him in the street,' he ordered. 'Let him start running.'

Kurnov's legs buckled and he tried to get back on to the floor, but the men held him easily, dragging his feet over the concrete.

Suddenly Perez spoke again. 'Of course, you'll try to explain everything, when you're finally caught,' he said, not bothering to turn back to the man. 'In an hour, this room will be what it always has been, a cellar. Our own forensic experts are going to clean it, so there'll be no evidence to support your story. The owner is a Jew, of course. He'll be amazed at any inquiries put to him. There's no way to prove your innocence, Heinrich. No way at all.'

Mosbacher paused, leaving the others initially to drag Kurnov from the room.

From the minute vestibule came the sound of Kurnov, whimpering.

'I was right,' said Mosbacher, positively. 'There was no justification for doing it this way.'

Perez turned to reply, but Mosbacher had already left the room.

Gerda Pöhl stood at her accustomed place at the window that morning, overlooking Duisburgerstrasse, drinking her coffee. He wouldn't come now, she thought. Herr Muntz had made a mistake. She'd benefited from it, though, she decided, walking into the bedroom and looking at the still-unworn suit. She'd put it on, she thought, when she visited Heini's grave at the weekend. And then linger over her coffee on the Kurfürstendamm, so that her new clothes would be noticed. She went into the kitchen, rinsed the cup and saucer and left them to drain, pausing before the refrigerator. She opened it, looking guiltily inside. She'd rationed herself to three slices a day, but it was nearly all gone, she saw. Heinrich had liked ham so much, she remembered.

The first injection three days before had made him sick. But then Bock, who had been cured of his heroin addiction five years earlier, had expected it. But it was better now. It was a wonderful sensation, like being supported on fluffy clouds. Nothing could hurt him or get to him, through the protection of the clouds, he thought, lying back in his apartment. He would control it this time, he told himself. It wouldn't get out of hand, like five years ago, threatening to interfere with his work.

He'd be sensible, restricting the injections. No more than three a day. It was stupid for doctors to argue about dependence leading to greater and greater doses. Three a day, that's all. The effect of the fix was subsiding, he recognized. Reality was coming at him, through the clouds, like seeing land far below an incoming aircraft. He wondered where Kurnov was: the conference ended today. He had expected contact. He *had* to know whether the Russian had recovered the contents of the box: his life might quite literally depend upon it. He looked at his watch. Nine-thirty. If there had been no call by eleven, he would have to go to the hotel, he knew. The prospect frightened him. He'd take another injection, he decided. It would be in addition to the number to which he had rationed himself, but there was a particular reason. He wouldn't do it again. Just this once. There wouldn't be any danger.

He jumped, startled, when the telephone rang. Kurnov, he decided, his mind still fogged. Smiling, he picked up the receiver, then winced at the Bavarian accent.

'It's all over, Helmut,' said Perez, at the other end. 'Frieden's dead ... they're all dead ... Kurnov's been exposed and is trying to escape ... the police know everything. They'll be coming for you soon. Run, Helmut, run.'

The surgeon stared down at the dead phone, then threw it away from him, as if it were contaminated with some infectious virus.

He dashed across the room, then stopped, frightened, not knowing why he was doing it. He needed another injection, he thought, immediately, turning towards the bathroom. Then he halted, positively. Heroin wasn't any good now. How they'd laugh and sneer, all those people who had sought his friendship and demanded secrecy for their operations. From outside the apartment, he heard the distant sound of a siren. Police car or ambulance? It was impossible to isolate. That's how they'd come, he thought. Several car-loads of police, forcing their way into the apartment or even worse, into the clinic, jostling and pushing him, anxious for it to be seen how they treated Nazis.

He turned away from the bathroom. He began to sob, and bite his lips together. The veranda doors stuck, and he had to pull several times before they slid aside. The sudden cold contrasted with the central heating of the apartment and made him gasp. He stood for several minutes, staring out over the skyline of Berlin. He shouldn't look down, he thought. If he looked down, he'd get frightened. And he couldn't stand there too long, either, otherwise he'd be driven back by the same fear. He tried breathing deeply, several times, but the emotion began to build up, breaking it into the sobs that had started as he crossed the lounge inside. Abruptly he grabbed the edge of the balcony, hesitated momentarily at the coldness of the metal, then vaulted over.

Far below, the waiting Israeli saw the body spread-eagle, then flutter down, as if it were flying. It seemed to take a long time to reach the ground.

He sighed, shaking his head. It was amazing, he thought, that Perez had so correctly assessed the behaviour of everyone. Strange how Mosbacher was objecting to it.

(19)

He screamed, once, as they half-carried him through the courtyard, his feet still dragging the ground in protest. It was Mosbacher who stifled the shout for help.

'Go ahead,' he said, from the left where he was supporting him. 'Make everyone look, Heinrich.'

The scientist was shoved, stumbling, into the Mercedes, which was already moving off before he struggled upright. They sat flanking him, looking straight ahead.

He tugged at Mosbacher's arm, desperately. 'I've got money. A lot of money. You can have it, all of it. Just help me.'

'I remember my mother saying something like that to the Nazis who took us away,' Mosbacher goaded.

Kurnov's fear over-rode the rebuke. 'Where are you taking me? What are you going to do? You must tell me.'

The scientist began staring left and right from the vehicle, anxious for landmarks. Suddenly he started to tremble, uncontrollably, like a man without clothes in a snow-storm. The men either side of him turned and smiled at the nervous reaction.

'It often starts like that, Heinrich,' said Mosbacher.

He couldn't recognize anything, the scientist realized. The Berlin he had known had disappeared, along with an ideology.

He felt the speed decrease and saw the Mercedes pulling into the curb. He strained out, looking for the indications of an official building. A police station. Or a Justice Ministry, he thought, forgetting in his apprehension that Bonn was the capital. He looked out on an ordinary street, full of shops and people.

Mosbacher turned.

'Time to learn what it's like to be a Jew, Heinrich,' he said. 'Start running.'

Kurnov tried to push himself back into the seat, his feet braced against the floor, but they pushed him forward from both sides and the passenger in the front seat leaned across, grasping the front of his coat. The driver got out and opened the door and reached in, too, pulling at his overcoat lapels. Kurnov grabbed at the door pillar. Behind Mosbacher said, quite calmly, 'People will start looking at you soon, Heinrich.'

The driver, less controlled than the other men, said, 'Let go that pillar, you bastard. Or I'll slam the door and break your hands.'

The man wanted to hurt him, Kurnov realized, his face only inches away. He let go and was expelled from the car in a rush, almost falling on the pavement. He swivelled, only half recovered and saw the Mercedes already moving off. He opened his mouth to shout, then stopped. People *were* looking, he realized. He stood tensed, awaiting the first yell of recognition. What would they do? Hit him? Or merely stand around, staring, until the authorities arrived? They'd panic, he decided, reacting with the customary crowd mentality, driven to mob violence. They'd beat him. He was sure of it.

Nothing happened. The people who had glanced casually as he fell from the car looked away. Momentarily, unable to understand it, he stood in the centre of the pavement as people washed around him. Then he realized the conspicuousness. Like a suddenly blinded man walking for the first time, Kurnov went to the side of the pavement and began to edge along, keeping close to the walls of buildings, as if they would provide protection. Hide, he told himself. He had to hide. Thank God it was winter and they had allowed him his overcoat. He shrugged the collar closer around him,

206

burrowing his chin low into it. Good enough, he reasoned. No one was going to take too much notice of a man huddled against the winter. He saw a street sign and looked up, anxiously. Dachdecker Weg. He was still in Buckow. They'd just driven around aimlessly, to confuse his sense of direction. There was a park nearby, he remembered. That would be the place to go. Neukölln Park. On the streets, he was close to people. In an open space, there would be safety. Goaded scientifically to the point of mental collapse, he snatched at omens, as he had when he first arrived in the city. He'd been on the streets for fifteen minutes, he calculated. And no one had even glanced at him. Perhaps the Jew had been lying. Perhaps the whole story had been an invention, a clumsy rather than clever attempt to break him. That was it. He had been bluffed out of Russia and now they had tried to trick him into a complete mental breakdown by extending the delusion. He'd even conducted such experiments himself, in Buchenwald. Perez had said he was following the precedents he had established. That was it. Another trick. But he was sure he could defeat them. Easy, he warned himself, the elation filling him. Too much confidence would be dangerous. He gripped his hands inside the pockets of the overcoat. That was irrational thinking: exactly what had to be avoided. He could only survive by being cleverer than they were. His advantage was knowing in minute detail what they had done. And what they hoped to achieve by having done it. They were trying to drive him insane. And as he knew it, he could resist them and win.

He recognized again the rehearsal and timing that had gone into Perez's explanation. Every word and every action had been calculated to the last degree of stress, to tilt him off his mental balance. But they'd overlooked one important factor. Clever men always did. They'd ignored the fact that he was a psychiatrist, someone perhaps better trained than Perez. Definitely better trained, he reassured himself. Certainly in behavioural stress.

If he could avoid panic, he could save his mind, he knew. That was the trick. Never for a moment lose control of his reasoning. And consider everything logically, forbidding any self-delusion.

How stupid he had been, he reflected, bitterly. Perez had been right. He had been manipulated as easily as a child's hand-puppet, performing to a carefully prepared script. If only he had stayed safely in Russia ...

He stopped the recrimination, fighting to regain control. His mind had slipped, he accepted, worriedly. Exactly what shouldn't have happened. That was how Perez would want him to think, undermining his self-control with personal anger, driving common sense away with his own exasperation.

Perez's story could easily have been concocted, he resumed again, the reasoning breaking away in another direction in a desperate search for the smallest degree of hope. Again he pushed the confidence back with logic. He had to be logical. He repeated the instructions to himself, like a child learning a calculation table. It didn't really matter whether the Nazis had been shot or not, he decided. Or whether the Russians had declared him a defector. So anxious was he for a lifeline he had erased from his mind the pictures and recorded confession. They were enough. More than enough. It would all be made available to the authorities, even if everything else was a lie. So arrest was inevitable. And the pictures would be published, if he were thought to be wandering in Berlin. So he *would* be hunted, like the Jews had been thirty-five years before. And the city *was* an island. There was no way he could get out. Why had he forgotten that? It was a ridiculous omission. Was it his mind blocking out the unacceptable? He'd recorded the tendency a hundred times, in every camp in which he had worked.

His tongue explored the now-aching cavity. If only the cyanide implant were still there, he thought. He would have used it. He would have had to. He couldn't stand capture. He knew he couldn't. He squeezed his eyes shut, visualizing what would happen. Arrest. Questioning. Mockery. Humiliation. A trial, where he would appear like a pet animal, for people to stare at. And then the imprisonment, the empty, sense-rotting incarceration in stinking cells where he would become sub-human, like they always did. He shuddered. He knew too well what happened to people in prisons to let it happen to him. And it would be imprisonment, he was sure. He would be tried in Germany, for war crimes. They'd ignore the Statute of Limitations, in his case. But they'd stop short of the death sentence. He'd probably be sent to Spandau, forced to listen to the gibbering of Rudolf Hess. The Russians would like that. It would give them a continuing excuse for the Four-Power presence in the city.

He became conscious of the bulge beneath his jacket and reached in, remembering the Russian passport. He pulled it out, covering it with his hand against any passerby recognizing it as a Soviet document. It identified him, he decided, immediately. If someone grabbed him, challenging his identity, he could argue. And perhaps escape. But not if he carried papers showing who he was. Ahead he saw a rubbish basket affixed to a lamp standard. He glanced around, ensuring he was still unobserved, then quickly dropped the passport in, hardly pausing in his stride. Once he was freed of the document, the unsteady elation flooded him again. Now no one could prove who he was. Not instantly, anyway. He turned into Buckowerdamm, sighing with relief at the sight of the park. Leafless trees shivered ahead of him in the winter cold. It was like a churchyard, he thought. The unexpected sight of his own face, staring back at him from a newspaper stand, was like a physical punch. He stopped, the gasp pulled from him. There were two pictures. One was clearly from the cellar confession. But the other was an official print, obviously older than the first. From Russia, he accepted. So it was true. Everything the Jew had said was true. He was inescapably trapped. But then he'd already known that, he reasoned. The refusal to accept reality annoyed him. It showed immaturity.

'Space Scientist is Nazi Murderer' said the hoarding. There were smaller headlines, but he was too far away to read them.

He turned, small sounds grunting from him, like a puppy nervous in a new house. He ran across the highway, twisting between cars, then forced himself to stop, aware of the attention he was attracting. Inside the park, he hurried over the grass, anxious to get into the middle, to an isolated part. He felt a choking sensation, like drowning. He coughed, near to vomiting, recognizing as he bent double the extent of the nervousness. No, he corrected. Not nervousness. Fear ... fear like the Jews said he would feel. Like they had felt. It was working, he told himself. Perez's torture was working. Because of the cold, the park was almost deserted. But he was hot. The feeling came in spasms, with the regularity of a heartbeat. The nausea was at the back of his throat and his skin began to irritate. He felt the perspiration break out over his face and back. He scratched, but the irritation seemed to increase. He looked down, concentrating for the first time since leaving the cellar on his own appearance. His suit had dried into concertina creases from the sweat that had soaked him during the confrontation with Perez. His shirt was creased and stained, too, and again he became aware of his own smell. He brought his hand to his face. After the surgery, his beard had never been heavy, but stubble stuck out in odd islands over his face. He looked disgusting, he knew. But his very appearance might be protection, he decided, still seeking escape. Immediately the pendulum swung, rejecting it. Perez *had* got to his mind, insidiously, like water finding its way under a stone. He'd always been so sure of the strength of his own mind. Now that confidence was washed away, as easily as a twig in a stream. He *had* been beaten, he accepted. There was no point in fighting. Or running. The apathy crept over him, numbing. Is this how they felt, those Jews who had been whipped and herded like cattle into pens for him to select? And those in the Russian camps, the people with blank eyes, sure of only one thing, their helplessness. Resistance flickered, like a candle in the wind. But there was a difference. Surely they'd withstood it much longer, he thought, critical of himself. He'd known men brought into the laboratory after six months, sometimes a year, all the time knowing they were to be experimented upon, who still weren't at the level to which he'd been reduced in hours. He groaned heavily, pulling the apathy around him like a blanket. So what? It didn't matter whether he was the weaker or stronger. He shivered, suddenly conscious of the cold. Instinctively he glanced at his watch, but found it missing. He must have been there at least an hour, he decided. Again the shrug. It still didn't give him an estimate of what time it was. Did that matter, either? He stood up, stamping the life into his feet and legs, moving slowly along the empty pathways. There was a sudden pain in his face, like a reminder, and again his tongue went to the extraction.

Without thought, he found himself on the edge of the park. He hesitated, his mind refusing to function. Still undecided, the erosion now well advanced, he pushed out into the street. A boy approached, looking at him, and the fear jumped immediately. The child went on and Kurnov stared over his shoulder, but there was no answering look. He released the breath, relaxing. But at what, he demanded, attempting to recover some control over himself. That there was no recognition? Or that there hadn't been the stare of realization that would have meant the end to the pointless meandering around the streets of a city he had once loved. Another newspaper poster shouted his name. He drew closer, hunched into the coat. Every newspaper looked the same, dominated by his photograph. The seller looked up and frowned, uncertainly. Kurnov hurried by, apprehensively. He imagined he heard a shout and immediately began running, blindly, pushing through the startled people until he reached a junction. He swerved to his right, listening for the following footsteps or shouts. Breath pumped from him and his chest hurt, like it had when he had climbed down the hotel fire-escape. How long ago that seemed! The first positive step of an unnecessary journey, he reflected. Oh God, how his injured leg hurt. He crossed the road, still hurrying, moving into a shopping arcade. There he stopped, looking behind. No one followed. Another false alarm. They said he'd run, frightened at anything, he remembered. The scare had momentarily blown away the apathy, and now thoughts were engaging more easily.

He was allowing them the satisfaction they had planned, he realized, suddenly. He was scurrying, stinking with his own fear, because they had told him that was what he was going to do. The anger flared in him. He'd long ago written a thesis on the characteristic of the Jewish people to accept oppression. There were isolated exceptions, of course. Warsaw. And Treblinka. But generally there had been little resistance. He'd sneered at it, he recalled, pointing it up as an inherent weakness in the race. And now he, Heinrich Köllman, one of the most feared and respected Nazis of the Third Reich, was doing exactly the same. He was behaving exactly like a Jew.

He'd deny them their final satisfaction, he decided. Again the cavity twitched, but this time he concentrated upon the pain. They'd revealed their fear by that extraction, he determined. And until now he had missed the clue. Their only fear was that he would have committed suicide to deprive them of the spectacle of a hunt, followed by a trial.

So he'd die. And beat them.

He tried to locate the street name, feeling for the first time the tiredness grab at him. He'd walked a long way, he realized, further than he could recall walking in one day. Mental fatigue was combining with the physical exhaustion, too. Geraerstrasse. There would be a U-Bahn station very soon. He hurried along, looking for the Underground. Now he had a purpose, he was more controlled. The idea of being the victor pleased him. It always had. He'd always enjoyed winning, Kurnov thought. Perhaps irrationally so. Certainly what little defeat he had so far experienced had always caused him too much anger.

It would hurt, he decided, suddenly, remembering his abhorrence of pain. He felt the sweat flush from him again. But only for a second, he rationalized. Just the briefest second, providing he was very careful about throwing himself completely beneath the train. So there could be no pulling back, no last-minute change of heart. If he baulked at the last moment, trying to twist away, then there *would* be horrific injuries. And pain. A lot of pain. He walked on, positively. It was almost as if he got courage from the determination to spite them. Just a second, he reassured himself again. Then it would all be over. Everything would be over.

He identified the station, immediately ahead. And a newspaper seller, next to the entrance. He hesitated, uncertainly. He'd forgotten the prominence of his photograph. It didn't matter. He'd have to pass. He waited until a group of people moved towards the station, then hurried up, tagging along behind and averting his face from the news-stand as he went by. Again he tensed for a shout, but nothing happened.

Inside, the warmth enveloped him and for a moment he paused, enjoying the comfort. He'd grown very cold in the park, he realized. Far below he heard the clatter of a train. Only a second, he thought again. He'd hardly feel anything. It would be just like the cyanide that he'd carried for so long and conditioned himself to use. Near the cash desk, he saw the tariff and smiled. The last laugh, he thought. He'd commit suicide with the money that the Jews had provided. He passed over the mark, turning his face as he received the ticket and the thirty pfennig change. The doubt began to snatch at him as he descended the stairs. In five minutes, maybe less, he'd be dead. He pictured the injuries his body would sustain under the wheels and actually stopped on the stairs, but the flow of people behind pushed him on. Perhaps it wouldn't be so quick. Anything could happen. Someone might see him move forward and try to grab him at the last moment, deflecting his fall. Perhaps the driver would even be alert enough to stop the train.

But he *had* to die. Had to. And where else, but in Berlin? Just as the Führer had done. He carried on down the stairs, trying to push back the fear. In five minutes. That's all. Just five minutes and it would all be over. Far away there was the rumble of an approaching train, like someone clearing their throat. The noise built up, gradually. It was as if his body had its own motivation, moving through people on the platform, while he stood aside, watching what was happening to himself. He gazed over the edge. One line would carry electricity, he realized, for the first time. It would burn. Would he feel the pain before the agony of the train? The noise was very loud now. Warm air gushed from the tunnel mouth, pushed ahead of the approaching vehicle. Three steps. That's all. Just three steps. Then fall forward, keeping his body stiff, so he would encounter both sets of wheels. Three steps. Only three steps. He'd be able to do it. The awareness of the courage came suddenly and the knowledge warmed him. He'd definitely be able to do it. From the blackness of the tunnel he saw approaching lights.

He took one step forward.

'That wouldn't be right, Heinrich, would it?'

He jerked around, noises clogging in his throat, the determination to die kicked away like a ladder being snatched from beneath a workman. Smiling at him was the man who'd ridden in the front of the Mercedes. And the driver who had threatened to crush his hands. They moved around, interposing themselves between him and the track, destroying the opportunity.

'Can't have you committing suicide,' said the driver, casually. 'That would be far too easy. You haven't run far enough yet. Not standing up to it at all well, are you?'

The train hissed into the platform and people surged forward. He pressed against them, eyes bulged at the two men. The bastards. The filthy, scheming bastards. All the time they'd followed him, ensuring that he was performed to their prepared scenario. Perez had probably filmed it, for later showing at the university ... 'and here's how he scuttled through the Berlin where he had once strutted in his S.S. jackboots ...'

And all the students would smile and giggle, knowing it was one of the jokes introduced to make their learning easier. He knew he was sobbing, but like the shaking in the Mercedes, he couldn't control it. Both men laughed at him. He edged back, away from them, pushed now by the disembarking passengers.

'And you'd better have this,' said the man who had been the passenger. 'Don't want any uncertainty about who you are, do we?'

The man tossed at him the Russian passport he'd tried to conceal in the rubbish basket. *Everything*, thought Kurnov, helplessly. They'd watched *everything*. The document struck him on the chest, then scattered on the floor.

'You've dropped something,' shouted the driver, over-loudly. Hurrying people hesitated and looked. Kurnov snatched it up, clutching it against him, hypnotized by their ridicule.

Then the dam broke. He turned and began running, as fast as he could, fighting against the tight breath and the pain in his legs, trying to take steps two at a time, pushing around people, uncaring of their shouts. At the barrier, he thrust out the unused ticket. The collector opened his mouth, but Kurnov shoved by, still running. But he was too tired. His feet began to stumble and he knew he would soon fall. And if he fell, he wouldn't be able to get up. He knew his legs would refuse to support him. So he'd be caught. He slowed, to a walk, but still the fatigue ached through him. It was like trying to walk through a weed-thick stream. He hadn't slept for almost forty-eight hours, he accepted. Or eaten, either. No one could go on, harried like he was being, for much longer. The idea of death pushed away, the need for sanctuary filled his mind. He looked behind, then to either side, wildly. There was no one obviously watching him. But they'd be there, he knew. They'd rehearsed it, very carefully, schooled by Perez with his conviction he could read every thought and anticipate every move. So they'd definitely be there, somewhere. Watching. And perhaps recording. The thoughts of being filmed annoyed him. He'd always filmed stress experiments, for later examination and analysis. And he remembered the reaction, when he'd shown them at Buchenwald or Auschwitz.

'Better than anything Chaplin could have done,' he remembered Bormann saying, on one occasion.

Now he was performing, for their amusement. He imagined the sniggering at his helplessness, the remarks about his appearance. It was obscene, he felt, like taking hidden pornographic photographs in a whore's bedroom. He snatched at his wavering determination. He had to break their control. He had to escape their surveillance.

That would upset them. Once they lost him, they couldn't manœuvre his collapse. Perez wasn't that good. He couldn't anticipate everything.

And he *would* die, he assured himself. He'd snatch the final victory to become just another tidy cross in the cemetery. Perhaps in St Thomas Kirchhof, like Heini.

He suddenly laughed aloud, ignoring the reaction from people around him. All along there had been an escape ... a hiding place. He'd even prepared it, when he had arrived in the city; but Perez had wiped his mind clean, like a teacher erasing instructions from a blackboard.

Kurnov paused, halted by a sudden, illogical thought. What a team they would have been, he mused, he and Perez. The combination of their minds would have been incredible. He fought against the idea, recognizing the symptom. It meant he was ceasing to oppose the man, switching his feelings to those of admiration. And once he allowed that feeling to settle, the domination would be almost complete. And he wouldn't allow the other man that control. He knew how to win because he had carefully discovered where Gerda lived. That's where he could hide. And sleep, too. That would spoil the bigoted account that Perez would deliver. '... And I regret, at this point, the Nazi was too clever for us and escaped ...'

He was going to prove himself superior to Perez, he knew. The challenge arranged itself in his mind. He *was* superior, he repeated, wondering at the need for reassurance. He'd prove it, definitely. Again the arrogance arrived on the back of euphoria.

It would be easy to fool Gerda, of course. She would not recognize him. He'd be a stranger to her. He'd have to be careful to avoid frightening her, though. She'd be convinced of his death, after all these years, so the reason he gave for suddenly appearing upon her doorstep would have to be convincing. He'd say he was a friend.

That was it. A friend whom Heinrich had always said could approach his wife. What about if she had read the newspapers? He thought back, trying to hurdle the gap of thirty years. She never had, ever. Her only interest was fashion magazines. How would he know where she lived? He discarded the problem, casually. He could manœuvre the announcement easily enough so that she would be too confused even to consider such doubt. Very easy to manœuvre, he thought again. Why? he wondered. Why had the thought appeared again? Did he have to prove his own ability to manipulate, to restore his crumbling confidence? Perhaps. So what? Daily everyone performed mental dance-steps to support their own ego. So Gerda — or the control of her — became another experiment. It was fitting she should prove some use after so long. As a wife, she had never been any use, just an embarrassment. He'd known the jokes that Goebbels and Himmler had made up about her. And of the damage to his progress to even higher honour in the Party her presence had caused. Yes, it was fitting she should belatedly help him. He looked around again, seeking the watchers. There would be cars, he knew. So there was no point in trying to leap suddenly into a passing taxi. And anyway, he had insufficient money. So there was no way. Yes, he contradicted, immediately. Yes, there was. The answer was in the U-Bahn. If he rode the Underground, there was no way any vehicle could pursue because they would not know a destination. Of course people on foot would follow. But he would have reduced the surveillance. And that would give him an advantage. Ahead, the station appeared. He smiled, buoyed by his reasoning. Once again he entered, purchased his ticket and moved easily down with the crowd.

On the platform, he stood far back from the track, studying the Underground map and the advertisements. Several people gathered between him and the line. One of them would be to prevent him making another dash forward. The realization gave him an idea and he smiled again. The approaching train grumbled nearer. Kurnov's eyes went from face to face seeking the slightest recognition, but no one responded to the attention. That was to be expected, decided Kurnov. The men watching him would be professionals, trained against exposing themselves. Would it work? he wondered. He stopped examining the crowd, aware of the risk of exposing himself. He huddled lower in his coat, anxious for the concealment it afforded. The danger would be greater on the train, he realized. A hat would help. He wondered if there would be one in Gerda's apartment.

The train came in, breathlessly. And suddenly Kurnov moved, lurching forward. Immediately he pulled back, but the movement had been sufficient. Two men directly in front had sprung together, forming a wall. So they were not professional after all, thought Kurnov. They stood, looking foolish, and Kurnov moved slowly around them, boarding the train.

The two Jews hesitated, uncertainly, angry at being shown-up. Just before the doors closed, one hurried in, moving down the train. As it took off from the station, Kurnov saw the second running back up the stairs.

The behaviour of the two men was important, judged Kurnov. It meant that despite the charade on the platform, the watchers were still under instructions not to expose him deliberately. The pendulum was swinging to his advantage, decided Kurnov, omen-seeking again. Quickly the confidence built up. He shrugged his collar higher, happy at the way the logic was presenting itself in his mind. Perez had failed to unsettle him to the degree intended, decided Kurnov. He had positioned himself carefully with his face towards the window, always conscious of the need for protection. But it was not very effective, he thought, gazing at his own reflection as the train bustled through the blackened tunnel. His crumpled appearance was mirrored to every occupant in the carriage.

He began counting. Three people were reading newspapers, two holding them in such a way that his picture was displayed, like a 'wanted' poster. And there was a discarded copy of *Die Welt* lying on a seat, again with his photograph uppermost. He pulled further into the window, lowering his head.

At the next station, the platform appeared against the door before which he was standing. He squeezed to one side, unwilling to move further into the carriage where he would be visible to all the other passengers. Several people coming aboard jostled him, annoyed at his refusal to retreat, and one woman stared directly at him, angrily. The perspiration broke out immediately, stoked by the nervousness, and he turned away, avoiding her.

He tried to recall the stops to the Tiergarten, wondering if he would be able to complete the journey.

He looked away from his own reflection, seeking the man who was obviously watching him. The Jew sat on a corner-seat, slumped miserably. Kurnov hoped the Israelis were as hard upon the operatives who made mistakes as the Nazis and the Russians.

Kurnov was suddenly aware that he was being watched, by someone else. Stupidly, he searched along the carriage, and saw it was the woman who had been annoyed at his barring her entry at the last station. Quickly, he jerked away. In the window's reflection he saw her look at the discarded *Die Welt*, then towards him. The initial look had been casual, without any reason. Now she frowned, going back to the newspaper, then up again for comparison. Kurnov turned completely away from her, risking exposure from the other direction. A station arrived, but entry was from the opposite door this time. It was getting crowded now, he thought, gratefully. T..e growing number of passengers gave him some protection from the woman. And the watching man. He felt pressure against him and stiffened. Behind there was a muttered apology and he glanced down, identifying a guitar case. There were several, all carried by chattering youngsters, long-haired and jeaned. There was even a double bass, he saw, fleetingly, before turning back to the window. An advantage, he decided. The cases and the people provided a definite barrier.

The woman was the biggest risk, Kurnov recognized. He edged around, staring from the corner of his eye. She had picked the newspaper up, intently studying the photograph, then going forward, trying to see his reflection better. Quickly he pulled around again. It would have to be the next station, he thought. Her uncertainty wouldn't last. The photographs were too good.

The tunnel wall began changing, growing lighter. He flexed his legs, surreptitiously. When the moment came, it would have to be sudden, but until then he had to appear relaxed and unprepared to move.

The station wall was before him now and he waited for the break that would mark the beginning of the platform. The station sign appeared and the hidden tension flowed away. Again the platform was against the opposite door. Very carefully he relaxed. The watching Jew was growing frightened. So big was the crush of people now that it was almost impossible for him to keep Kurnov in view. The Israeli stood, surrendering his seat, pushing up on tiptoe to see over the heads of those who had intervened. The woman was completely hidden, too. The train jerked out. Kurnov readied himself once more, right against the door. It would have to be timed to the second, he thought. Too soon and the man would be behind him. Too late and the opportunity would be missed. He was sure he could not travel to a further stop without challenge.

Again he located the woman. She was standing now, leaning over towards the window, trying determinedly to see his face properly. For a few seconds their eyes touched, the looks bounced back by the window. Conviction registered. And shock, too. Her eyes stared and she opened her mouth. He hunched, waiting for the scream, but there was no sound. Her mouth moved, trying to assemble the words. The platform gradually unwound alongside and the doors opened. He pulled to one side, letting the disembarking passengers ebb around him. Ironically, it was the woman who made his escape work. She began waving her arms, trying to gesture to the man sitting alongside. He glared up, irritated. Kurnov stayed near the open doors, tensed for them to close, watching her tug at the man's arm and indicate towards the opening. The Israeli could stand it no longer, getting up and trying to squeeze past the musical instruments. Then the woman finally shouted. Once the block was broken, the sounds screamed out, seizing everyone. Instinctively, the Jew stopped and turned. And at that moment, the doors began to close. The observer turned back, hurriedly, but the crowd were moving against him, trying to see the reason for the woman's yells.

Kurnov had timed it perfectly. As he stepped through, the rubber lining of the door actually tugged at his coat, but not sufficiently to activate their automatic reopening. He swivelled, to see the Jew pressed against the door. Behind him, the woman was shouting and gesticulating. Other people seemed to be shouting, looking bewildered at one another, but no sound was audible. Like human goldfish, thought Kurnov, laughing aloud in delight. Even that gesture encouraged him. There had been no hysteria in the sound, he decided. Perhaps such euphoria would be acceptable, he reflected. He'd done it! He hurried from the station, even the tiredness receding at the knowledge that he'd broken their observation.

Immediately outside, he moved into the backstreets, changing direction several times. It would only be minutes before the man got off at the next station, but he had more to worry about now than just Jewish surveillance. Within minutes of the woman's account, supported perhaps by others who had identified him once he had cleared the train, the district would be blocked by police. He paused, stopped by a sudden thought. The police would be able to make extensive sweeps and move faster than he could on foot. He smiled as an idea settled in his mind.

There was an obvious way to clear out of the area in a hurry. Ahead he saw the sign and quickly hurried down into the U-Bahn again, knowing it was the last place where they would seek him.

$\left(20\right)$

For two hours he hid in the Tiergarten, growing increasingly colder as night approached. Gerda would have to be home before he made an approach, he had decided, reluctantly. He could only risk once running the gauntlet before the concierge. What else did such people do all day, but watch television or read newspapers? The caretaker would be bound to recognize him unless he was careful. So he stuck by his earlier decision, seeking safety in open spaces. He kept carefully from other people and not once in the two hours was there any risk of identification. The only problem was the cold. It became so bad that an ache started in his legs and feet, but even then he resisted moving from the park prematurely, enjoying the personal experiment in will power. It was further proof he could withstand what Perez had done to him. Six o'clock was sounding from an unseen clock before he moved out into the streets again. He hunched down into his coat, needing the warmth generated in his body by the movement. The darkness was a help, too, he decided, walking through the streets without the nervousness he had felt during the day.

He found Duisburgerstrasse easily, hesitating on the opposite side of the road. There was no way to isolate her apartment to determine from a lighted window if Gerda was home. A friend, he thought, rehearsing his story. He'd say he was a friend of her husband's. She'd always been stupid. She wouldn't question too closely, exposing the obvious emptiness. Positively he pushed across the road, stopping immediately outside the entrance. The door was closed but not locked, he saw, gratefully. Inside an uncovered bulb gave a yellow, tired light. Softly he opened the door, tensed against any sound. The concierge's office was to the right, fronted by a small counter. The office door was open and there was a light burning in the room behind. Faintly, he could hear the scuffling of the woman behind the door. Probably eating, he guessed. Silently, he eased across the vestibule, his eyes always on the opening. He heard voices and halted, then smiled, recognizing from the formality of the words that she was watching television. Excellent. She would be distracted, careless of the hall. Quickly he hurried across, dodging around the stair-well He stared back, waiting for the challenge. Nothing. He smiled again, happily. Still walking carefully to avoid sound, he mounted the stairs, testing each step before putting his weight fully down, pausing at every turn to ensure the landing was empty. His leg began to ache again. He was desperately tired, he realized.

Gerda's apartment was on the third floor, he discovered. For several moments, he stood before the door, gazing at the number. He was very frightened, he accepted. He'd been a fool not to prepare properly a reason for suddenly confronting the woman to whom he would appear a scruffy, dishevelled stranger. She'd panic, he thought, trying to remember her reaction to sudden surprises. Yes, she'd definitely panic. She might scream, even. What if she put a burglar-chain across the door and refused to admit him? His stomach lurched at another thought. What if she had married again and there was a man inside? Pöhl could be a married name as easily as an assumed one. Or she might have a companion, some woman whom she had befriended and lived with for company or financial help. He swayed, dizzy from fear and fatigue and exhaustion and hunger.

It didn't matter, he dismissed. Having got this far, he had to make an approach. There was nowhere else to go, no hiding-place he could otherwise choose. It would be very easy to cry, he realized. Perez was a bastard.

Hesitantly, the first attempt hardly making any sound, he knocked at the door.

Inside, Gerda jumped, over-reacting, like a stranger in a foreign country being shouted at by an official. It could only be Heinrich, she determined, instantly. Herr Muntz had said the approach might come any time. And there had been that strange call to the office that morning, with no explanation for why he could not come in. Three appointments had had to be cancelled and she was sure they'd lost at least two clients. Only Heinrich's reappearance could have caused Herr Muntz to behave like that.

She sat, her body rejecting any movement. Again there was the knock, louder this time. She stared down, immediately. She wore her oldest suit, the one shining with use, and there was a stain where a piece of fat from the almost exhausted ham had fallen upon her already grubby blouse an hour before.

She started towards the bedroom, but the knock came again, insistently. She hadn't time, she knew. If she delayed, he might go away, imagining she were not in. She hurried her hands to her hair, squeezing and pushing the collapsing bun at the nape of her neck. Her lip trembled with emotion and annoyance. She had so wanted to be beautiful when he came. Perhaps once he was inside the apartment she would be able to change.

Outside Kurnov heard her doubtful footsteps. He'd been listening, ear to the door. No conversation. At least she was alone. Trying to subdue the noise, in case she detected the caller was a man, he cleared his throat, preparing to speak first. He would have to be quick, to quell her fear.

The door lock clicked, but it didn't open immediately. Gerda pulled it uncertainly, apprehensive of what would confront her.

The two frightened people stared unspeakingly at each other. Gerda reacted first, her carefully held face breaking with disappointment when she saw the man was not who she had been expecting. Since that morning in the lawyer's office, she had created a mental image of how Heinrich would re-appear. Illogically, she had imagined him no older than when she had last seen him. And smart, very smart. He always had been. Perhaps a businessman's black suit and overcoat. Or maybe a leather topcoat. He always had liked the leather uniform coats.

But this wasn't him. She felt cheated. Her face twisted at the grubby old man who stood before her, his body held to one side as if he were about to collapse. The smooth, almost artificial face was spotted with isolated patches of beard, like dunes on a sandy shore, and his eyes were staring, fixedly, as if he were in shock. She began to close the door, feeling frightened.

'Frau Pöhl ...' blurted Kurnov. He hadn't spoken immediately, as he had planned. And now he had started badly. Quickly he corrected himself, knowing the key. ' ... Frau Köllman ... please ... '

Gerda stopped, alert but still unsure. So he *was* connected with her husband. Representing him, perhaps. Herr Muntz had said he might send a friend. He was obviously someone in the Party, otherwise he would not have known her true name.

Immediately she reopened the door, beckoning him in, and instantly Kurnov became unsettled by her reaction. Why hadn't she asked questions, demanded explanations? He nervously stopped inside the door, prepared to turn to run from what might confront him.

The flat was badly furnished, he saw, nearly every piece of furniture aged and worn. Obviously it was beyond her means, but Gerda would want to live here because it was fashionable and people might be impressed. She always had been stupidly snobbish. There were three doorways leading from the main room and he looked towards each, but no other person appeared. So she *was* alone. And there was no sign of a television or any newspaper. Hence the absence of startled, terrified recognition. At last things were going his way.

'Frau Köllman ...' he tried again, but Gerda interrupted, anxious to prove herself.

'I know why you're here,' she announced, smiling at him.

Kurnov interpreted the look as one of triumph and stared back, eyes searching the apartment again.

'What ... ?' he stumbled, confused.

'Herr Muntz told me ... warned me I might get an approach to help Heinrich ... I was expecting it ...'

'Muntz ... ?'

What a stupid man, she thought. How he must irritate Heinrich with his inability to grasp quickly what was being explained to him.

'Herr Muntz ... a fine man ... a loyal Party member,' she enlarged, enjoying the role, savouring the memory of how she had once been able to treat people in the disdainful way she was behaving towards the visitor. 'Here, in Berlin. He's with the Organisation der Ehmaligen S.S. Angehörgen.'

Kurnov groped against the door, feeling the support go from his legs. The Nazis had him! He'd escaped one trap to walk into another. And this one was worse than any other ... far worse.

'No wait ...' he began, weakly gesturing with one hand. If he didn't sit down soon, he'd fall, he knew.

Gerda looked at the cheap clock on the mantelpiece.

'I must telephone him,' she hurried on. 'I made a promise that if there were any contact, I'd call him immediately. The Party want to help Heinrich. They know he's in trouble.'

Kurnov blinked, finding difficulty in focusing. She *was* alone. And the Nazis *didn't* know yet. He strained to try to understand the rambling woman, remaining before the door to prevent her leaving. Again the hand moved, aimlessly.

'Wait,' he repeated. Desperately he began talking, mouthing the thoughts without consideration, as soon as they came to him. 'Don't call anyone ... not yet. There's a lot to discuss ... I've lots of messages from Heinrich ... Plenty of time for telephone calls later ...'

His mind was running ahead, trying to work out what had happened. There wasn't a trap, he guessed. From what she had said, he reasoned they had just inveigled her as a dupe, knowing her stupidity and confident she would perform exactly as instructed. He *was* safe. Gulping air, he pushed away from the door.

'I'm very tired,' he said, plaintively. 'And hungry. Heinrich promised you'd help ...'

She wavered uncertainly. She *had* undertaken to notify Herr Muntz immediately. But the man swaying before her did seem exhausted. And he had had contact with Heinrich perhaps only hours or days before. Another thought intruded, one that had occurred frequently since her conversation with the lawyer. She wanted desperately to know where her husband had been, why he'd chosen to appear again, and why he'd never contacted her, all these years. Half an hour wouldn't matter, she convinced herself. Just thirty minutes. That wouldn't be long to encompass thirty years.

'Please ...' she gestured to a chair. Damn, she suddenly thought. Why had she eaten all that ham?

'Brandy?' she offered. 'Or coffee?'

Kurnov nodded, settling in the chair. Tiredness pressed in upon him, like a weight.

'Both?' she queried.

Again he nodded. It was almost too much effort to speak any more. Had the Jews felt like this, he wondered, driven to the point of not caring whether they lived or died? It was very easy to give up, accepted Kurnov. The slightest setback destroyed any confidence he built up.

She handed him the liquor. He needed both hands to hold it and choked on the first sip. His eyes began to water, but he drank again, enjoying the sensation as the drink suffused his body.

'And food,' he said, urgently, his voice hoarse from the brandy. 'I'm very hungry. Anything.'

She moved away behind him, and he heard crockery and cutlery rattling. He leaned back in the chair, eyes closed, the hand holding the drink supported by the arm-rest. The Jews had come closer than he had realized to breaking him, he decided. If he hadn't taken the precaution of locating Gerda, by now he would have been screaming in the streets outside, his mind twisted by the stress. Almost, he decided. But not quite. And that was the important difference.

With difficulty, he opened his eyes, then moved to the edge of the seat. He'd kept ahead so far by being cleverer than they were. But it was too soon to relax.

He stumbled to the dresser where Gerda had the drinks, refilling the glass, then using the excuse quickly to examine the apartment more closely than he had so far been able to do. It *was* empty, he confirmed. His face twitched at the squalor of it. Certainly it was neatly kept, he conceded. But then Gerda always had been tidy. He remembered when she had had closets of clothes she had listed them in a tiny notebook always kept in the top left-hand drawer of her dressing-table. How different everything here was from the luxury of the Berlin house she had once occupied. All this furniture was cheap and second-hand, the legs of the bed and table tilted haphazardly, like a young foal first learning to stand. The stuffing was bulged in nearly every seat-back and had actually burst through in some cases. In the bedroom he saw a suit hanging on the outside of the cupboard, covered with plastic. It looked new. He frowned, wondering why she kept it like that. The dressing-table once occupied by silver-backed brushes and every cosmetic that could be bought or looted from Paris was now bare, and verdigris whirls discoloured the mirror. The bedroom floorboards were uncovered, he saw, apart from what looked like a hand-made rug on one side of the bed.

He turned back into the living-room, moving to the chair in which he had first sat. It was the best in the room, he realized.

Little of value to steal, he assessed. It hardly mattered. He couldn't take the chance of going to a pawn shop, anyway. It would have to be money. From the condition of the flat, and the messy, untidy way she was dressed, he didn't think there would be much of that, either.

In the kitchen, Gerda shaved what she could salvage from the ham, chopping the surviving sausage finely to make it appear more. She added sauerkraut and bread, then started mixing the coffee.

How dreadful he was, she thought. She nibbled her lip, sadly. Heinrich must be in serious trouble, to associate with a man like that. Would Heinrich be as scruffy and ugly? she wondered.

She hoped not. Heinrich had always been such a fine, upright man.

'The peacock strut of a gentleman officer,' she recalled Bormann once saying. How proud she'd been.

She arranged the meal carefully on a tray, laying everything upon tray-cloths. At least he would see how her husband was used to being treated. Kurnov stared at the food greedily, snatching at the bread before she had placed the tray on the low table before him, knocking some of the sausage from the plate. He crammed his mouth, gulping the food, ignoring the criticism in her face.

'There's wine,' she offered.

He grunted, unable to talk.

She struggled with the cork. Heinrich would have opened it, she thought. Crumbs stuck in his throat and he coughed an ugly sound.

'How well do you know my husband?' she asked.

Sure of herself, she had always been able to conjure a demanding arrogance, remembered Kurnov. He was eating slower now, knowing he would have to control himself to digest the meal. He sipped the wine, arranging the story he had prepared while she was in the kitchen. It was perfect, he had decided.

'Very well,' he asserted, swallowing. 'His best friend.'

The sausage tasted stale, he thought. And the ham was dry, too.

'How ... ?'

'Poor Heinrich,' said Kurnov, surely. 'He's suffered very badly. Very badly indeed.'

Immediately Gerda's attitude faltered, as he had known it would.

'Tell me ...'

'At the end we were captured, a group of us, by the Russians ...'

'Did they discover what ... ?'

'No,' said Kurnov, immediately. 'No, we managed to get away from the camp so there was no link. There were months of being moved from camp to camp. They never bothered with a trial or anything like that. They just used us all as slaves ...'

'Heinrich ... a slave?' She shuddered.

Kurnov nodded, happy at the effect his story was having.

'We've been shuttled everywhere, over the years. East Germany first, then Poland ... even the Ukraine ...'

She sat heavily in a sagging chair opposite, head down. She was very near to tears, he thought.

'My poor darling,' she said, almost to herself.

'Then they began to break up the camps,' he continued, easily. 'We were back in East Germany by then. Suddenly, for the first time in years, the authorities started taking greater interest in our backgrounds ... something to do with resettlement ... official inquiries were opened ...'

She looked up, concentrating. Her eyes were wet, he saw.

'It was obvious from the questions what was happening. And that, after all these years, there was a risk of our being exposed. Thank God the camp was on the point of disbandment. Security was lax ...'

'So you escaped?'

Kurnov nodded and Gerda smiled. That sounded like Heinrich. No matter how much hardship or deprivation, his spirit would not have been broken.

'Tell me,' she prompted, smiling in anticipation of a story that would prove her husband's courage.

Kurnov shook his head. A good liar told no more lies than were necessary. Thank God she was so stupid, he thought. The account didn't sound as convincing as he had planned.

'It's too long,' he avoided. 'Perhaps tomorrow.'

'But where is he?'

Kurnov sighed. She was so malleable, she would accept anything, he decided.

'Still behind the Wall,' he announced.

Her face contorted angrily, and the words burst out.

'Why? Why didn't you bring him with you? He could be caught, imprisoned again ...'

He raised the limp hand, trying to quieten her.

'No', he said. 'No, he's quite safe.'

She shook her head, refusing the assurance.

'Heinrich is frightened he would be recognized, even

after all these years,' said Kurnov. Still she looked unsure.

'He's actually safer, where he is. He sent me across to contact the Party ... we had addresses ... ,' he added.

'But not the name of Herr Muntz?' she intoned, suddenly suspicious.

'Is it likely that we would be provided with the identity of the leaders, until we had been thoroughly checked?' he fenced, easily. She nodded, satisfied.

'When can he come across?' she asked.

Kurnov shrugged, his eyes closing despite the conscious effort to stay awake.

'Herr Muntz,' declared Gerda, positively. 'He'll know what to do. I'll go to Herr Muntz, immediately.'

'No,' Kurnov jerked awake, nervously. He'd handled it badly, he thought.

'Please ... a moment ...' he faltered on. 'I need rest. I cannot answer the questions they would want satisfied now. I've spent three days, without sleep or food, trying to reach here to help Heinrich. Let me rest, a few hours. A bath, perhaps ...'

'I'll tell Herr Muntz not to come for several hours,' offered Gerda.

'Do you think they could wait, knowing one of the heroes of the Third Reich was so near?'

He was putting forward a poor argument, he knew, but it was impossible to assemble his thoughts. She was looking at him uncertainly, unsettled by his attitude. Soon doubts would begin. She offered more wine and he accepted, even though it would accelerate the sleep that was washing over him.

'Heinrich and I devised a plan,' he ad-libbed, desperately. 'We didn't know how long it was going to take for me to make contact. He isn't going to appear at the meeting point for another three days. It would be pointless, contacting Herr Muntz tonight. We could achieve nothing.'

It was a vacuous argument, he accepted. The sudden change in the woman's attitude disturbed him. It wasn't going to be so easy after all.

'Who are you?' she asked, abruptly.

She *was* suspicious, he determined.

'Reinhart,' he said, immediately. The name had provided good protection for a long time, so why not utilize it again? It was a background upon which he could easily be questioned. 'Klaus Reinhart.'

She frowned, searching for a memory, then nodded. An utterly lonely woman, Gerda was more aware of the events and people in her life of thirty years before than she was of the preceding day.

'I recall the name,' she admitted. Immediately, she added, 'But I don't recollect your being a friend of my husband. Rather the reverse.'

Oh God, another error. He'd forgotten telling her about Reinhart, all those years ago. Why the hell should she have remembered, anyway?

'At Buchenwald I was a doctor, nothing more,' agreed Kurnov. 'It's only been since then ... forced to live for so long as we have ... that we've come so close ...'

Still she looked doubtful, he thought. To talk further would only create fresh questions. He struggled towards the edge of the chair. His body felt heavy. Every movement was a conscious effort.

'Frau Köllman ... ,' he said, respectfully, anticipating she would respond to such an approach. 'I've travelled for so long without sleep. Or the facilities even to wash my face. Perhaps a bath ...'

She nodded, indicating the nearest door.

'I'll get towels.'

Too quick, he judged. She wanted him out of the room, so she could contact that bloody Nazi. As she went into the bedroom, he looked towards the door leading into the hallway. Thank God. There was a key in the lock. As quickly as he could move his leaden body he went over, securing the door and putting the key into his pocket. He moved away, appearing to greet her as she returned from the bedroom. He was aware of her close attention. She was examining him minutely, looking at his hair, then his face, going over his body and even looking closely at his hands when he reached out for the towels. He grabbed them quickly, trying to avert the examination.

'I'll only be a few minutes, Frau Köllman,' he said, moving towards the bathroom. 'Perhaps it would be possible for another coffee when I'm finished?'

She nodded, head still to one side, her face blank.

Inside the bathroom he pressed against the door, listening. Her footsteps receded and he heard the muffled clatter of crockery again.

He turned on the taps and started undressing, gratefully. His smelling, stained clothes felt like another skin. They even seemed difficult to divest. He stared into the mirror, shocked by his appearance. He looked like a madman, he thought, a dishevelled, glaring-eyed madman. A night's sleep. That's all he needed, a good night's sleep. His body was numbed with fatigue so there was no feeling in his legs. It was like walking on cotton wool. The bath would help, he thought, groaning at the pleasure as he lowered himself into the water. The woman worried him. The suspicion was building up, he knew, like a snowball rolling down a hill. He looked around the cramped cubicle, seeking a weapon. There would be no way he could sleep without subduing her first. The idea of harming his wife came quite dispassionately, without any remorse.

There was nothing heavy enough to render her unconscious, he realized sadly.

In the kitchen, Gerda tidily stacked the plates in the drainer frame, then wiped her hands.

There was something wrong, she knew. She couldn't isolate it, but she could not lose the feeling that the man's account was untrue. She shuddered, suddenly frightened. Heinrich had hated Reinhart, she remembered. A bad German, he'd called him, a traitor, and he'd had to discipline the man a hundred times. She frowned, regressing along familiar paths, trying to recall. He'd even demanded Reinhart's arrest and trial, she thought. Yes, she was quite sure of it.

Herr Muntz should know. Determinedly she went back into the living-room, but moved softly, so the man would not hear. By the bathroom, she listened, intently, hearing the sound of the water. She smiled, moving on into the bedroom to get her frayed cloth coat from the cupboard. The door creaked slightly and she looked back, hesitantly. Still just the sound of someone bathing. She put the coat on as she went across the room, walking fast, needing to quit the apartment even though she could not identify her fear.

There was a strangled, frightened sound as she tugged at the locked door. Unable to understand what had happened, she kept pulling until it rattled in the frame. Then the fear came up like a solid feeling in her throat, blocking her lungs. Finally she backed into the room, staring at the door, disbelievingly shaking her head. Why lock it? It was pointless. Nothing made any sense. She turned to the bathroom, eyes staring, trying to pin the thoughts that butterflied through her mind. Who was he? And why had he locked her in? Who on earth, apart from Herr Muntz, knew her name? The Jews? Could it be the Jews, come to get her after all this time?

His carelessly constructed story unwound in her mind, but this time the faults glared. No one, she decided. No one at all. Well, almost no one ... but not even the Jews ...

She began moving slowly, head erect, hypnotically drawn towards the closed door, from behind which she could still faintly detect the sound of his movements. It couldn't be, she thought. Again she was reminded of the similarities that had occurred to her as she had emerged from the bedroom thirty minutes before, handing him the towel. She felt faint, as if the band were being slowly tightened around her chest, like the feeling she had experienced in her meeting with Herr Muntz. It wasn't possible. *He* wouldn't have treated her so cruelly. At the door, she stopped, not knowing what to do. Feeling suddenly foolish, she stooped, trying to squint through the keyhole. In her fear, she almost giggled. He had his back to her, leisurely drying himself. His skin was old and sagging, like a lizard, she thought, but there was an odd line around his throat, almost like a collar. He turned, twisting to dry his back and she screamed, unable to stop herself. She saw him stop at the sound, but then she was falling, going backwards, helplessly, her mind locked on the distinctive scar that Heinrich had carried on his thigh since the Hamburg car crash, and which she remembered so well. The door opened and he stood there, unclothed, staring down at her. His face, the face she didn't know, was entirely without expression.

'Heinrich ...' she mumbled, bewildered. '... My darling ... what ... ?' she stopped, listening to her own voice. My darling ... ? Was that so? But she didn't know the man who stood over her ... he was as strange as his face.

'... Help me ...' she pleaded. '... I don't understand ...'

The thoughts rushed into her head, like water filling a hollow on the seashore. It *was* Heinrich. He was back. There would be a reason for the surgery. It didn't matter. The explanation could come later. She would learn to live with that face. What did a face matter? He'd come back. That was the important thing. She wasn't going to be alone any more. Back. At last. No more loneliness No more poverty. Perhaps even dresses again.

She reached out, imploringly, smiling up at him. Kurnov looked down at the old woman. How ugly, he thought. Stupid. And ugly.

He moved forward and she offered her hand, to be pulled up, but he spread the towel he held, like a cloak. She frowned, unable to comprehend, and then everything went black as he threw it over her face and she felt the weight and dampness of his body. She tried to hold him, thinking it was an embrace, and then felt the chain he had torn from the hand-basin looping around her neck and realized for the first time how the air was cut off by the towel over her head. She tried to scream, but the sound choked away. He was so heavy ... so heavy ... why ... why was he doing it ... she loved him ... it didn't matter about the new face ... really it didn't ...

'... Please ...' she tried, but the sound was smothered and a few seconds later she lapsed into unconsciousness.

Kurnov lay on her, utterly exhausted, long after she had ceased struggling and he knew she was dead. At last he got to his knees, then finally upright, drained by the brief fight. Her body was covered in the towel, so that only her legs showed, exposed where her skirt had ridden up. He freed one arm and jerked her towards the bathroom. She was very heavy and it took a long time. He moved in short spurts. Everything took so much effort. He wedged her against the side of the bath, knowing he was very near complete collapse. Stumbling, unable even to see properly, he half fell from the bathroom, grabbing a chair in the living-room. It didn't stop the collapse. He couldn't stand now, he knew. On his hands and knees he crawled into the bedroom. As he went past the wardrobe, his back hit the suit Gerda had bought but never worn. The plastic gripped at his dampened, warm skin and it fell off, on top of him.

He gasped, frightened, throwing it off in a heap. He knelt for several moments by the bed, concentrating his ebbing strength, then lurched up, throwing himself over it. He was asleep before his body settled.

It had happened, just as Mavetsky had feared.

'How can he have vanished?' demanded Shepalin.

Mavetsky looked away, refusing to meet the chairman's accusation. No one else came to help. Bastards.

'Too many things are happening that we can't tie together,' said the minister, desperately. Responsibility was being directed against him from every side, he knew. The entire Praesidium had decided he should be the scapegoat. Suvlov had even been sent back to Berlin, not arrested and put into a camp, as Mavetsky had expected.

'Every Nazi from whom we might have got a lead has been killed,' added Mavetsky.

'I *want* Russia to be in a position of handing Kurnov over,' insisted Shepalin. 'We've scored an enormous propaganda victory so far. It must continue.'

'I'll try,' shrugged Mavetsky, hopelessly. But he couldn't, he knew. There was nothing he could do. Nothing at all. Except hope that the agents he'd flooded into the city would stumble across something.

'You'd better,' warned Shepalin, softly.

(21)

It was an agonizing pain, reaching deep into his unconsciousness, driving through his head. He struggled, trying to escape, but he was pinned firmly down. He could feel the hands upon his arms and legs and others holding his head, preventing almost any movement. He shouted and tried to twist away, realizing his ear lobes were being squeezed, to make him awaken. He didn't want to wake up. He wanted to sleep, forever. Go away, please let me sleep, he thought. Still the searing pain continued.

Initially his eyes fogged, refusing to see. Then the light penetrated and he heard the familiar voice and blinked, fixing his vision.

There were four around the bed, moving away from him now he was conscious. Perez was at the bottom, smiling down.

'We can't allow sleep, can we, Heinrich?' he said, mocking. 'Amazing how quickly the human body and mind can recover, after a little sleep. You established that years ago, didn't you? There's too many people looking for you to let you hide away here.'

Kurnov began moaning, head-shaking his refusal to accept their presence.

'... Alone,' he pleaded. 'Leave me alone. I'm sorry ... really ... very sorry ... it was orders ... I did everything under orders ... didn't want to do it ... made to, by the S.S. If I hadn't, they would have killed me ... had to obey orders ...'

Perez and Mosbacher exchanged looks. The burly

241

Israeli seemed disgusted, not by the man on the bed, but by what was happening in the room. There was a fifth person there, realized Kurnov, standing back against the door. There was a hand-held movie camera recording everything.

'A genuine murder, Heinrich,' went on Perez, ignoring Mosbacher's criticism. Always that goading, jeering tone, thought Kurnov. He hunched himself away from the psychiatrist, drawing his knees in front of him and locking his arms around them, so that his body was clenched into a foetal position.

' ... No ... ,' he said. ' ... Please no ... just kill me ... please kill me ... please ...'

'... You made people run under greater stress than this, Heinrich,' said Perez, remorselessly. 'You know you did ...'

'... How ...?'

Perez laughed, confident now of his absolute control.

'We never lost you, Heinrich. There were three on the platform, not two. We followed you all the time. Not that we had to. We've known about Gerda for years ... Saw you follow her here days ago. It was obviously the place where you'd go to ground.'

He tossed an object in his hand.

'We even had a key to the apartment,' he said.

Mosbacher moved at the side of the bed, anxious to quit the room.

'I hope you're finally satisfied,' said Mosbacher, to Perez, 'Now you've done exactly what that swine practised years ago.'

Perez's smile died and he looked up at his friend.

'Your family died in the same way,' he reminded.

Mosbacher looked at Perez, contemptuously. 'This isn't the way I want them avenged,' he said.

He moved away, towards the door. 'We'd better go.'

Perez paused, uncertain whether to continue the argument, looking at his watch.

'We've telephoned the police, Heinrich,' he said, coming back to the man on the bed. '... like any good neighbour who had heard screams and indications of a struggle ...'

They began moving from the room.

'... I'd say you've got about ten minutes to get out ... just ten minutes to start running again ...' concluded Perez.

Kurnov stared up at his tormentor, who laughed from the doorway. At that moment, Kurnov's mind snapped. He threw back his head and let out a long, wailing scream, more animal than human.

'Satisfied now?' demanded Mosbacher, sickened. Perez didn't reply, leading the party from the flat.

'Orderly!'

Where the hell was the man? Not the first time he'd had to be disciplined. It was incredible how everyone was reacting, just because of a minor setback on the Eastern Front and an isolated reversal in Normandy. The Führer had told them the truth ... reinforcements were being drafted into the areas. By winter, all the ground would be recovered and more besides. They'd spend Christmas in Moscow ... by spring, the invasion of England would be launched. Then the doubters would regret their cowardice. Names were being collected, he knew. Lists already existed. The Führer would have his revenge, just like he had after the July outrage in 1944.

'Orderly!'

He looked around the room frowning, unable to recognize it. Where was he? He saw for the first time that he was naked, and instinctively covered himself with a sheet. Everything was cheap and shabby. He giggled. A whore's bedroom. That was it. He must be in a whore's room. No wonder the orderly wasn't there. Bloody schnapps. Impossible to remember anything after

243

a few schnapps. He looked around for his clothes. Dirty bitch must have stolen them. He got off the bed, wondering why he felt so weak. Amazing. Almost impossible to walk. He lurched into the living-room, holding the door-edge for support. It looked familiar, but he couldn't recall why he should know it.

'Anyone here?'

He stared down at Gerda's crumpled figure on the bathroom floor, stirring it with his foot. Who was she? With difficulty, he tugged the towel from around her head. Been strangled, he diagnosed, professionally, looking at the contorted, swollen face. She was very old. Surely he hadn't gone with her? Definitely have to stop drinking so much. Played havoc with the memory. Everyone drank a lot now. Cowardly. Far too many people running and drinking. Even denying membership of the Party. But the Führer knew. He had the lists. Embarrassing to be found in a room with a dead whore, he decided. Despite everything, law and order still existed in the capital. Quite right, too. Where was his uniform? He saw clothing on the bathroom chair and picked it up, distastefully. Not his, surely? Filthy, smelly shirt and suit. And civilian, too. Not his. Couldn't be. Have to wear something, though. He would be recognized by all of the guards at the camp. They'd know better than to try to stop him. No trouble to get admitted without a uniform. He carried the clothing into the main room and started to dress. God, how it smelled! Appeared to fit, though. His face crumpled as his mind tried to grasp reality, but it eluded him, like hurrying images seen through a fog. Sure he knew the room. And the woman, lying over there. Always the fog swirled when he thought he was about to remember. He looked down at himself, offended by the suit, feeling through the pockets, seeking identification. He pulled the Russian passport from his pocket and stared at it. 'Vladimir Kurnov', he read, moving to the picture. Sure he knew the man. Positive. Damn the difficulty in remembering. Definitely have to stop drinking. Wouldn't be good to have a Russian document in his possession, he thought. Sign of a traitor. Get his name on one of the Führer's lists that way. He tossed it on the couch. Better get out. It was very confusing. Obviously dangerous to stay. Time he got back.

He went out into the passageway, moving slowly, seeking the exit. He walked with his shoulder brushing the wall, grateful for the support. He was ill, he decided. So difficult to move. See a doctor when he got back. Working too hard. That was the problem. Too few left like himself prepared any more to work hard, to make the effort when it was necessary.

He stumbled, stiff-legged, down the stairs, stopping several times to recover his breath, careless of the noise. He felt sick, too. Probably the drink.

'Hey.'

He turned at the shout, seeing the woman gazing at him over the counter. The Madam, he decided. Wonder if he'd paid. Bound to have done. Wouldn't have let him into the brothel otherwise.

'Where have you been?' she demanded.

Who did she think she was talking to? Didn't know her place. No one did any more. He jerked his arm upwards, vaguely, not bothering to answer her.

'I want to know ... ,' began the woman, then stopped. 'Oh my God ...' she said, the words jumping from her. She groped backwards into the doorway of her tiny office, holding the edge as if she were about to dodge behind it. He smiled. So she'd recognized him. About time. He had intended taking the address and reporting the brothel to the local S.S. office. Wouldn't now. No point in causing unnecessary difficulty. She'd been lucky, though. Never know how lucky she'd been. Everyone had their names on lists these days.

He pushed his hands over his civilian clothes.

'Misplaced my uniform,' he said. No wonder she hadn't recognized him immediately as an officer, dressed like this. He smiled, openly.

'Don't worry,' he said. 'Won't report you.'

Why were his thoughts and words coming so disjointed? he wondered. Bloody alcohol. Definitely have to stop.

She cringed further back into her room, watching him cross the small vestibule to the door. Immediately outside in the street, he stopped, looking around in bewilderment, unable to recognize anything. Berlin? Yes, definitely Berlin, he thought, going slowly up the Duisburgerstrasse towards Brandenburgische.

Vaguely he heard the sound of sirens. Probably an ambulance going to the scene of another cowardly air-attack upon innocent civilians. When the setbacks had been overcome and they'd occupied London, the Führer intended putting on trial the people who had ordered the indiscriminate bombing of civilian targets, he knew.

He turned, seeing vehicles arrive far down the road. Was it the Madam, gesturing? He couldn't see. Too far away.

On the main thoroughfare, his confusion grew. What had happened? No uniforms. And the lights. Too many lights. Hadn't they heard of the blackout? No wonder there were the sounds of so many ambulances. Impossible for bombers to miss targets like this. Why no uniforms? Discarded, that was it. Everyone was throwing away their uniforms and running. Cowards, all cowards.

'Cowards,' he shouted, aloud.

There were sniggers, but no one stopped. In the Kurfürstendamm he stood, watching the swirl of cars and people. The Führer should know. He'd tell him. The Führer had always liked him, inviting him to the Bunker and to Berchtesgaden. Even called him the architect of the super-race. Yes, he'd tell him. There had to be lists. That was the way to keep discipline. Impose the regulations and laws. Keep lists.

He heard the sirens again and looked around, trying to isolate the burning buildings. Must be several streets away, he decided. Main roads would be jammed, he thought, with fire engines and rescue vehicles. He moved into the side streets, moving surely through the darkened road, squinting at the lights. Momentarily the fog in his mind receded and he huddled against the wall, frightened without knowing the reason. Then it swept in again. He pushed away from the wall, surprised to find himself there. From an adjoining street, he heard the metallic voice of a public address system and thought he caught a name he remembered. '... Kurnov ...' he heard. He stopped, making a conscious effort to recollect, then shook his head, dismissively. Didn't matter. Had to tell the Führer about the relaxation of the regulations. Across the darkened street he saw people hurrying and nodded. The half-heard announcement would have been from the radio street-van, warning them to prepare for another air-raid, he guessed. Have to hurry. Had to reach the Bunker before the raid started. Mustn't get delayed. Führer had to know. The vans were nearer now, enabling odd words to be heard.

'... Murder ... avoid approach ...'

It *was* murder. Cold-blooded murder. Why didn't they turn off their lights? Idiots. Not taking proper precautions. Keep away from tottering buildings. Turn off the lights. They'd be avenged, though. Lists were being prepared. Ahead he saw a jumble of cars. Road blocks. Damn. Dangerous buildings, probably. No papers. And the Führer had to be warned. He dodged into an alley. The darkened office buildings would have an exit into the next street. Bound to have. Complete darkness. Impossible to see. He crashed forward, into rubbish bins. Didn't matter. Good blackout. Important. Less possibility of getting hit. Shouts around him. Brave, these civilian firemen. Landwehr, too. Risked death every night. He'd tell the Führer. Important to praise. Good for morale. He emerged on to a parallel street, sighing. Not blocked. Understandable. Too many men needed for reinforcements. Even forming units from foreign nationals now. Didn't agree with that. Tainted the purity of the cause. Didn't matter. Only a temporary measure. Führer knew what he was doing.

Potsdamerplatz. He smiled, recognizing the thoroughfare. Not far from the Bunker now. Quieter here. To be expected, obviously. Essential to guarantee the blackout, so near the Bunker.

All around were the tall, deserted buildings, blinded by their bricked-up windows. Hadn't known they were bricking up houses for protection. Couldn't see the point. Must remember to ask why. He was suddenly confronted by the Wall and stood, confused again. Berlin. Not Buchenwald. So why the wall? Didn't make sense. He went closer, touching the rough breeze-blocks, like a blind man trying to determine his surroundings. Wasn't his camp. Just barbed wire there. The administration and research buildings were concrete, certainly, but they were inside the wire. And he hadn't come through the gate. Had he? He frowned, unable to remember, turning to look behind him. No. Certainly not. He was going to the Bunker, not the camp. Going to the Bunker. To warn the Führer. Protective wall. That was it. They'd built a protective wall around the Bunker. Couldn't remember it being there before. When was his last visit? He pressed his head against the concrete. Couldn't remember. Didn't matter. Protective wall. Very sensible. He began groping along, seeking an opening. No break. Climb over that was it. Get into the inner compound. No danger. He was well known. They'd recognize him, without identification. First-name terms with all of them. He began dragging upwards, feeling for handholds in the rough brickwork, grunting as his fingers slipped, splitting the nails. It had happened before, recently, he thought. Where had he climbed recently? Wouldn't come. Bloody schnapps. He fell twice, skinning his shins the second time. He sat slumped at the bottom of the wall, limbs weighted by tiredness.

Far away he heard the persistent sirens. Getting nearer. Meant the raids were coming closer. Führer had to be warned. He began scrambling up again, urged by the sudden, desperate knowledge that if he fell he would not again be able to attempt the climb. He drove his fingers into the cracks, ignoring the pain, the effort coming from him in sharp, gagging sounds. Had to do it. Had to warn the Führer. As his hand covered the top he sobbed with relief, hanging there. Made it. Führer would be grateful. Barbed wire. Should have expected it. He felt carefully, wedging his hands between the spikes, so he could use the wire for support, pulling his legs up to perch precariously on top. He looked to where the Bunker should have been visible. Odd. Just a hump in the ground. Camouflage. That was it. Cleverly hidden. He glanced back, into West Berlin, seeing the sodium glow reflected as an orange blur against the low cloud. God, it was a bad raid tonight. Funny he hadn't been aware of the explosions. Wrong wind-direction, probably.

The searchlight hit him like a physical blow and he swayed, nearly falling. He snatched out and felt the barb bite into the palm of his hand and groaned with the pain.

'Don't shoot,' he screamed, urgently. They'd be under orders to protect the Führer, quite ruthlessly, he knew. 'Don't shoot. It's me, Köllman. Heinrich Köllman. Important I see the Führer.'

There seemed to be searchlights from either side. He waved his free arm, hesitantly, his balance tottering.

'Blackout,' he shouted. 'Too dangerous. Stop the lights.'

Behind him he thought he detected a vehicle with a red marker revolving on the roof, but the other lights were blinding, so he couldn't be sure. There were voices telling him to come back, but he ignored them. Just firemen and Landwehr. Didn't know how important it was to get to the Führer. Wouldn't understand. Limited mentality. Only good for menial work.

'Got to see the Führer,' he shouted down to them.

He clambered over the wire, trying to judge the distance to the ground. They'd have to bring a ladder. He looked up, to call for one, and the movement dislodged him. He fell, feeling the wire rip at his clothing like a hand trying to pull him back. He landed with a sickening jolt and lay, open-eyed, hawking the air back into his lungs. His wrist hurt and was twisted beneath him. Why didn't they come to help? Where was everybody? He'd tell the Führer. Make sure names were on the list.

Fifty yards away, the Russians and East Germans who had had a street-by-street account of Kurnov's progress towards the Wall from people whom they regarded as agents but who were, in fact, carefully planted members of Perez's team, watched the prostrate figure fixed in the beam of the searchlight. From the other side of the Wall, the West German police-car spotlight went out and the occupants ran to the observation posts looking into East Berlin.

'Get up, Heinrich Köllman,' shouted Suvlov, formally. He wore his uniform, which made him seem more imposing. There might be photographs from over the Wall, he knew. He was smiling, confident the expression would be misunderstood by everyone around him.

He'd recovered, decided the Russian colonel. He would be known as the man who had captured the Nazi. A total disaster had been turned into complete victory.

He grabbed a megaphone from the man standing next to him. An officer hurried up, reporting that the electronic mines had all been turned off, so there would be no danger in moving forward to get the man.

'Let him crawl to us,' said Suvlov. He switched on the megaphone, knowing his voice would be heard over the wall and that the arrest would be fully reported in the Western press.

'Heinrich Köllman, you are a prisoner of the Soviet Union,' he shouted. Should he have added, 'and the German Democratic Republic'? Perhaps. But diplomatic niceties didn't matter. Later perhaps. But not now.

The old man pushed up, trying to shade his eyes against the light with one hand. The other was hugged across his chest, as if he were injured. He squinted, unable to see anything.

Very confusing. Not what he had expected. Russians. Definitely Russians. Recognized the accent. How? Didn't matter. Definitely Russians. So he was too late. Was he dead? Was the Führer dead? Or captured? Neither. Would have escaped. Obviously be a plan. He would have been too clever for them. Escaped to regroup further south, with the reinforcements. Of course he had.

Only a temporary setback.

He couldn't feel his legs and swayed, staggering slightly backwards. Careful. Mustn't collapse. Mustn't show weakness. Had to demonstrate superiority. That was important.

He came forward, his body moving stiffly, puppet-like, and after a few steps his mouth opened and he threw back his head. Suvlov put his head to one side, but couldn't identify the words.

'What's he saying?' he demanded from the men who had given the news about the mines. Before there could be an answer, the old man got nearer and they were all able to hear. He sang croakingly, but still discernibly.

He was off-key, but the tune of the Hörst Wessel song was easily recognizable.

> '... And comrades whom reaction and Red
> Front has slaughtered
> In spirit march with us and ne'er shall die ...'

From behind there was the click of a rifle-bolt.

'No!' ordered Suvlov, urgently. 'That's what he wants, to be shot.'

Faltering, breath driven from him by the effort of walking, the mass murderer sang on.

> 'For brown battalions clear the streets of others,
> Clear us a way and each Storm Trooper cheer,
> The Swastika brings hope to all our myriad
> brothers,
> The day of freedom and of bread is here.'

He was close now, his feet scuffing over the rough ground, blinking in an attempt to see them. Impossible. They were just black blurs.

'For the last time, Reveille has been sounded, for battle ...' he began again, but his voice trailed away at the awareness of so many men in uniform. Lucky he was in civilian clothes. Wouldn't know who he was. No documents. He'd lie. Be easy, with so much confusion everywhere. No difficulty getting lost in all the prisoner-of-war camps that would be created. He'd beat them. Be easy.

'Heinrich Köllman?' challenged Suvlov.

The scientist looked at the uniformed man. Difficult to recognize the rank from his shoulder epaulettes.

'No,' he denied, positively. 'I'm ...'

He halted, confused. He couldn't think of another name. He looked around the half-circle of soldiers. And burst into tears.

It was over a year later, long after the remedial plastic surgery and the allocation of the Chair of Psychiatry at the Hebrew University in Jerusalem, that Uri Perez was asked the question at the end of a lecture. It came from a student who watched the film, shot from one of the abandoned houses on the West side of the Wall, showing Köllman walking forward to confront the Russians.

'Having once been in one of Köllman's camps, and then having evolved the scheme that trapped him, you had an enormous personal involvement,' said the boy whom Perez had selected as one of the brightest in the course. 'What satisfaction did *you* feel, seeing everything work so completely.'

Although he had answered the question to himself many times Perez hesitated. There really wasn't another reply, he decided, finally.

'None,' he insisted, definitely. 'Not the slightest satisfaction. In fact, I experienced the most overwhelming feeling of pity.'

He stayed at his desk, long after the lecture hall had emptied. Why had he never been able to convince Mosbacher, he wondered, regretfully. Perhaps, if he had, they would still be friends.